Whatever June Coffin says, goes—literally. And it's not just because she's a chain smoking rebel. As a Siren, June has the ability to force people to obey any command she voices. But in a world where those with supernatural powers quickly become lab rats for science, she'd rather look out for herself than fight on the front lines...until her similarly gifted twin brother, Jason, is captured by Chicago's Institute of Supernatural Research.

To save Jason, June has no choice but to enter a hidden world of conspiracy, murder—and strange bedfellows—including a widowed paranormal advocate whose memory June accidentally erased, and a fiery paranormal separatist leader. Soon the lines between attraction and strategic alliance become blurred. But in a city exploding with paranormal crossfire, and her brother's life at stake, June will have to face her inner demons and finally take a stand.

Visit us at www.kensingtonbooks.com

I0667081

Books by Megan Morgan

Siren Song Series
The Wicked City

Published by Kensington Publishing Corporation

The Wicked City

Siren Song Series

Megan Morgan

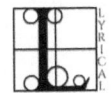

LYRICAL PRESS
Kensington Publishing Corp.
www.kensingtonbooks.com

Lyrical Press books are published by
Kensington Publishing Corp. 119 West 40th Street New York, NY 10018

All Kensington titles, imprints, and distributed lines are available at special quantity discounts for bulk purchases for sales promotion, premiums, fund-raising, and educational or institutional use.

Special book excerpts or customized printings can also be created to fit specific needs. For details, write or phone the office of the Kensington Special Sales Manager:
Kensington Publishing Corp.
119 West 40th Street
New York, NY 10018
Attn. Special Sales Department. Phone: 1-800-221-2647.

Kensington and the K logo Reg. U.S. Pat. & TM Off.
Lyrical Press and the L logo are trademarks of Kensington Publishing Corp.

First Electronic Edition: March 2015
eISBN-13: 978-1-61650-683-4
eISBN-10: 1-61650-683-0

First Print Edition: March 2015
ISBN-13: 978-1-61650-684-1
ISBN-10: 1-1-61650-684-9

To Abe Schaffer, my first reader and fan.

Acknowledgements

To my family and friends who have supported me in every effort over the years. Thank you for listening to me, encouraging me, and believing in me. Also to my wonderful son Cain, who is by far my greatest piece of work.

Foreword

This book has gone through so many changes and rewrites since the original story I started seven years ago, the first draft and what you're about to read are not even comparable. Along the way I lost characters, picked up new ones, invented pieces of story, dropped what didn't work, made connections, and cut loose ends. The protagonist of this story started out as an incidental male background character in the very first draft. Look at her go now!

However, this story, no matter how much it has changed, has always been set in Chicago. I love the Windy City with all my heart and try to visit as many times as I can each year--hopefully, I'll live there one day. Many of the city details are things I've personally seen and been close to. Some are the result of loving and dedicated research. Chicago is the ultimate city for urban fantasy, as it's vast, dazzling, awe-inspiring, a little dangerous, and a lot sexy. If you've never been there, I hope I can give you a clear picture with my words.

June Coffin is a character built from the ashes of other characters I had to dismantle along the way, and she is, at last, the perfect person to tell this story. She's a reluctant heroine battling with the things that make her who she is, a character who has to find the courage to balance past pain with the need to accept the dark parts of herself in order to move forward. Despite her reluctance, she doesn't take crap and she doesn't mind expressing her opinion. She's deeply complex because I've put her layers on one by one, until I found out who she was. I hope you'll feel the same way about her and enjoy this story told through her eyes--the story I was trying to tell all along, I just had to find it.

Thank you for reading.

Chapter 1

The first time June Coffin saw Micha Bellevue, he was giving a lecture at the Chicago Institute for Supernatural Research. June and her brother Jason weren't yet prisoners of the unholy place and June had sneaked into a conference room. Though the subject of the lecture—something insipid about paranormal rights in the workplace—didn't interest her, the lecturer certainly did. Micha was tall and rugged yet boyishly handsome, all her weaknesses. *Meesha*, not *Mi-ca*, much easier to yell in bed. He had sandy brown hair with gold highlights, cut shaggy with a swoopy fringe. He also had sky blue eyes and a crooked smile.

June, in contrast, was five-four, lean, and petite. Her father once called her "diminutive," and she'd hated the word ever since. She had a flowing mane of jet-black hair, though at the moment it lacked volume or luster and she'd been keeping it in a ponytail. Her eyes were vivid green, nearly iridescent, but their color was real, unlike her hair. She was also over-fond of tattoos and piercings.

She was Micha's exact opposite, which was fine, because she believed people needed to explore sexual pursuits outside their peer groups.

In the fifteen minutes she spoke to Micha after the lecture at the Institute, the lovely man revealed himself to be full of ostentatious ideas and painfully corny jokes. A bit later, June stood in an atrium, smoking a cigarette while he led a string of eager young supernatural neophytes across the courtyard below. She narrowed her eyes against the smoke curling around her face. *I'm so gonna hit that.* She hadn't, not yet, for huge moral reasons.

Namely, because Micha had a wife.

Except, his wife currently lay trussed up in her casket, awaiting her funeral service in the morning, and June had kind of helped put her in it.

But right now they also had this issue with the gun.

Hanging out with dead people on a Sunday night didn't rank high on June's to-do list, despite her last name. But as she stood in a darkened funeral parlor staring at the tall, buxom, red-haired woman with said gun, she realized how much her priorities had changed.

"What the hell is that?" June's question was rhetorical, but she still wanted an answer.

"It's a Glock." The redhead—whose name was Cindy—said this coolly, as if she were describing a pair of shoes. Cindy had dressed all in black for the occasion, like a cat burglar.

The three of them—June, Micha, and Ms. Congeniality herself—weren't in the funeral home to steal anything. Even after the events of the preceding week, June wasn't cracked enough to snatch a body.

"Why do you have it?" June asked. "We don't *need* a gun."

The whimpering aged gentleman on his knees next to Cindy probably welcomed this news but clearly was no less frightened, as Cindy had the muzzle pressed against his temple. The man wore a handsome silk robe with wide lapels, the kind rich guys sported in movies. Were all funeral directors so dashing in their choice of nightclothes?

"I brought it just in case," Cindy said.

"Why would we need to shoot someone in a funeral home?" June raised her voice, no longer worried about being quiet. The director had probably heard them clamoring through the window at the rear of the house. June possessed some nifty skills: she was an excellent self-taught artist, she could shoot whiskey with the boys like she was one of them, and she could make wicked smoke rings. However, grace and athletics eluded her.

"I don't think he's armed," June said. "I doubt you need to defend a funeral home."

"You never know," Micha said behind her. "Necrophiliacs probably like to break into funeral homes."

June closed her eyes; she counted to five, and then ten, but when she opened her eyes again, she wasn't any calmer.

"I won't hurt you," the man on the floor said in a small, pitiful voice. "Just take what you want and go."

June stepped forward and waved a hand at Cindy, shooing away the gun. June had never touched a gun in her life. She had never needed to.

Cindy lowered the gun and stepped back. "I was just trying to help." She spoke with the petulance of an admonished child. A child who didn't get to play with her deadly weapon.

June knelt. The paunchy balding man was shaking, his eyes wide.

"It's all right." A heavy energy, curled in June's stomach like a sleeping cat, rose to her sternum and surged upward again to warmly coat her throat. "Just sit there and relax and think about your favorite things until we're gone."

The man's body sagged. His face slackened. He pivoted to the side and sat down on his bottom with a shuddering thump, his gaze gone distant and dreamy. A smile tugged at the corners of his mouth.

June stood.

"There. Isn't that awesome? Supernatural powers and stuff?" She didn't enjoy throwing around her "hypnotic voice phenomenon," as the scientists liked to call it, but invasive persuasion seemed far less cruel than criminal menacing.

Cindy pushed the gun forcefully into a holster on her hip. June winced, afraid it might go off, but thankfully—or perhaps regrettably—it didn't. June had failed to notice Cindy was wearing a holster, probably because she'd been too busy figuring out how to break into a funeral home.

"Come on," June said. "Let's get this done."

She stepped past the oblivious man on the floor. Micha followed.

The casket, tucked into a bank of flowers and wreaths, rested atop a short dais like a morbid confectionery in a baking contest. June slid her hand along the side of the casket to find a latch. She did *not* want to do this. Despite the mind-obliterating madness she'd survived recently, corpses still jangled her nerves.

"Gah." She lifted the lid a few inches.

She turned into a baby around corpses, despite knowing they weren't going to sit up and strangle her. Earlier, when she'd voiced speculative, mostly joking concern about the dead getting their revenge, Cindy pointed out scientific research had proven zombies non-existent.

"Turn a light on." June took a bracing breath and opened the lid farther. She expected a bad smell, but a faintly chemical, perfume-y odor wafted out.

"Here." Cindy slid up beside her.

A pale bluish light illuminated the space around them and fell on the still, poised figure inside the casket. Cindy held her cell phone aloft, screen lit. June paused.

"What?" Cindy's eyes shone in the faint light.

"I think if you try, you could be a little more disrespectful. Maybe you'd like to shoot her a couple times? Turn on a light!"

"You're the one breaking into her casket." Cindy tapped the screen to renew the light. "We can't turn on a light. Someone might see. Hurry up. This is freaking me out."

"It's freaking you out?" June opened the lid fully. She snatched the phone from Cindy and held it closer to the body to get the grim task over with.

Micha's wife, the esteemed Mrs. Rose Bellevue, had been a lovely woman. Had. Been. She had high delicate cheekbones, plump lips, and dusky skin—the times June had seen her alive, anyway. Her dark hair was fixed in a neat knot atop her head, loose curls spilling onto the white pillow beneath her. A tiny smile touched her lips. Her long-fingered hands rested delicately on her stomach, manicured nails gleaming. She wore a white dress with a boxy neckline and lace sleeves. She looked like an angel instead of a zombie, thank God.

June waited for Micha's response, sort of hoping, sort of not. "Well?"

Micha leaned closer and peered at her face. The light on the phone dimmed. June jabbed the screen, and a moment later a faint jingle came out of the phone.

"Give me that." Cindy yanked the phone from her and looked at the screen. "You just dialed my boyfriend. Good work."

June was aghast. "I can't believe anyone would date you."

"*One* of them."

Cindy disconnected the call and shone the light back on Rose's face. June ground her teeth and pulled a breath through her nose.

After a tense, silent moment, Micha stood upright. "No. I don't recognize her." He shrugged. "Pretty, though. I must have game."

June smoothed a hand over her hair. The strands were greasy and limp and she winced. She hadn't had a shower in more days than she wanted to contemplate.

"All right," June said. "It was worth a try. Let's split, before we get caught. We'll go through the front door this time."

Cindy lowered her phone and patted her hip. "If we have to fight our way out, I'm ready."

"Yes, if the legions of undead try to block our escape."

June carefully closed the lid of the casket, turned, and walked down the aisle, past rows of couches and folding chairs. The funeral would be huge. She had to get the hell out of the place, away from the woman's dead body and her own guilt. She needed to get the hell out of Chicago, but she couldn't. Not yet.

Not until she got her brother back.

* * * *

Cindy had an apartment in West Lakeview. She told June that's where they were, but June didn't care if they were on the moon. She felt like she *was* on the moon, in some bizarre alternate reality, even if all signs pointed to being on earth. Cindy also had a tortoiseshell cat named Serendipity—Dipity for short—that liked to sit on June.

June lay in bed in Cindy's guest room, a small white box with little decoration or furniture—a twin bed, a sagging sofa, and a hulking, ugly wooden dresser. Dipity sat on June's stomach, kneading her belly as she prepared her for—who knew? Dinner, probably. One paw, then the other. Over and over. Knead, knead. Knead, knead. A cigarette dangled from the corner of June's mouth, one eye open as she peered through the smoke, past the bowl she was utilizing as an ashtray on her chest.

"Will you lay the hell down?" June snarled.

Dipity did, folding herself into a loaf and gazing at June with wide, accusing yellow eyes. Dipity moved up and down as June breathed.

Soft slapping footsteps sounded in the hallway. Cindy peeked around the doorframe. "Did you say something?"

Dipity looked up at Cindy.

"I was talking to your damn cat," June said.

Cindy stepped into the room. June found her pretty in an overbearing sense: Amazonian and bodacious, leggy and curvy in a way most guys liked. All the things June wasn't.

"She likes you." Cindy wore white pajama pants and a pink T-shirt stretched tight across her ample bosom. "It must be your charming personality. Or you smell like Micha."

June glanced over at the sofa. Micha had his back to them, covers bunched around his waist, his white T-shirt twisted and hair a tousled, mottled mess of brown and gold. Despite Cindy's friendship with Micha, she pointed out repeatedly that she was not a "paranormal activist" like him. June didn't blame Cindy for wanting to be clear. June had actively avoided paranormal activists until she committed the grave mistake of coming to Chicago.

"He's been sleeping a lot." Cindy indicated Micha. "Is that one of the side effects?"

June ground her cigarette out in the bowl and sat the bowl next to her hip. "Hell if I know. I've never accidentally messed up someone's mind so bad I couldn't reverse it."

Cindy left the room. She returned shortly with a newspaper.

"Look at this." She walked to the bed and thrust the paper at June.

She gave June the Paranormal section of the *Chicago Tribune*. June had been reading it every day for some mention of Jason. She'd also been reading news online, on Cindy's laptop. The Chicago Institute for Supernatural Research, the first and biggest facility to be given government approval for paranormal research, kept the city alive with supernatural intrigue and gave bloggers something to endlessly blather about. The Institute's presence didn't mean folks in Chicago were hugging their neighborhood telepath, however. The freaks still got persecuted, like in Sacramento where June lived.

The headline on the first page said: HAVE THE SIREN TWINS LEFT CHICAGO? INSTITUTE NOT FORTHCOMING.

June's heart jumped and then sank again after she read the article. The reporter speculated she and Jason had fled, "shaken profoundly by the horrific and untimely death of the Institute's top vampire researcher, Rose Bellevue, her vicious murder still a hot topic of rampant speculation." The article went on to say paranormal citizens were pointing fingers at a normalist group called the Secular Normalists of Chicago or SNC, "a dastardly force polluting this city with misinformation and blatant ignorance."

June could end the speculation, if she dared come out of hiding.

The article also said police were still investigating the possible kidnapping of Micha Bellevue, Rose's husband and one of the paranormal community's most lauded advocates: "last year's recipient of the J.B. Rhine Award for Advocacy, friend of many paranormal people. His generous admirers hope fervently for his safety and the punishment of those involved in this horrendous crime."

June had seen plenty of bloggers speculating Micha had something to do with Rose's death and was on the run, and one particularly amusing guy was convinced Micha had been abducted by the CIA. June could be sneaky, but she wasn't on level with the government.

"I can't believe how lurid this shit is." June tossed the paper on top of Dipity. She emitted an angry mewl and got up. "Reads like a tabloid."

"Ethan Roberts." Cindy lifted the paper off her cat. "He's been the lead paranormal reporter for the *Tribune* for years. He might be colorful, but he knows what he's talking about." She tucked the paper under her arm. "My friend will be here soon. So haul your ass out of bed and get dressed."

Dipity jumped off June and padded slowly around the bed.

"I tried to warn him." Cindy looked over at Micha. "All those years he thought the Institute could do no wrong. He sure took it up the ass without lube this time."

June didn't comment.

"It sucks, though." Cindy dropped her voice a little. "He didn't deserve to lose Rose."

"Look at it this way. Now he can be an advocate for the right people. Knowledge is power. Fight the Man. Rah rah."

June sat up. Dipity moved behind her and rubbed across her back in a sleek caress. Cats forgave easily.

Cindy turned toward the door.

"Hey," June said.

Cindy stopped.

"What's the SNC? I keep seeing them pop up in these articles."

Cindy scrunched up her face. "They're a paranormal...protest group. Can't say 'hate group' since the treaty. The Secular Normalists of Chicago. They wanted to set themselves apart from the Bible-thumpers and fundies, but they still like to beat us up."

"I didn't realize they needed an organized group to do that. Where I come from, that's called a gang."

"It was founded by this guy named Alan Jenkins. He died like five years ago and his son Aaron took over. Aaron says he wants to clean up his father's dirt." She pursed her lips. "I don't believe him."

"Quite a city you got here."

Dipity hopped off the bed and landed on the floor with a thump.

"I don't know how you sleep at night," June said.

"With one eye open." Cindy turned and left the room. Dipity streaked after her.

Micha, undoubtedly having been awake for the entire conversation, stirred and rolled partially onto his back and twisted his head around. He gazed at her with bleary, unfocused eyes. She fought the urge to walk over to the sofa and lovingly smooth his hair back; then grab a fistful.

"I like your ink," Micha said groggily. "I have some. On my back."

June blinked and stretched her exposed arms. She had countless hours and thousands of dollars worth of tattoos up and down her arms, across her chest, some on her back, one down her left side. A lot she'd done herself. She also had multiple piercings: six in one ear, four in the other—minus the gauges—one in her tongue too, not to mention a few other places. A "rebel," her mother called her. She caused soccer moms to cross the street on a regular basis, even when doing nothing more malevolent than smoking a Parliament while holding a latte and texting.

"Thanks," she said. "You'll have to show me sometime."

Micha rolled fully onto his back and stretched, arms over his head, long legs stiffening beneath the blanket. He didn't fit on the sofa, but he'd insisted on taking it, like a gentleman.

"God, what time is it?" he asked.

"A little after nine." She needed to say something but took a moment to choose her words carefully. "I feel bad about you missing your wife's funeral today. But until I figure out how to fix what I've done to your head, I can't send you back into the wild. Let them keep thinking you've been kidnapped by the CIA or whatever. I have a feeling if you surfaced right now you'd fall into the Institute's net anyway."

Micha put his hands over his face. The light caught on his gold wedding band.

"I'm so confused," he murmured through his fingers. "Not only about this woman who's supposed to be my wife, but about the Institute." He took his hands away. "I supported them. I thought they were doing the right thing. I believed they were helping the maligned and oppressed."

June couldn't believe he'd used the words "maligned and oppressed" in seriousness.

"I've done so many seminars there," Micha said. "I've lauded them as a safe haven and a place for paranormal people to understand themselves and help others understand them. When I think of all the people I've sent there…"

The sunlight blazing on the white walls magnified the color of his eyes, making them some inane interior decorating color like *cerulean*. They were desperate though, dimmed with worry and care, darkened and dulled by sadness.

"Well"—she wasn't good at placating—"a lot of people thought Hitler was doing the right thing until they found out the truth. Didn't make them criminals."

Instead of seeming relieved, Micha blanched, his eyes going wide. She popped her tongue into her cheek and looked around for her smokes. Smooth. *Real* smooth.

Chapter 2

Cindy changed into a brown shirt-dress thing, black leggings, and fuzzy brown boots. The colors looked good with her pale skin and shock of short, choppy brilliant red hair. At least she knew how to dress. She made some tea and proceeded to slosh a shot of Jack Daniels into her cup. June looked at the clock on the wall—just after ten a.m.

"My nerves are shot," Cindy said.

They were sitting in her living room, June in a chair, Cindy on a big cushy stool. The kitchen and living room flowed into each other, small and sparsely decorated and as colorless as the bedroom. June didn't mind. She could handle minimalism.

"I'll take your word for it," June said. "But who puts Jack Daniels in tea? That's not even right."

"I have an excitable condition. It keeps me calm. Trust me, you don't want it to get out of hand."

"Trust her." Micha sat on the couch, legs tucked under him. He looked wide-eyed and tousled and stupidly cute.

June wanted to hug him and tell him she didn't mean to call him a Nazi. And maybe give him an apologetic hand job.

"Let's get down to business." Cindy plunked the bottle of whiskey on the black lacquer coffee table in front of her.

June was tempted to snatch the bottle and take a swig. Without the tea. She hated tea.

"June," Cindy said, "this is Robbie Beecher."

Cindy's friend was a slender sharp-shouldered man, with neck-length dark brown hair. Cute, but not exactly June's cup of…well, straight Jack Daniels. He wore all black—black pants and a black sweater under a black tailored jacket, fashionable, suave. He smiled at June and she couldn't stop herself from flinching. He had a wide mouth and thin lips, making him appear to have too many teeth, like a shark. She and her friend Diego in Sacramento would classify him as a "surprise horse face."

"Robbie's deaf," Cindy said.

"Well that's inconvenient." June sighed.

"It's all right," Robbie spoke up, voice smooth, words well pronounced, not at all like the slow, labored speech of the deaf. "I'm a powerful telepath. I can hear your voice in my head. That's how I can speak so well, since you're wondering. And thank you for the compliment." He smiled a tiny toothless smile.

"Most telepaths are courteous enough not to stick their faces in other people's heads," June said.

"I need to read your mind to hear your voice."

"I wasn't talking when I was thinking about your huge mouth."

Cindy pursed her lips together, and took a drink of her tea.

"Robbie's a member of the Paranormal Alliance, just like Cindy," Micha said. "He's a powerful telekinetic in addition to being a telepath. The Institute has solicited him for years. He's also compiling an enormous collection of pre-research era supernatural documentation."

June blinked a few times. "What?"

"Books and other written works documenting supernatural phenomena throughout history," Robbie clarified. "Back when they still thought vampires turned into bats and gypsies put curses on you. I have quite the collection. The Institute would love to get their hands on it."

She detected smugness.

"How titillating," June said. *How very goddamn boring* she thought at Robbie.

Robbie flicked his gaze to the bottle on the coffee table; it slid smoothly across the surface and stopped at the edge, in front of her.

"Hey!" Cindy lurched forward.

"There," Robbie said. "Since you want some."

June hated telepaths.

A smile tugged at the corner of Micha's mouth, and his eyes glittered as he glanced at June.

"Oh, you won't get any of *that*," Robbie said.

June really, really hated telepaths. "I might not be telekinetic, but I can throw something at you."

"Guys," Cindy said. "Can we stick to the subject? As Micha *said*, Robbie's a member of the Paranormal Alliance, like I am."

"Great," June said. "I'm not clear on what the hell that is, but let's pretend it's going to get my brother out of the Institute, since you keep bringing it up."

Cindy plunked her teacup on the table. "The Paranormal Alliance is the only organized group in Chicago made up entirely of paranormal humans. We hate the Institute." She focused a sour, tight-lipped look on Micha. "And Institute *lovers*."

"They're supposed to be doing some greater good for their people," Micha said, "but they mostly spend their time harassing the Institute. They have a lot of reasons. Some don't trust the Institute. Some don't like that they're uncovering paranormal secrets. Some believe their culture should be kept underground as it's always been, away from the 'normals.'"

June resisted the impulse to point out they had the right idea. He probably had enough salt in his wounds.

"I don't like the Institute," Robbie said. "I've never trusted them. Do you know ninety percent of the Institute's staff is non-paranormal? What does that say?"

Micha opened his mouth, but then snapped it shut.

"So these guys are your friends." June looked between them, brow furrowed. "But you're an activist who supports—supported—the Institute?"

"I believe a good activist understands all sides of a conflict." Micha spoke reasonably. "We may have differing views, but we both want safety and rights for the paranormal. That's all I've ever wanted."

"We've known Micha forever," Cindy said. "And he's right, we both want the same thing when it boils down to it. But"—she leaned forward, eyeing Micha—"we don't allow normals into the Paranormal Alliance."

"Not that I *want* in it," Micha said.

It sounded like a war, but instead of two countries fighting, it was sixty of them, all with their own set of self-righteous ideals. People like Micha wanted equal rights for everyone. And June hated everyone equally.

"So you guys are extremists," she said to Cindy. "Kind of like that SNC group. Just on the flip side."

Cindy gaped. "We are *not* like them!"

She sprang up and charged at June. June braced herself, calculating quickly she could take Cindy out at the knees with a swipe of her leg, maybe, if she acted fast enough. Cindy stopped in front of her, though, and snatched up the bottle.

"We've never used violence to get our point across," Cindy said.

Behind Cindy, Robbie made a shifty glance to the side.

"Go sit down." June, leg lifted defensively, bobbed her foot at Cindy. "Get outta my face."

"Watch your mouth." Cindy pointed a finger at her.

June scowled after her as she retreated, and then narrowed her eyes at Robbie, finding something strange about the way he'd reacted to Cindy's statement. Maybe he wanted to bash a few skulls in. She could get behind that.

"So can you help us or not?" Micha asked. "We have to get June's brother out of the Institute."

Cindy sat back down on her stool and twisted the cap off the whiskey bottle. "Don't worry. We're gonna take you to see someone." She took a drink straight out of the bottle.

"Someone powerful," Robbie said. "His name is Sam Haain."

Micha groaned and slapped a hand to his forehead. "Oh God. Not him."

"Yes, him." Cindy sat up straight with a bright smile.

"Who's Sam Haain?" June asked.

Micha lowered his hand. "He's the leader of the Paranormal Alliance. If you want to know why his members are so…adamant, it's because their dogma and paranoia trickles down from the top. I don't know if Sam Haain is his real name. Maybe his mother had a terrible sense of humor. But he certainly enjoys being the ominous specter of the disenfranchised and mistreated."

June didn't know why, but the way Micha talked heated her panties up. Normally, if someone were in her tattoo shop spouting crap like that, she would tattoo "loser" across his forehead and shove him out the door. Maybe having a hot body to distract from the piousness made all the difference.

She reminded herself today was Micha's wife's funeral and she needed to be respectful.

"Sam is a very effectual man," Cindy said, overloud. "Are you calling us zealots?"

"The last thing I want to do right now is talk to Sam Haain." Micha deftly sidestepped the question. "There's got to be another way."

"You name it." Cindy shrugged.

"Sam is our best bet right now, Micha," Robbie said. "We had to do a lot of groveling to get him to agree to this meeting."

"Now, I don't buy that at all." Micha snorted. "Sam Haain is always looking for an opportunity to be affronted."

"I think he handles the bullshit in this city quite gracefully," Cindy said. "He's had to deal with people hating and fearing us ever since the

Institute opened, and he, unlike you, never bought into their 'benevolence.' I admire his poise and rationale."

"Two constructs I've never associated with Sam Haain," Micha said, "but if you say so."

"Sam has all kinds of connections," Robbie explained. "With city officials, the media, independent researchers… Not all paranormal scientists work for or believe in the Institute."

June actually knew this, but she figured Robbie could dig around in her brain like a gopher and pillage her childhood memories. The Institute was a big scary entity, but the world had always been full of scientists studying the paranormal who didn't need the government to tell them to go ahead. Chicago just decided to make everything official.

"Great." June lifted her hands. "So this guy is going to, what? Bust into the Institute with guns blazing? Help me get Jason out of there?"

"I hope not," Micha muttered.

"You have to speak to him," Robbie said. "This afternoon, Navy Pier. He won't meet anywhere else."

"I want to go, too." Micha sat forward. "Much as Sam Haain rankles me, I want to hear what he has to say."

"You can't go out in public." Cindy gasped, wide-eyed. "I know you don't remember, but they killed your wife, Micha. That makes you next on their list. I didn't even think you should have gone out last night, and that was sneaking around, not out in public."

"They expect me to be hiding. They won't look for me in a public place. Besides, today is my wife's funeral, right? So they'll probably be watching for me there."

"He's got a point," June said.

Cindy slammed her cup down on the table. "All right then." She got to her feet. "We'll just have a parade right down Michigan Avenue."

"Awesome." June got up. "I'll twirl a baton."

* * * *

Chicago was a living metropolis, a brilliantly modern and majestically primeval creature breathing and teeming and issuing forth a steady cacophony of human noise. Under the stark winter light, the buildings loomed as monoliths, an overwhelming collection of glittering glass, gleaming steel, and earthy stone. At street level, the world was narrow and claustrophobic, life chugging along under the shadows of the great towers like thick blood pulsing through deep, dark veins.

It was beautiful and horrible at the same time. Like most great monsters.

"Where's Sears Tower?" June craned her neck, trying to see out the moon roof of Cindy's car. She had seen the skyline from the freeway, the tallest building in the country rising like an obsidian deity amongst a gray court.

"You can't see it from Michigan Avenue." Micha sat next to her in the backseat. "And it's Willis Tower now."

"What?"

"Willis Group Holdings moved into it. It's called Willis Tower now."

"Are you serious? It's an American icon."

"They renamed Comiskey Park 'U.S. Cellular Field.'" Micha shrugged. "Corporations buy things; they change the names. If you think you're shocked and outraged, you should hear the people who live here."

"Killing traditions," June said. "Your city is pretty good at that."

"What's that supposed to mean?"

"I don't know. Maybe you should ask all the pissed off paranormal people."

Robbie, sitting in the front passenger seat, turned his head and shot a close-lipped smile at her. June mouthed *turn around*. He did.

"Not that I'll get to go up it," June said, "but are you outside on top of the *Willis Tower*?"

"No." Cindy snorted. "It's glassed in."

"So no spitting over the edge," June said.

"It would never reach the ground from that high up." Cindy rolled her eyes in the mirror.

"And it would be so windy up there you wouldn't be able to stand," Robbie added.

"Quit bringing me down. What's next? You're gonna tell me there's no God?"

They crept along slowly, the streets choked with cars and the sidewalks alive with pedestrians even in the intense, blustery cold. They passed over a wide stone bridge, and June sat up. The water beneath the bridge was murky green and choked with a mosaic of ice chunks.

"Is water supposed to be that color?" she asked.

Micha sat up as well. "They dye it even greener for St. Patrick's Day."

"Sounds totally safe."

"It is safe. The original stuff they used was flourescein, but it was harmful to the organisms in the river, so they changed it."

"I bet it's still flourescein." She relaxed against the seat. "When three-eyed fish start washing up on the banks, you'll know."

"Mmm, three-eyed fish." Micha tilted his head and gave her a crooked smile. "Extra eyeballs means extra delicious."

June was titillated—yes, titillated—to be called out on her sarcasm.

"Just imagine," Robbie spoke up. "Once, none of this was here. It was just a peaceful river flowing through the wilderness. No people, no buildings, no cars, no pollution. You couldn't look at it and imagine that someday civilization would rise up on its decimated banks and all this terrible progress would stand where once there were trees and hills."

Everyone stared at him, even Cindy.

"I wish we'd brought the Jack Daniels with us." June envisioned smashing the bottle over Robbie's head.

Robbie looked over his shoulder at her.

"What's Sacramento like?" Micha asked.

June shrugged. "Smaller. Brighter. More laid back."

"Is there a prevalent paranormal community there?"

"Not really. It's not as out in the open as it is here."

"Do they have organizations for paranormal people?"

"I don't get into that stuff." The buildings crawled past. "Ending up here is a reminder why."

"I read in the *Tribune*," Micha said, "you were discovered by an entertainment reporter."

She snorted. "Yeah. This girl from a local rag came into my shop to get some work done. I've known her for a long time, did most of her ink. She was talking about supernatural stuff, and I let it slip, told her about Jason and me. I thought I could trust her. Then she went and wrote a frickin' article about it." She fidgeted, looking down at her fingers. "Jason was pissed. Hell, I was pissed. He's an actor, and he thought if it got out it would hurt his career, thought people would assume he's charming his way into roles. Not that he would ever do that."

"If he did, he'd have an Oscar by now," Micha said. "A million of them."

"Still, I didn't think anyone read that stupid paper, certainly not people in Chicago."

"The Institute is vigilant," Micha said. "They keep a sharp eye out for the smallest things. The paranormal is still an underground community for many reasons, so they have to canvas far and wide. And your power is uncommon, being an aural captivator, a Siren." He scoffed. "'Siren' is such a misleading term, though. Sirens are mythological creatures. Hypnotic voice phenomenon isn't gender specific, either."

"Thank you, Mr. Encyclopedia. I don't give a damn. I should have kept my mouth shut. That's what I get for trusting people. I don't understand why you like being so involved in it."

"My family had a lot of paranormal friends when I was growing up. Before it was recognized scientifically. Back then it was all about getting people to accept it as a reality. People like my mother campaigned for her friends to get recognition. Now I'm trying to convince people not to hurt them."

"So you inherited a legacy."

"And my family is paranormal." He waved this off as if it were a lesser reason. "My sisters both have paranormal abilities. So does one of my aunts. Marked telepathy and mild telekinesis, but Emily, my oldest sister, is also a pyrokinetic."

"A pyrokinetic? She sets things on fire with her mind? Like that Drew Barrymore movie?"

Micha's voice darkened. "It's not *exactly* like that. She can make certain substances heat up. If they're flammable, yes, they can catch on fire. It's not easy to do, though."

"So you're the odd one out. In this case, the white sheep of the family."

"It bothered me when I was younger. I guess I felt left out. But not many people in this city *want* to be paranormal."

June turned her attention back out her window. A building with a diamond-shaped roof loomed over them, and she craned her neck. "Well, go ahead and feel like you're doing something noble. Me, I don't shove it in everyone's face. It's my damn business."

"It's hard, isn't it?" Cindy said. "I mean, you're persecuted on two fronts. Society is so goddamn prejudiced, it hurts. Why can't people just be who they are, be the way they were made?"

June narrowed her eyes. "Two fronts?"

"I mean, your preference. You're still harassed for that, I'm sure."

"My what?"

Robbie looked at Cindy, frowning. "She's not a lesbian, Cindy."

Cindy glanced in the mirror at June, brow furrowed. "You're not?"

June goggled at her. "No!"

"I—you were checking out my rack, though. And the leather, and all the tattoos, I thought…"

"Oh my God," June said.

Micha started snickering. June scowled at him. He snickered more. Robbie rubbed the bridge of his nose.

"I have some wonderful lesbian friends," June said. "But no, just because I have tattoos doesn't mean I don't like cocks. Straight women can have tattoos, you know. And I happen to like leather. It's sexy."

Cindy shrugged and mumbled, "Sorry."

An awkward silence fell, though Micha had his lips pressed in a tight line, rubbing his jaw.

June looked back out the window. She narrowed her eyes. "Is that Millennium Park?"

"Yes." Micha's voice was tight with stifled laughter.

Jason had been looking forward to visiting Millennium Park. He loved sculpture. She could see him sitting on the plane, book open in his lap, rattling on about his favorite sculptors. He thought she didn't listen, but she did. Anish Kapoor's *Cloud Gate* in Chicago. His *Sky Mirrors* were in front of Nottingham Playhouse and Rockefeller Center. His piece *Taratantara* stood outside the Baltic flour mills. She could take a test on Jason's favorite sculptors and pass with flying colors.

She hoped she'd still get a chance to.

When they reached Navy Pier, the place looked like a carnival, complete with a Ferris wheel and the entrance boasting a huge lit-up sign akin to a funhouse. She sensed not much fun would go down, despite appearances. Cindy parked the car on the street in front and swiveled around.

"Robbie will stay here with the car. I'll come with you to meet him."

"Good idea," June said. "You know where he is, after all. Unless we're gonna just wander around like idiots."

"I don't, actually. Sam doesn't like to be predictable. But don't worry. We'll find him." Cindy paused. "I'm really sorry about—"

"It's cool." June held a hand up and quirked the corner of her mouth. "You do have a great rack."

They had to walk through what looked like a shopping mall to get to the outer part of the pier—a broad concrete walkway empty of people, the steady wind off the lake making the January cold *fucking* cold. The wind cut through June's T-shirt like a thousand evil icy razor blades and forced her to zip up her jacket. The immense plane of bleak and choppy water was filled with big ice chunks like the ones she'd seen in the river. Farther out, solid sheets spread like snowy islands. The city stood across the water, thrust in a jagged line against the stark sky.

"First time I've seen any of the Great Lakes." June's teeth chattered.

"Really?" Cindy asked. "I've never seen the ocean."

"I guess neither of us is a world traveler, huh?"

Micha huddled into his coat. "Let's walk down to the end."

June kept a cautious eye out as they started down the pier. They saw no one else, as all other people in the city were smart enough not to be walking next to the lake in freezing temperatures.

"So what do you do when you're not fighting the good fight?" June asked Micha, trying to keep her mind off the fact her face had already gone numb. They'd been acquainted nearly a week, but with fearing for their lives and June grievously worried about her brother and spending every waking minute trying to figure out a way to rescue him, they hadn't made much small talk. She knew little about Micha beyond him being altruistic and sexy.

"I'm an administrator at the College of Paranormal Science. That's where the Institute gets most its staff. I run a couple non-profit organizations too. Keeps me pretty busy. In fact, things are probably falling apart without me right now."

"And you?" she asked Cindy to be polite.

"Bartender," she grunted from inside her coat. "Some of us can't be constant heroes."

"Bartenders have always been my heroes," June said.

They passed by the closed patios of restaurants, kiosks shut down for the season, moored boats, and a glass building called the Shakespeare Theatre. They were walking briskly to keep from freezing to death. After what seemed like a terrifically long, ridiculously cold time, they reached a round ochre building with a huge dome and two towers rising on either side.

Beyond was the end of the pier, the area deserted save for two people. They stood against the stone railing at the end, facing the water.

"Is that—" Micha slowed.

"It's either who we're looking for or a star-crossed couple contemplating suicide," June said. "No other reason to be hanging out here in East Frozen Hell."

Flags on a series of flagpoles popped in the wind. The place felt eerie and empty, thrust out into the void of frozen water. In the distance, a lighthouse loomed, caught in the ice.

"It's him." Cindy picked up the pace.

June flexed her stiff fingers inside her jacket pockets. She couldn't feel her feet, even in her expensive weather-resistant leather boots. She needed to hear some good news, the promise someone could help. One of the figures was a man—tall, broad-shouldered, wearing a black coat, and the other one was short and tiny, a woman dressed all in white.

The couple turned in unison as they approached.

Chapter 3

"Sam?" Cindy said.

The man—Sam Haain, apparently—had a square jaw, a heavy menacing brow, straight black hair past his shoulders, and dark eyes. He was tanned and appeared perhaps not entirely Caucasian. He wore a black pea coat and a maroon scarf. The woman was narrow-faced and pale and had short platinum blond hair. She was wrapped in a fuzzy white coat and looked like a little snowball. She seemed a gentle light next to the man's brooding darkness.

The sight of them was unaccountably unnerving—two lonely, strange figures pressed against the backdrop of the gray, blank world around them.

"Finally." Sam gave an exaggerated shiver. "I'm freezing my cock off out here."

June didn't detect an accent, but he sounded overfull of testosterone.

"We didn't have to meet here, you know," Cindy said. "This is June Coffin, Sam. And that's Micha Bellevue."

"The activist." Sam gave Micha a once-over, thick lips pulled in a grimace. He then jerked his head toward the little white girl. "My bodyguard," he said, without a hint of irony. "Muse Sagan."

Muse stared at June with her wide silvery eyes, irises washed out like the winter sky. She had a facial tick, the corner of her mouth jerking.

"She's good." Muse nodded. Her voice was breathy and scratchy.

"What?" June asked, a little creeped out.

"She's a telepath," Cindy said. "We had Robbie check her out already, Sam. I wouldn't have brought her here without having her scanned first."

June turned on Cindy. "You—"

"We had to make sure your story was legit!"

Sam focused on June, his eyes hard and appraising. "Welcome to Hell, Siren. Aural captivator, whatever it is the normals call you."

"My name is June."

"I know what your name is." He stepped forward. "June Coffin. Is that your real name?"

She clenched her jaw. She got tired of people's reactions to her name.

"Yes, it's my real name. My brother is the actor. Your 'bodyguard' should have already known that."

"Your brother. Cindy tells me he's in the Institute's slimy grip."

"He is."

"What's going on at the Institute is incredibly complex, Siren. You've gotten yourself mixed up in a much bigger and more convoluted game than you could ever imagine."

"I don't give a damn. My brother is being held prisoner there. I want to know how to get him out. Whatever else is going on isn't my problem."

"But it is mine." Sam drew his hands from his coat pockets. They were swaddled in thick, knitted gloves, the same color as his scarf.

June wanted to steal them.

"Last I heard, you were at the Institute with your brother. Yet here you are." Sam turned his attention to Micha. "And here *you* are, though I heard you disappeared."

"I busted out four days ago," June said. "Unfortunately, Jason was caught trying to escape with me."

"And they…killed my wife," Micha said. "That's what I'm told, anyway."

Muse cleared her throat, a disgustingly wet, unladylike sound. The corner of her mouth still twitched.

"His mind is all messed up." Muse sounded like an eighty-year-old woman who had been smoking two packs a day for fifty years. "What happened to you?" she demanded of Micha.

"I happened to him," June said.

Muse flashed her gaze to June.

"I would love to see the Institute blown up," Sam said. "I would even provide the dynamite. I've never let them put their filthy hands on me. Why would you let them touch you or your brother? Maybe you got what you deserved, Siren."

"June." She gritted her teeth. "And a lot of persuasion and a boatload of money was involved. I didn't come here to justify anything to you. I need to get my brother out of the Institute, and they said you could help."

"Oh, really? Because I can't."

"What do you mean?"

"Much as I would like to rip the Institute apart piece by little piece, I don't have any power over them. At least not right now. I certainly can't just walk in their doors and get him out for you."

"What are we doing here then?" She snarled at Cindy. "Why did you say he could help?"

"Sam," Cindy pleaded. "I know you might not be able to do anything directly, but maybe you know someone who can. Surely if you agreed to this meeting you had something in mind."

"Do you know how many sad-eyed, beleaguered fools come begging for my help per day?" Sam asked. "Why should I help this yapping little pipsqueak? She got herself in this mess."

June lost her composure. "I will kick your ass, I swear to God. All the shit I've been through the past few days, I don't need anyone else's bullshit, certainly not some swaggering asshole I don't even know! I will stab you in the face if you say one more—"

Muse cleared her throat. "She doesn't have a knife, Sam."

"You." June pointed at her. "You, I will pick up and throw over that railing."

Sam grabbed June's finger with his gloved hand, looking her in the eye. He was quite a bit taller than she, but then, everyone was. He leaned in close, and she caught a faint whiff of understated musky cologne on the cold wind.

"You passed the first test." Sam let go of her finger.

June stared at him.

"I don't help those who can't help themselves," he said. "Come to my door whimpering and crying, I will kick you like a stray dog. Come ready to fight, we can do business."

June closed her eyes for a moment and then opened them. "Great. Now can we—"

"Do you know what this is?" Sam flung his arms out. "All of this?"

He spun in a circle, scarf dangling, his hair moving in the wind. Muse watched him placidly. Cindy watched him too, hands clasped and eyes wide.

"Uh," June said.

Sam turned back to them, arms still extended. "Do. You. Know. What. This. Is?"

June looked around, figuring she had to either entertain the madman or remain on the pier forever, encased in a block of ice. "A lake?"

"It's my world." Sam darted forward and got right in her face.

June took a step back, eyes wide.

"This is…" Sam turned slowly to Micha. "Our world. It belongs to the paranormal, it always has, and it always will."

Micha clenched his jaw.

"The Paranormal Alliance will own this city when the Institute is finally in ashes." Sam lowered his arms. "I will gladly do anything to help undermine them and lead them to their inevitable fiery end. So if you aren't a blithering child, if you're willing to fight the fight, then yes, I will help you, but"—he held up a finger—"there will be a price. You will owe me something."

June shifted. "I—they took my wallet at the Institute. But when I get back to California…"

Sam chuckled and pushed a gloved hand through his hair, which was healthy-looking and thick. He was handsome; she finally had the mindset to notice.

"I don't want money," Sam said. "I don't need money."

"What do you want, then?"

"I'll tell you, when the time comes. You have more tests to pass."

June scowled. "I'm not jumping through any hoops for you."

"Oh yes, you are." He clapped his gloved hands together. "We need to leave here. Go somewhere warmer. And less public."

"We could have been somewhere warmer and less public to begin with." June huffed, jerking her jacket around her.

"He needed to be able to escape." Micha turned around next to her shoulder and sang softly, "Para-noia."

June's suspicion had been growing since Sam first spoke. The dude was insane. Yet her only hope currently rested on him.

Sam demanded they ferry him in Cindy's car, though he wouldn't say where they were going. Muse sat in the front seat between Cindy and Robbie and Sam in the back, Micha in the middle. Micha's knee rested against June's leg. He smelled like the frigid air of the pier, and his hair was tousled from the wind. Micha caught her eye and smiled, coyly. She shifted and tugged her jacket across her body. They were all silent as Cindy drove down Michigan Avenue per Sam's instructions.

"Here." Sam pointed.

Cindy pulled the car up in front of one of the many towering buildings on the street and slid into a valet area.

"We're already taking a huge risk being out like this," Cindy said. "Can't we go back to my place?"

"We'll be safe here," Sam said. "This is our territory, and you know the rules."

June didn't know the rules, but she figured they might be in Sam's head anyway, for some game he played with himself.

"Muse." Sam poked her shoulder. "I want you and Robbie to take the car and go on patrol. Make sure no one's been watching us. Don't come back until I call you."

"This is my car!" Cindy protested.

"You're a member of this organization," Sam said. "That means this is my car."

"The Communist manifesto of the Paranormal Alliance," Micha muttered under his breath.

June opened the door. Sam, Micha, and June got out. Cindy got out as well, practically snarling, and Robbie got out and went around the car to the driver's side. The valet attendants sprang forward but withdrew when Sam raised a hand.

June looked up. The building had a glass façade that reflected the sky. Despite the building's height, a skyscraper and an ebony obelisk nearby dwarfed the structure. In Chicago, no matter how impressive something appeared, something else was right next door to one-up it like a competitive asshole sibling.

She turned. Muse was inside the car and Robbie outside the driver's side window, the two exchanging a round of sign language. Sam caught June's eye.

"Their powers cancel each other out. He can't read her mind."

"Isn't she lucky?"

"You know, you can build defenses against telepaths. I only allow them to see as much as I want of my own mind. But it takes discipline and vigilance."

"I'll have to fit some lessons into my busy schedule."

The entryway of the building glowed. A red rug lay out to guide them to a set of doors. A doorman opened one with a flourish.

"Welcome back, Mr. Haain."

"Harry." Sam nodded.

Inside, they faced a bank of elevators.

"We're going to the twelfth floor," Sam said. "To the lobby, and then up to a room I have here. Beyond these doors, you are guaranteed safety at all times." He eyed Micha. "Even you."

"The lobby's on the twelfth floor?" June asked. "You know it's a fancy hotel when you have to go up to get in."

The elevator sported a marble floor and a chandelier, the light reflected all around in mirrored walls. They could pay for the bulbs by selling sunglasses to passengers before they got on. The operator largely ignored their presence, aside for some small talk with Sam.

The ridiculous elevator proved only a taste, as the lobby took first prize for most overblown room of the century—more extravagant chandeliers, furniture suited for royalty, and gleaming tile floors. A single lamp probably cost more than every inch of ink on June's body. She expected to see the Queen lounging in one of the chairs, possibly being fed grapes.

A fountain rose in the middle of the room, with an elegant sculpture of several great bronze birds taking flight above the gushing water.

"Nice place," Micha murmured.

They strode across the lobby toward another bank of elevators.

"I should bring Rose here for our anniversary," he said.

June stopped in her tracks. "What?"

Micha nearly fell over her. The rest of them stopped and June gaped at Micha.

"You just mentioned Rose," Cindy said.

"I did?"

"Is your memory coming back?" June panicked. This wasn't a good time for Micha to remember his dead wife and proceed into a meltdown.

"I don't—" Micha scratched at his scalp. "I don't even know what I just said. What…was it?"

"You said you should bring Rose here for your anniversary," Cindy said.

"Oh." Micha furrowed his brow. "I thought you said she was dead?"

"Hello!" Sam called out, drawing their attention. He stood a few feet away and gestured dramatically toward the elevators.

In the second elevator, as opulent as the first, June stole furtive glances at Micha. He was frowning, brows drawn down, staring at the floor. How would he react when he realized he would have no more anniversaries? Her guilt warred with the urge to hold and comfort him, to dry his inevitable tears and provide all the sex he would otherwise be deprived of with his wife gone.

I really am a crass bitch. She scowled at her reflection in the mirrored wall.

After exiting the elevator, Sam led them down a hallway to a door at the end and unlocked it with a key card. The room was as overstated as the rest of the hotel.

Tiffany lamps, jewel-toned sofas, and cream-colored carpet filled the space, the décor bright, sophisticated, and chic. A wall of windows looked out on a spectacular view of the lake, the sky monochrome and thick with clouds above the dark water.

"Holy shit," Cindy said. "Sam, is this what you've been doing with all the fundraising money?"

Sam pulled off his scarf. "Sit your ass down. I'll have some food sent up." He pointed to the sofas.

The three sat down, June and Micha on one, Cindy on another across from them. June swiveled.

"Fancy digs here," June remarked. "Oh look, there's even a bar."

Sam took his coat and gloves off and tossed them in a chair. June arched an eyebrow, unable to stop herself.

Sam wore a dark green V-neck sweater and a pair of jeans, both formfitting, on a form worth showing off. He was broad and muscled and had nice hips and long legs. She was torn. She liked tall, light-haired, blue-eyed, goofy men. Oh, to hell with that. She liked men. And lately, she'd been suffering from a distinct lack of them in her life. Maybe that was why she was making such poor decisions.

"I know you have terribly important things to talk about, June," Sam said. "But first we need to understand each other. That's why I brought you here, so we can talk and understand. But first, what do you like to drink?"

June wanted a beer.

Her choice arrived in a dark green bottle, a goblet with a gold rim provided to drink it from. Sam also ordered coffee and tea. June had no qualms about drinking from the fancy glass while they sipped from their little teacups. Cindy had a whiskey on the rocks. June appreciated a woman who actively, unabashedly cultivated her alcoholism, grating as Cindy could otherwise be.

Sam also ordered an array of snack food, and June was glad to partake, as she hadn't eaten anything since Cindy ordered Chinese takeout the night before. She had to be careful what she put in her mouth, though. She had an assortment of annoying and ever-growing food allergies. Not the kind trendy people used to annoy waiters in restaurants, real ones that could be debilitating and miserable. She knew which beers were gluten-free, too.

"You have a ridiculous amount of tattoos." Sam sat down across from her, on the sofa with Cindy.

June had taken off her jacket and was wearing a short-sleeved scoop neck T-shirt. She extended her arms, like she had for Micha, goblet clutched in her left hand. Myriad artwork curled around her biceps and flowed down her forearms. The right arm held more.

"Chaos on my right. I did a lot of them myself. I'm ambidextrous, but I'm better with my left hand."

She hadn't done all of them herself. The one on the underside of her right arm, a black-and-white portrait of a little girl, had been done by her friend and the co-owner of her shop, Diego.

Cindy smirked. "Apparently some people think having a bunch of tattoos makes you a lesbian, so I hear."

June picked up the cap from her beer bottle and threw it at Cindy. She flinched out of the way and chuckled as it just missed her head.

Sam sat his cup on the table beside him and gazed at June. She took a drink from her goblet.

"Tell me what happened at the Institute," Sam said.

June lowered the goblet. "Do you mind if I smoke?"

"It's a non-smoking room."

"That's not what I asked." The pesky smoke detector was on the other side of the room, above the wet bar. Far enough. She delved into the pocket of her jacket that she'd draped over the arm of the sofa.

"By all means," Sam said, "do whatever the hell you want."

"Thanks."

She lit up and took a long, delicious drag. She blew the smoke out the corner of her mouth, away from Micha. She needed something to brace her nerves before she hashed over the story again. She'd had to tell the whole sordid tale to Cindy the night they met.

"When we first got to the Institute, we were in a pretty bad mood." June grabbed her empty bottle. "I'd let our secret slip. Jason was pissed, and I was pretty pissed off myself. But Jason always wanted to visit Chicago, so he was trying to make the best of it. And they were really cool to us, at first. Gave us a nice room, TV, all that crap, even if it was a bit like a hospital. Good food, even. They were nice enough to have special stuff made up for me since I'm allergic to half the food on the planet."

Micha raised his eyebrows. "Food allergies?"

"Yeah, it's kinda ridiculous. I have to watch myself. I don't make a huge deal out of it, though. I can usually find something. And you know, it makes me healthier. I can't eat a lot of junk."

"But you smoke like a chimney," Cindy said. "Very conscious of your health."

June held up the cigarette perched between her index and middle fingers. "I'm not allergic to cigarettes."

Sam continued staring at June like he intended to use his gaze to burn a hole through her chest.

"Anyway, it was all stuff we expected at first. They asked us questions, took our history, gave us a psychological evaluation. They had a field day with me, let me tell you."

From the corner of her eye, she saw Micha grin.

"We were allowed to roam around. Couldn't leave the building, they said for security reasons, but we were allowed to go anywhere not restricted. That's how I met him." June jerked her head toward Micha. "I saw him giving a lecture in a conference room, thought it was interesting, so I waited around and said hello to him after." She left out the fact Micha's body had been the only thing she found "interesting."

"His wife was there, and he introduced us. That's how I knew her, later." She paused. Here, the story took a dark turn.

"They started doing tests. Recording our voices, MRIs, x-rays. Then they wanted blood samples, and for some reason—I don't know, it was the way they were acting—that put a red flag up for me. I asked them what the hell they wanted our blood for, but they wouldn't give me a straight answer. So of course that just made me ask more questions. And the more questions I asked, the more uncomfortable they got."

Sam leaned forward, placed his elbows on his knees, and clasped his hands under his chin.

"Then Jason got upset. He wouldn't do any more recordings. He's got issues about using his power." She paused again. "They got hostile and sequestered him in our room and took all our shit—our clothes, our wallets, our cell phones. I only had my jacket because I was outside smoking when it all went down. When I came back, they told me to get in the room with him. I knew something was going down and we were in trouble, so I started planning a way to get out."

"What did you do?" Sam asked.

"They came in to give us food after a while, two guys. They were wearing these special noise canceling headphones; they'd been using them every time they did a test on us." She snorted. "Didn't stop the one from going down like a load of bricks when Jason punched him. The other one just got out of the way. We ran out of there, got in an elevator. I didn't know where to go, the elevator didn't go all the way to the ground, so I just hit the lowest floor."

She tucked the bottle in her lap. The cigarette burned away in her hand.

"When the doors opened, she was standing there, his wife, Rose. She must have been getting ready to go home or something. I didn't know if she would help us. I told her they were chasing us, and she got this look on her face, like…she knew. Like she'd been waiting for something to happen."

Micha furrowed his brow.

"She said 'come on.' We got in this other elevator. It went down to a parking garage."

"The vampire research floor," Sam said. "It has access to an underground parking garage, so the vampires don't have to expose themselves to sunlight. Trust me. I've got more blueprints of that place than the people who built it."

"When we got down there, it was too late," June said. "These security guards popped up out of nowhere." She stared down at the glowing end of her cigarette emitting a slow ribbon of smoke. "They took a shot, just like that. Shooting at us like if we got out it would be the end of the world. They didn't even try to subdue us. I felt the heat off the bullet. Went right past me and into her."

She saw Rose's face again—her wide, shocked eyes, her dark red mouth opening in a scream. Her blood splattering the trunk of the car behind her.

"They grabbed Jason, but I ran. I should have stopped. But I ran instead. I don't know how I got away, just hiding behind cars until I found a way out."

Micha still looked confused.

"When I calmed down enough to think, I went through my pockets. All I had was my smokes and Micha's card. He'd given it to me when I talked to him. So I hustled some change and called him from a pay phone. I'd just watched his wife die, and he was the only person I could call." She took a long drag. She blew the smoke out slowly.

"Go on," Sam said.

"I hid until he picked me up. I was out of my skull. I was sure they'd killed Jason. I didn't know what to do. I needed Micha to help me, so I made a bad decision. Not the first one that night."

"You enchanted him." Sam sat up straight.

She nodded. "I made him forget he was married, in case someone called him while we were together. I just wanted him to get me somewhere safe, then I was gonna take it off him. But I couldn't. It was stuck."

"You were emotional when you did it," Sam said. "That gives it power."

She pushed the stub of her cigarette into the bottle, and it sizzled faintly as it hit the bottom.

"Micha took me to her place." She indicated Cindy. "She hid me out. Us. Since Micha has a big gaping hole in his memory concerning his wife, who was just murdered, we thought things might be a little difficult for him."

"I don't remember this woman they're telling me is my wife." Micha's voice was odd, flat yet tremulous. "I feel like I'm going mad. There's pictures of her in all the papers. Hell, there's pictures of her in my phone. But I don't remember being with her. How can I not remember my own wife?"

The desperate edge in his voice made June's stomach lurch.

"It'll wear off," Cindy said. "Maybe it's best you don't know right now. It's saving you from a lot of despair, so you can save your own life."

"I feel like someone is playing a big joke on me." Micha looked down at his hands. "I can remember everything else—my work, my life, my family. There's just these big empty spots where I know things used to fit, and I suppose that's where she goes, but she's a stranger to me."

June swallowed thickly. "Micha, I'm sorry…"

Sam clapped his hands together, cutting through the moment. "Stop it. We have no time for bullshit and pity. Regret is a useless emotion." He focused on June. "Your power is 'stupid strong,' as the kids say."

"I don't think the kids say that." She set her bottle aside.

"Whatever the hell they say, you have an impressive amount of whatever it is you have. That's why the Institute wants to stick a huge scientific dildo up you."

June twisted her lips.

"They took one look at your eyes," Sam said, "and they knew."

"My eyes? What about my eyes?"

"They're very green," Cindy said.

"I thought you were wearing contacts the first time I met you," Micha said.

"I know they're really green. I've had them my entire life."

"Your eyes are connected to your brain," Sam said. "The stronger your power, the more your eyes are affected." He widened his own at her, dark and gleaming. "How powerful are you? Aural captivators are rare, but not undocumented. I've heard about the Siren Song."

"That's a myth," she said sharply.

"What's a Siren Song?" Cindy asked.

"A strong enough aural captivator," Sam said, "can harm a person with their voice. Maybe even kill them. So they say."

"Are you going to help me or not?" June sat forward. "Or are we just gonna talk shit all day? If you can't do anything for me, tell me, so I can find someone who can."

"Yes, I'm going to help you. But you have to give me a little time. Right now, go get some air and calm down. I need to make some phone calls."

The room had a balcony. She took Sam's advice and went out for another cigarette. Towers loomed around her like watchful giants, the world buzzing around their bases far below. The air ripped and pulled at her hair and clothes.

After a few minutes, Micha stepped out, not wearing a coat. He walked to the railing where she stood. June finished her cigarette and flicked the butt out into the wind.

"I'm not angry at you," Micha said. "I know you didn't mean to hurt me."

"Yeah, and how do you know that? You don't know me."

"I think you wouldn't look at me the way you do if you didn't feel some remorse."

She didn't respond.

Micha jerked his chin outward. "What do you think of it? Chicago?"

She bent over and rested her arms on the railing.

"Doesn't matter what I think of it. Jason, he'd be acting like a stupid tourist right now. It's not like L.A., where he lives. For one, you don't have as many pretentious douche bags walking around."

Micha chuckled. "You just haven't been to the right places yet." He shifted toward her. "This is a true metropolis. Something to behold. Intimidating sometimes, but majestic. A testament to what humans can create. It's an entity, you know. We as entities create other entities. That's what humans do."

"You're not from here, are you? No one talks about where they live like that."

"I am, actually. I guess I'm just not jaded."

June almost said "you will be," but Micha didn't need any more negativity.

"So your brother is an actor in L.A.?" Micha said. "You and I haven't really talked much, have we?"

"It's not been a very good time for socializing. And yes, he is. He does more grunt work at studios than acting right now, but he's working on it." *Was* working on it? She pushed the terrible thought away.

"Has he been in any movies?"

"He's done some extra work. A few commercials. Had a small part in a TV pilot, but it never got picked up."

"You know, it's okay that you ran."

She squinted against the wind. Micha's hair fluttered over his forehead, his own eyes squinted as well.

"Tell my brother that."

"Out here, on the run, you still have a chance to save him. In there, if you'd let them catch you? You'd *both* be screwed."

Her hands trembled from the cold. Or emotion. Or both.

"Right now both our lives are messed up," Micha said. "But we have to figure out the right thing to do before more people get hurt. Before anyone else goes down because of this."

Putting the needs of others first. She being selfish as she was, she didn't know if she could ever tolerate someone like that.

"You're a good man, Micha."

"You don't know that. You don't know me."

The air whistled around the balcony and pushed under her shirt like a solid icy mass.

"Why don't we go back inside?" Micha motioned to the door. "It's cold out here."

She stood up and turned away from the railing. "All right."

Back inside, Cindy had a fresh glass of whiskey. Sam leaned on the back of the sofa he'd been sitting on, cell phone to his ear, hip jutted out. June walked around him and discreetly checked him out, or so she thought.

"I saw that," Sam murmured.

She shrugged and flopped down in her spot next to Micha on the other sofa.

Sam lowered the phone and pressed it against his shoulder. "June, who was the lead researcher on your study?"

She struggled to recall. "John…McKormic? I think. Short guy, balding. Obnoxious."

"Do you know him?" Sam asked Micha.

"I know who he is," Micha said. "I've talked to him at fundraisers. He's a brilliant man, created more efficient research techniques, made them more streamlined and specific."

"So jacking my blood was his idea." June scowled.

Sam placed the phone back to his ear. "John McKormic? Do you know him?" A pause as he listened. "Yes. Send someone to have a chat with him, someone who can get some information. Send a witch if you have to."

Cindy jerked her head around.

"Find out if the other Coffin twin is alive," Sam said. "Call me back at this number."

Sam took the phone from his ear and clicked off. "So you know this guy, Micha? This researcher?"

"We're not best friends or anything, but he knows me. I'm sure he knew my…wife, too, if she worked at the Institute."

"Well then, we need to make sure he doesn't see you, since he'll recognize you. You're staying here at the hotel until further notice, with June."

"We're staying here?" June asked.

"You want my help, you get my protection. Package deal."

"So benevolent," June said. "We could just go in and shoot up the place, too. Cindy would love to help with that, I'm sure."

She shot June a glare.

"Completely realistic," Sam replied. "You'll keep your ass here until otherwise told not to."

June saluted him. "Aye aye, Captain."

"Good, you passed your second test. We're getting somewhere."

"What was the second test?" June asked.

"Doing what I tell you to, without question. Cute *and* smart. Cindy, I'm having Robbie come pick you up."

"I am *not* cute," June said.

Chapter 4

A huge flat screen TV hung on the wall between the two sofas; June sprawled on one, Micha the other. They were watching a news program. She couldn't pay attention though. Everything about her current situation bothered her—lying down, watching TV, cozy and safe while somewhere, in the depths of the foreign city surrounding her, her brother languished as a prisoner. If he still lived at all.

Sam's bodyguard, Muse, had returned about an hour before, and she and Sam left together, Sam declaring he had "important business" to take care of. He gave them strict instructions not to leave the room in his absence. June had no intention of wandering around the hotel showing off a lack of common sense or taking a stroll down Michigan Avenue with a big target on her back.

"Does Sam live in this hotel or something?" June asked.

Micha wasn't watching TV, either. He was stretched out, shoes off, arm propped on the back of the sofa. "I don't know." He sounded distracted and distant. "I don't know a lot about Sam. Just that he's gregarious. I mostly try to avoid him. I've only actually met him once before today."

"Why doesn't he like you?"

"Because I'm a normal. He doesn't think I should be sticking my nose in paranormal affairs."

"But you help paranormal people, right? All that activism stuff?"

"Not to his specifications."

She gazed at the ceiling, at the dull afternoon light stretched across the swirled plaster. "So what's Sam's specialty? Besides belligerence? And clearly being insane. What's his super-duper special paranormal power?"

"Not really sure about that, either. People say he doesn't have any abilities. He's just crazy and thinks he does. I know he's got something, though, or his followers wouldn't flock to him. He told a reporter one time his ability depends on subterfuge. It works better if no one knows about it."

She rolled her eyes. "Well, he's clearly not a mind reader, or he wouldn't need that little girl. You think they're screwing?"

"It's hard to tell."

They were quiet for a minute, the TV droning away on the wall, newscasters jabbering back and forth.

"I've been thinking about the Institute," Micha's voice was soft.

"I'm trying not to."

"All the years I worked with them, all the times I've been there..." He didn't sound particularly distressed, more wondering than hurt. "They brought you there from the airport?"

"Yeah, they sent a driver to pick us up."

"Did you see the big sculpture out front, in the courtyard?"

She tried to recall the details of their arrival. A small crowd of protestors had been gathered out in front of the tall, white building and they drew most of her attention. Some of them looked bored, sitting on the curb with their signs propped against their legs. The driver explained with a chuckle they were always around, every day, though they had little reason to get excited unless someone important or a news station showed up. The sculpture Micha was referring to rose from a broad circular fountain in the middle of the courtyard—a huge, granite angel with arms and wings gloriously spread. The sculpture was pretty. Jason had certainly seemed fascinated by it.

"Yeah," she said. "Sorta. I was paying more attention to the protestors."

"It's called *Benevolence*."

She snorted. "It should be called *Irony*."

"A lot of people don't like that the Institute is in the Illinois Medical District. Detractors say the Institute can't be classified as a medical facility because they don't do medical research. Supporters counter they study human physiology there, which makes it a medical facility."

"If we're lucky," June said, "they'll blow it up. Then everyone'll be happy."

Micha was silent. The revelation had to be difficult for him, his once happy place now a fortress of villainous bullshit. Unfortunately, Micha needed to learn no good deed went unpunished.

"How did you discover your abilities?" Micha asked.

She welcomed the change of subject, even if the subject they switched to wasn't one she enjoyed discussing.

"Hell if I remember." She hoped the words sounded casual enough that Micha wouldn't pick up on the lie. "People didn't know as much about supernatural stuff when I was a kid, so Jason and I didn't know we were different for a while."

"What made you realize it?"

She shrugged. "We were spoiled. Kids, teachers, even our parents, they'd just do whatever we wanted. We didn't think it was strange. Then around second or third grade, people started noticing we were weird." An old anxiety stirred in her gut. "Around that time we found out for ourselves we were screwed up."

"People always find out. One way or another. I saw how my sisters were treated."

"Yeah. Our parents split up because of us. Always fighting about discipline, about all the stress we put on them. They must have thought they were losing their minds. My dad hated us. He was afraid of us. Me, especially. Jason quit using his power around the time we realized we had it."

Micha turned his face to her, frowning. "That must have been rough."

"Yeah, well. When we were fifteen, we moved with our mom from Rhode Island to California to get away from him. She got an offer from an opera company in Los Angeles. Singing's her passion. Fitting, huh?"

Micha smiled faintly.

"California gave me a place to rebel like crazy. I lied about my age, got an apprenticeship in a tattoo shop, learned my skills. Then I filled my head with holes and covered my skin with ink. My mother was relieved, I think. Normal teenage bullshit versus being a freak of nature."

"You're not a freak of nature. Paranormal abilities are not a disease."

"It's easy for you to say that." She tried to keep the bile out of her voice. Micha probably heard it enough. "Our mother got this guy to come over to our apartment and talk to us a couple times a week. He was impervious to our abilities, so he could teach us how to control them. That was when, you know, all this stuff started to become 'science.'"

"Was he a vampire?"

"A vampire?"

"Vampires can block most paranormal abilities."

"Hell, I don't know." She heaved herself into a sitting position. "Doesn't matter, though. It was what it was. It is what it is."

"Eloquently put."

She sat quiet for a moment, knees drawn up, elbows resting on them. "What about you? What was it like being the odd one out?"

"You don't want to hear about that."

"I asked, didn't I?"

Micha rubbed his face. "It's boring and inconsequential. Another time."

"Unfair. After I just told you my darkest secrets."

"Life isn't fair. And you wouldn't want it to be. That would mean all the bad stuff happens because you deserve it."

She grinned. "It's a good thing you're hot. Otherwise, by now I would have punched you in the face for all these gems of wisdom you keep flinging at me."

Micha sat up too, on one elbow. "So are you in a relationship? Got a special lady?"

"Oh my God, stop."

Micha laughed.

She feared she might actually blush. "No. I don't want a boyfriend. Not right now."

"I don't remember introducing you to my wife. I do remember meeting you. I remember what I thought of you when I met you."

"You thought I was an uncouth, nasty little punk girl, didn't you? Most people do. You probably still think that. Because I am."

"I thought you were absolutely fascinating, and I still do."

"I bet you say that to all the supernatural girls."

"I don't."

"You don't really know me, Micha. You don't really know yourself right now."

Micha sat up fully and swung his long legs over the side of the sofa. "There you go with 'you don't know me' again. I know you'd like me to kiss you."

Heat swiftly shot up her neck and into her cheeks. "Why do you think that?"

Micha opened his mouth, but then hesitated, before titling his head and giving her a smile. "I can tell. I have amnesia, but I'm not stripped of my perceptions."

"Oh really? So you're into dirty punk girls?" She struggled not to start mocking, her natural defense mechanism. "'Cause whether you know it or not, you were married to a very austere, beautiful woman."

"I don't have a type. I think you're interesting."

She winced. "Oh God. Wrong, *wrong* answer. You have no idea how wrong."

"Is it?" Micha sat back and patted the cushion beside him. "Why don't you come over here?"

Very bold. She could appreciate that. But...

"Micha, you have no idea the guilt I would suffer if I made a pass at you right now."

"It's a good time, though. I don't remember my wife."

"What kind of girl do you think I am?"

"What kind of guy do you think I'm not? I can't remember, so it's now or never."

This had to be the worst, most obscene, wonderful logic she had ever heard, like allowing drunkenness to facilitate getting it on with a best friend you'd been wanting for years. The consequences ran the gamut from amazing to horrible—and she knew from experience.

"Come here," Micha repeated, softer. "I won't hate you even if my memory comes back."

"Micha."

"Come. Here."

The tone of his voice, a hook in the gut, and she was caught by chemical urges.

She lost the ability to gauge the good idea-ness of the situation somewhere between her sofa and Micha's sofa, upon which she found herself instantly tangled with him and kissing hungrily. He pushed her back and crawled on top of her. So much for romance. His lips were incredibly soft, silky and wet, agonizingly intimate. He gripped her hair, and she liked the gesture. She kissed him harder, parted his lips, and plunged her tongue into his mouth. The barbell through her tongue clicked against his teeth. She had no conscious control over her hands, letting them roam without timidity, over his broad shoulders, down the curve of his back, onto his ass. Micha slid his hands down her sides to the top of her jeans.

"You have a nice body," Micha murmured against her mouth, when they eased up on the kiss. "Nice and..."

He dug his fingertips in above her hipbones, under her shirt, clearly at a loss for an adjective and making her forget how to speak English as well. He slid a hand lower, and his fingers crept under the edge of her waistband.

"And an amazing ass," he added. "Anyone ever tell you that?"

The only words she could find in her hormone-scrambled brain made no sense, words like "Kentucky" and "racquetball." "I think so?"

Micha chuckled.

Of course, the door opened.

The two of them scrambled apart like naughty teenagers caught in a backseat. Judging by the look on Sam's face, they hadn't moved fast enough.

"That's what his ability is," June muttered. "Cockblocking."

"I'm glad to see you two kept yourselves entertained." Sam spoke pointedly.

Muse walked in behind him. June tried desperately to think of something else in case Muse turned out to be as much of an invasive jerk as Robbie, sticking her nose in other people's heads. June pictured her mother's little flower garden behind her house, but suddenly Micha was pushing her into the tulips and getting on top of her.

Sam walked between the two sofas. He stopped and stood over her. He had a newspaper in his hands.

"I have news, good and bad," he said. "I'd give you a choice of which to hear first, but the bad won't make sense without the good."

She tensed. "What is it? I don't think I can handle any more bad news."

Sam thrust the paper at her, a magazine-type deal. An entertainment paper. She took the offering tentatively. Muse sat on the opposite sofa and clasped her hands in her lap, watching them. The corner of her mouth jerked. She blinked rapidly.

"That him?" Sam asked. "I mean, obviously you're fraternal."

The headline at the top of the page said, MYSTERY TWINS ARE IN TOWN. Underneath the headline were separate pictures of her and Jason.

"I don't know how they got one of Jason's head shots," June said, "but yeah, that's him." Her picture was from one of the advertisements for her shop. She didn't care how they got it. She did wonder what the hell made them "mysterious."

"They ran those pictures in the *Tribune* earlier this week," Micha said. "You have no idea how tenacious reporters in this city can be, especially Ethan Roberts."

June looked up at Sam, her stomach jumping. "He's alive, isn't he? You saw him."

"I didn't. But the telepath who talked to John McKormic did."

She dropped the paper in her lap. She feared she might do something stupid, like start crying. "Did he look all right? Is he okay?"

"I don't know the state of health he's in, but he's definitely alive. My spy couldn't talk to Mr. McKormic too long without arousing suspicion."

Micha gripped June's shoulder.

"Wait… What's the bad news?" Her stomach dropped.

"The bad news is, I don't know how the hell we're going to get him out of there." Sam scowled darkly, as if this were more a personal affront to him than an agonizing revelation for her. "They're keeping him in the Special Projects department, which is under heavy security. And I don't have any people in the Institute who have clearance for that floor. They're extremely paranoid about who has access."

"I'll go in there myself if I have to," June said. "I have to get him out."

"Sure you will. Going in there is not going to save him. The only thing that'll happen is you'll be caught as well."

She wanted to punch something, hard. Hard enough to break all the bones in her hand, make the pain distract her from the horrible sickness in her stomach, the certainty she had made the wrong decision running away. Micha still had his hand on her shoulder, and he squeezed again, tighter.

"Just hold on to your panties," Sam said. "I'll come up with something. I'm the smartest man in this city."

* * * *

Evening fell, the world outside the windows murky and dotted with glittering lights. Micha had dozed off on one of the sofas. Sam had been making phone calls—she assumed—beyond a set of closed French doors on the other side of the room. He had sent Muse off on another mysterious "patrol." June couldn't stay still, pacing and smoking, getting dangerously close to running out of cigarettes. Finally, the doors opened and Sam strode out. She glimpsed a bedroom beyond.

"There's going to be a press conference in half an hour," Sam said. "They're going to talk about Rose Bellevue."

Some political talk show was on right now. "That ought to be interesting." Maybe they would talk about her and Jason as well.

"Eric Greerson wants to say something, since today was her funeral. So kind of him."

"Who's Eric Greerson?"

Sam made a face, as if something vile had been shoved under his nose. "Eric Greerson is the head of the Institute. The second one in the decade it's been open. The former head, Michael Paulson, was known for being indecisive and didn't like confrontation with dissidents, so they replaced him. Eric is just another fool in what's sure to be a long line of them. He doesn't know what's going on at the Institute right under his nose."

"Are you sure about that?"

"I've met him. He's a self-righteous asshole. He believes in what the normals running the Institute want the place to stand for. The Institute's governing board keeps the PR machine rolling so they can continue blinding the public. Eric's their pawn. There's a legend he threw a huge party for the Institute's supporters the day Alan Jenkins died. Probably untrue. Or I like to believe it is, since I didn't get an invite."

She recalled what Cindy had told her that morning in her apartment. "Alan Jenkins. That's the guy who ran the SNC?"

"Yes, before his son Aaron took over and we hammered out our treaty. Not that the treaty makes us best friends. But I force myself to tolerate him." He walked over to the sofas. "I want to see this press conference."

"We need to get my brother out of the Institute," she reminded him.

"Give me time."

"I don't have time. My brother doesn't have time."

"And I don't have a magic wand." Sam stood between the sofas, in front of the TV. "We're going to order some food and sit down and watch this press conference. You want a beer? You sound like you could use a beer."

"Fuck beer. Give me some wine."

"Wine?" Sam raised both eyebrows, then narrowed his eyes. "Red or white?" He clearly believed he was dealing with an amateur.

"I'm sure a fancy hole like this has a Paul Hobbs Cabernet Sauvignon. That's *red*."

While Sam called room service, June gently shook Micha awake. She didn't want him to starve.

Micha opened his eyes and it seemed for a moment he didn't recognize her. Then he shifted and winced.

"Hey." His voice was gravelly. "How long have I been asleep?" He sat up on one elbow, looking around.

"Not long." She sat down on the edge of the sofa and touched his knee. "You all right?"

He rubbed the side of his head. "A little disoriented." He slipped his hand down his neck, squinting at the TV. "I feel weird, like I might be coming down with something."

"Disoriented could be my fault, but my power doesn't make people sick. I think you probably just need to eat."

The food arrived, as well as the wine.

"Do you know how much that stuff costs?" Sam asked.

"Yes, I do." June swirled the wine in her glass and took a sip. Full bodied. Well-balanced. "Don't assume shit about me."

June wasn't interested in the press conference, but clearly couldn't escape. Micha sat next to her on the sofa, nibbling on a piece of bread.

Sam sat on the opposite sofa. On the screen, Eric Greerson appeared as a thin, narrow-shouldered man with silver hair and a solemn face. He stood at a podium, surrounded by several official-looking people.

"As you all know," he said, "today we laid to rest one of the finest researchers the Institute for Supernatural Research has ever known, our head vampire researcher, Rose Bellevue. Her death was the result of a brutal murder, the perpetrators of which are still to be found. The police are working in close contact with us. We are also attempting to find her husband, the well-known paranormal activist Micha Bellevue, who, in conjunction with her death, has gone missing."

June was cringing for Micha, but Micha just stared blankly at the screen.

"We have very little information, unfortunately," Eric said. "Security footage shows intruders bypassing the Institute's security systems and attaining access to the vampire research floor. We believe they were specifically targeting her, but because their faces are covered we cannot identify them."

June gaped. "That's not what happened!"

"Do you really think they'd let Eric give the police the real footage?" Sam said. "Someone doctored it, of course."

"We're sending a special group of our own choosing to Old Town to gather information. The police are aware of this, but are not leading, nor condoning, this separate investigation."

"Of course." Sam scoffed. "They think militant vampires did it."

"What's in Old Town?" June asked.

"The Nocturnal District," Micha spoke up. "A place where vampires hang out. Everything's open from dusk 'til dawn. The less PC refer to it as 'Blood Row.'"

"The old vampires, and some of the young ones, aren't happy with his wife's discovery," Sam said. "Not that I blame them. They don't like having their mystique ruined. It makes a good cover for the Institute, though."

"I'm only vaguely aware of what she did," June admitted. "I think I might have read about it somewhere."

"Like the nosy little normal she was, she isolated the bacteria responsible for vampirism," Sam said. "Found out the bacteria creates enzymes that cause accelerated cell reproduction, which is why they can live indefinitely unless an essential organ is destroyed. It also affects their skin cells; that's why they're sensitive to sunlight."

"It won't kill them," Micha said. "It'll just make them sick with prolonged exposure."

"The reason vampires have other abilities has more to do with the structure of their society," Sam went on. "They almost always choose people who already have some level of paranormal ability. However, once they turn, they become impervious to everyone else's abilities. Scientists are still not sure why. I'm sure some other normal will come along and pick up where she left off so we can all find out."

June wasn't into the biology crap supernatural people liked to go on about these days, but the explanation intrigued her. "So why do they drink blood?"

"If they don't," Micha said, "the bacteria will deplete their own blood." Apparently he could remember the science, just not the scientist. "The fresh blood gives it an environment to live in. Since the discovery, they've actually found transfusions sustain them better than drinking. Some vampires have decided to be more humane and stop feeding altogether in favor of transfusions."

"A kinder, gentler vampire." June sucked in a breath. "Jesus Christ."

"You seriously don't know any of this?" Sam shook his head. "You've never picked up a copy of *Paranormal Scientific Weekly*?"

"No. You ever pick up a copy of *Inked*?"

"She was looking for a cure," Micha said softly.

The two of them looked at him. June's skin crawled.

"What makes you think vampires want to be cured?" Sam asked him.

"A few of them do. Some of them don't realize what they're getting into. You have to educate non-vampires as well. It's an infection, so there's a possibility you can get it from things other than bites or ingesting infected blood. There's a small chance it can be sexually transmitted."

"The next great STD." June stood. "I can't watch any more of this. I need a smoke."

She hoped she would feel better after a cigarette. She didn't. She hoped she would feel better after she ate. She didn't. She glowered at Sam every chance she got.

"I have to figure out a plan," Sam told her. "You have to be patient."

"I can't be patient. My brother might have been alive when your spy saw him in that dude's head, but that doesn't mean he'll stay that way."

"If you think you could pass the time more easily in a coma, I'll be glad to put you in one."

"I'd like to see you try, tough guy."

Sam planned to leave for the night and once again instructed them not to wander out of the room. They were allowed to call room service, but he told them not to pick up the phone if it rang.

"I won't contact either of you by phone, ever," he said. "It's too dangerous."

"So you're just gonna leave us here," June said.

"You'll be safe. I keep refugees here all the time. I don't need to hang out and baby sit; I'll be back in the morning. Besides, don't you two want to be alone?"

June scowled. "Good night."

They made sleeping arrangements after Sam left. Micha inspected the bedroom. "There's a huge bed. We can both sleep in here."

June was harboring more than a touch of guilt. "No, that's all right. You take it. I'll sleep out here on one of the sofas."

"That's silly." Micha walked out through the French doors. "I've been sleeping on a sofa all week. It sucks."

"I know, it's just…" She didn't know what it was "just."

She searched for some pillows and blankets and located said items in a closet near the door. Micha didn't argue further. He stood and watched while she made up a bed for herself on one of the sofas.

"Are you feeling better?" she asked, avoiding his gaze.

"I guess so."

She unfurled a blanket. "Glad one of us is." She hesitated before saying, "I thought for a second earlier you were remembering your wife. Is anything coming back to you?"

"Hm. I…remember coffee."

"Coffee?"

"I always took a thermos of coffee to seminars. The swill they serve at those things is awful. I think she made it for me. I was always raving about it. I seem to remember telling people she made it."

June sat down on the sofa. "I guess that's a start." She had another knife fight with her guilt and once again, it stabbed her in the eye. "Guess we better try to get some sleep."

"Yeah. Guess so."

June was convinced she would never be able to fall asleep given the turmoil in her head, but her body, exhausted by stress and many previous nights of scant and sketchy sleep, decided otherwise.

Chapter 5

Unsurprisingly, a series of frightening and disjointed dreams descended as soon as June fell asleep. She dreamt of being chased through the corridors of the Institute; she found her brother in a room, but couldn't convince him to leave with her. Then she stood on the pier and something dark and sinister crawled out of the shadows toward her, but she couldn't run.

She abruptly woke with no clear notion of how long she'd been asleep. A lamp shone in the corner, the only light in the room, yellow and muted. She could faintly hear Micha's breathing in the other room, a sound she'd gotten familiar with over the past week. The air above the blanket was cold.

Then she caught something from the corner of her eye.

Her body reacted before her mind processed what she saw. She jerked away, flattening herself against the back of the sofa, her first assumption someone from the Institute had gotten into the room. The intruder was indeed from the Institute, though not on their current employee roster.

Rose Bellevue stood next to the sofa. She wore the white blouse, jeans, and powder blue tennis shoes she'd been wearing the night June saw her murdered—no blood on her, or visible wounds. She did look like a corpse though, like someone had propped her dead body up on a stick. Her dark eyes were empty and lifeless. She was horrifyingly eerie, completely still, her chest not rising and falling with breath.

June assumed in blind terror Rose had come back to haunt her for June's role in her death and for kissing her husband.

June tried to push out a scream, but couldn't get her throat to open or her lungs to expand. "What the hell?" she gasped out.

Rose lifted her hand. The dark lines on her palm contrasted against the paleness of her skin.

"I was a means to their end." Her voice was as hollow as her eyes, emotionless and strange. "Find the truth," she whispered. She didn't move, her hand still lifted—her left one, sporting a gold wedding band.

June tried to speak, to yell, but again found no air in her lungs.

Rose lowered her hand and gazed toward the windows, motionless. How long would she stand there? A terrible notion swept over June. What if she never left?

Then the spell broke. Rose disappeared, and June jerked out of her frozen state.

She fell off the sofa and emitted a rather pathetic yelp when she hit the floor. She immediately scrambled up and went for a weapon. She snatched a Tiffany lamp from the table closest to the sofa and brandished it in front of her, turning in a swift circle.

"The *hell* was that?" she yelled.

Micha stumbled out of the bedroom a moment later, bleary-eyed, in a white T-shirt and dark blue boxer-briefs.

"What's going on?" he asked.

"I saw your wife."

"What?"

"I saw your fucking wife!"

"She's…dead?"

"I know she's dead." June quickly set the lamp down. Trying to smack a ghost with an expensive piece of art was stupid. "I thought I was dreaming. She was standing over me. She lifted her hand and I saw her wedding ring. She spoke to me. She said 'I was a means to their end.'"

"A means to their end?"

"Then she just disappeared. She was wearing a white shirt and jeans and blue tennis shoes. That's what she was wearing the night she died. Gah." She clawed at herself, trying to get the crawling feeling off her skin. "I hate ghosts."

"Maybe it was just a dream."

"She was standing right there." She pointed at the sofa. "Right next to me. And I was *awake*. It wasn't a dream. Don't you feel how cold it is?"

"Are you sensitive to spirits?" Micha asked. "Have you ever communicated with the dead before?"

"No. I hate the dead."

"Well, you don't necessarily have to be sensitive to see a ghost. Or it could be some late-stage abilities kicking in." This seemed to interest him more than the prospect of his wife's ghost.

June stared at the spot where she'd seen her, almost expecting her to reappear, this time with a letter opener to stick in her jugular.

"If you really saw her," Micha said, "and even if you only dreamt her, she's clearly trying to give you a message. What do you think 'a means to their end' means?"

"At this point it could mean a lot of things. Who knows?"

Micha helped her check the entire room, but they found no sign of anyone, ethereal or otherwise. After their search, June went to the balcony and smoked a cigarette to calm her nerves. When she stepped back in, she peeked through the French doors while taking off her jacket. The bedroom was as big as the outer room, and Micha sat on the enormous bed with the covers pooled around his waist.

"Come here." He beckoned.

June stepped into the room. A huge vanity spanned one wall, the mirror reflecting the bed and cream-colored walls. Another flat screen TV hung on the wall across from the bed.

"You all right?" Micha asked.

"Yeah." She padded over to the bed, arms crossed.

"You still seem spooked."

"Yeah, well, we might be safe from the Institute here, but you can't exactly keep the wandering dead out, can you? Kinda unnerving."

Micha gazed at her. She wasn't fazed by people staring, as her ink drew a lot of attention. Micha was probably looking at her nipple piercings, though. They were rather prominent against her tank top at the moment.

"Do you think it was really a ghost?" he asked.

"I don't want to think about it." She uncrossed her arms and smoothed her hands over her hips. She prayed Rose wouldn't pop out of a wall.

"You want me to order something from room service, since Sam said we could?" Micha turned toward the phone on the stand next to the bed. "Something to calm your nerves? Hot tea, or some of that fancy wine Sam was pissed about? What was that?"

"I don't drink *tea*, and it was Cabernet Sauvignon. But I'm not exactly in the mood for wine."

Micha picked up the handset. "How about some decaf coffee with a shot of whiskey? It'll help you sleep."

She rocked on her heels. "Yeah, I could go for that."

The clock next to the bed said 1:52, yet their request was taken; that meant either room service went on all night in fancy hotels, or they kept a light on for Sam's guests. June sat on the bed. Micha went to the door when their order arrived, not bothering to put pants on.

A heavy hand had poured the whiskey and the liquid burned her throat and chest, which she'd been hoping for.

"I don't think I can handle much more of this shit," she said.

Micha, back in bed under the covers, had a cup of tea. He took a sip. "I don't think you have to worry about a ghost. She may have a message, but she can't do anything. The dead are just that, dead."

She glanced down at her cup, at her reflection in the dark liquid. She looked tired. "Do you think I'll get him out? Jason?"

"Yes."

She looked up.

"And I'm not just saying that." Micha smiled.

"Thanks," she said softly.

They were silent for a few minutes. June took a big drink of her coffee and winced. The burn focused her thoughts.

"So," she said. "What do you think is gonna happen to you? I guess you can't hide forever."

"Does it matter?"

"Yes, it matters."

"I guess only time will tell."

She took another drink. The whiskey trickled down her spine and a tingling heat spread outward, over her limbs. Optimism crept in, just a little. "Yeah, I guess it will."

"You wanna sleep in here with me now?" Micha set his cup aside.

"Like a little kid hiding from monsters in her parents' room?"

"I'm a little freaked out, too."

"You just want me in bed with you."

Micha arched an eyebrow. "That bother you?"

"I feel guilty about what I did earlier. Especially now with your wife showing up."

Micha scooted down and lay back against the pillows. He stretched out and folded his arms above his head. His T-shirt rode up, giving her a glimpse of tight, smooth skin.

"I'm just asking if you want to sleep in here so neither of us will be spooked," he said. "What's on your dirty mind?"

"Oh, that's not fair."

"What isn't?"

"That." She gestured at his body.

Micha pulled the covers down next to him. "I promise I won't touch you, if you feel that bad about it."

She slid off the bed. "Screw it then. I'll go back to the sofa."

"You're the one who just got all pious!"

She plunked her cup down on the bedside stand next to Micha's. She picked his up and sniffed. The smell of whiskey filled her nostrils. Bourbon, actually. Fruitier.

"Lush." She put the cup down. "I knew you weren't just sipping tea."

Micha stretched out, one arm behind his head, the other still holding the covers back. "Get in bed."

* * * *

June awoke to sunlight and the sound of a television. She shifted and found her body both warm and comfortable, which almost made up for the light and noise. For a moment the shit-storm her life had become remained silent, her mind blissfully blank. Then she opened her eyes and all the bad stuff rushed in. Ghosts. The Institute. Jason. Bullshit.

She lifted her head and winced at the light. Apparently, fancy hotels couldn't afford curtains after they got done making the gold toilets. But they had curtains, her bedmate apparently didn't believe in them.

Her bedmate.

Micha lay beside her, several pillows elevating his head, covers pulled up to his chest. He held the TV remote. "Morning. I didn't wake you with the TV, did I?"

June smacked her lips. The taste of whiskey lingered in her mouth. "What time is it?"

Micha rolled his head on the pillows and looked at the clock on the other side of him. "Eight thirty-six."

She pushed herself up on one elbow. Her usual morning processes kicked in: the craving for nicotine, firing up like a jet engine; a few coughs to clear her lungs and remind her that if the Institute didn't kill her, her habit would; the nagging need to empty her bladder.

"What are you watching?" She squinted at the TV. A silver-haired man was talking about reforming something while a stock ticker scrolled across the bottom of the screen, next to a box showing the weather forecast. Today would be cold.

"The news," Micha said. "It's pretty biased here, but you take what you can get."

June shifted and winced. She didn't like sleeping in jeans. "Don't worry. It's like that everywhere."

"The news in this city, especially when it comes to the paranormal, is incredibly biased. One way or another. It's either long on sanctimony and short on facts, or long on criticism and short on sympathy." He thrust the remote at the TV. "All they do is argue."

"Those bastards." She sat up fully.

"Aaron Jenkins will be on this morning. He wants to talk about Rose's death, too."

June shuffled through the layers of confusion and drama in her head to recall the name. Aaron Jenkins. Current leader of the SNC. "I don't wanna miss that. So I'm gonna go piss and smoke."

Micha smiled.

"What?" she asked.

"Nothing."

"What?"

Micha chuckled. "Your bed head is cute. You look frightening and charming at the same time."

She reached up and raked her fingers through her hair. Disgusting. Definitely shower day. If she wanted to punish Micha for being a tease, she had probably done it by marinating the bed in her funk all night. She threw the covers back and got up.

"Did you see anything last night?" Micha asked. "After you came in here?"

"Is there a puddle of piss in the bed?"

She looked around for her smokes. They were in her jacket, by the balcony door. She made a quick attempt to tug her jeans out of her crotch.

"Don't make fun of me," she said. "I hate it when my jeans crawl up where they're not supposed to be."

"I'm not making fun of you."

"Not sleeping in them again. If I'm here tonight, I'm sleeping in my underwear like you, and you better still behave yourself."

"Jeans *are* uncomfortable to sleep in."

"And when I get a frontal wedgie, it sucks." She hobbled around the bed and passed in front of the TV. "I have a clitoral piercing. It rubs. Uncomfortable as hell."

"A—" He widened his eyes.

"Clitoral piercing. I have a ring through the hood of my clit. I'm gonna go smoke." She left Micha lying on the bed, staring after her.

She peed, smoked a cigarette on the balcony, and returned to the warmth of the bed.

"Order me some coffee." She snuggled under the blankets.

Micha reached over and picked up the phone. "Breakfast? Some eggs?"

"Allergic." She sat up, fluffed her pillow, and lay back down.

"Pancakes?"

"If they're gluten-free."

"Damn."

"See if they have any veggie bacon. Vegetarian stuff I can usually work with."

Micha curled his lip. "Veggie bacon? Are you allergic to meat as well?"

"No, I'm just used to the vegetarian version of everything. I know, it's deplorable. Isn't that one of those big words you like?"

Micha chuckled. "Good thing you're not allergic to booze."

"Yes, a woman has to have her vices. I still give blowjobs in train stations, too."

Micha blinked at her.

"I'm kidding. That only happened once. Gimme my breakfast."

Micha placed an order. Tea, coffee, eggs, and pancakes for himself, and of course, they had a large vegetarian selection being such a fancy joint, and they had veggie bacon. The interview with Aaron Jenkins came on right after Micha placed the order, and he turned up the TV.

Aaron didn't hold a press conference like Eric Greerson had, taking his interview in what looked like an office. A middle-aged man with thick sandy blond hair and a sturdy jaw, he had the air of a politician, sporting a burgundy tie and a neat black jacket. He struck her as oddly familiar, but she couldn't place why. The young woman interviewing him had upswept brown hair and thick-framed glasses. At the bottom of the screen, they flashed her name: Amy Mahoning, Investigative Reporter. She started by asking Aaron what his feelings were on the latest tragedy in the paranormal community.

"I think it's horrifying." His voice matched his suave appearance. "Though many think my organization would revel in the loss of such a key figure in the paranormal community, that's simply not true. My father's legacy and the image people have of the Secular Normalists are things I wish to transform. I did not approve of my father's methods, nor the dogma he extolled in his lifetime."

"So why do these acts continue today?" Amy asked. "Why do people still point fingers at your organization?"

"I do not sanction acts of violence, and I do not run the SNC on the principle of violence. However, because of my father's ways, the habit of blaming us for anything tragic that happens in the paranormal community is unfortunately still present even after five years. The acts that have been attributed to our group since my father's death were not committed by our members, and if they were, they were not approved by me."

"There are plenty of accusations that you're running the group in the same way," Amy said.

"And these are wholly untrue allegations. In trying to clean up the marred legacy my father left behind, I resent strongly that some people are placing the blame for Mrs. Bellevue's death on our group without sufficient proof."

"Who is blaming you, Mr. Jenkins? Mr. Greerson has stated he believes her murder to be the act of militant vampires."

"Pick up a paper, Miss Mahoning." His voice turned icy. "Pull your average Chicagoan off the street and ask him."

"If the disgusting acts of violence, property damage, and menacing over the years since your father's death were not done by your group, who *was* responsible?"

"There are much worse groups out there. We don't even consider ourselves anti-paranormal. We simply want our views considered. Those who would subscribe to violent ideals are quickly eradicated from our ranks, even more so today under my leadership. Unfortunately, my father did not discourage discrimination and fear mongering. He looked the other way or didn't punish those who committed such acts, which I don't agree with. I am committed to instituting new rules that allow no tolerance for such behavior. I want our group to get our message out peacefully."

"And what is your message, in your words, Mr. Jenkins?" Amy asked.

"We do not wish the paranormal community harm or want them eradicated. We are simply calling for the Institute to provide results of their research. We want answers. It's not prudent that so many programs and so much money be channeled into causes for conditions that aren't even substantially documented or proven."

"What are you saying, Mr. Jenkins? That the paranormal is an elaborate hoax?" Amy reared back a little, eyeing him.

Aaron fixed her with his chilled gaze. "The average member of the paranormal community is probably unaware that the Institute does not publish nor publicly disclose the results of nearly eighty percent of its research. It can only get away with this because it's privately funded and has no committee or agency to report to."

"That true?" June asked Micha.

"I don't really know. I've heard that before."

"We simply want the Institute to disclose its research," Aaron said. "We oppose special privileges and programs for members of the paranormal community until their conditions are clearly established and defined. If these people are expected to integrate into society and be accepted, we deserve a clear definition of their situation and needs."

"What about other groups who oppose the paranormal on religious and moral grounds?" Amy asked. "Do you share their feelings?"

"We can't be responsible for their behavior. That's why we're a secular group. The ideas these other groups have are their own, and they do things for their own reasons. We simply want answers and honesty."

"They can never stay on topic." Micha sat up and pushed back the covers. "This was supposed to be about Rose. Here's that bias I was talking about."

"He obviously knows some shit is up with the Institute," June said.

Micha got out of bed. "Nothing in this city is black and white." He walked to the bathroom.

The food arrived. While they were eating in bed, the door to the room opened, and they both froze, until they heard Sam's voice. A moment later, Sam appeared in the bedroom doorway and stopped, staring at them. He wore his coat and scarf. Other voices, feminine ones, came from the outer room.

"It's all right." June lifted her cup of coffee. "It's not what it looks like. We're just having breakfast after a long night of rough sex."

"Lovely," Sam said. "Put some clothes on and get out here."

Cindy appeared at his side, in her coat as well. "Well," she said, hands on her hips, "I see you guys are getting cozy."

"It's a big bed." June took a bite of her bacon. "Ain't the only thing that's big."

Micha chucked a piece of real bacon over onto June's plate.

"Ugh." She picked the offending piece of meat up between thumb and forefinger and flung it off the bed.

"Just get out here," Sam told them, and left the doorway.

Cindy gazed at them another moment, her eyes predatory and shining, like she wanted to crawl in bed with them, until Micha waved her off.

"That…was creepy," June said.

"You have no idea."

Micha put his pants on. Out in the main room, Cindy sat next to Muse on one of the sofas. Muse wore a white fitted dress, white leggings, and white boots. She was running her fingers through her hair, making it stand up, lips drawn across her teeth in a grimace. She slackened her expression when she saw June looking at her. Sam had draped his scarf over a chair but still had his coat on. He eyed the bed June had made up on the other sofa. She wished they *had* gotten it on to make all the scrutiny worth it.

"Nice to see you again," June said to Cindy, to create a distraction.

Cindy shrugged, sat forward, and worked her coat off. "Sam called me, had Robbie come pick me up." She nodded at a duffel bag at her feet. "Micha, Muse went by your apartment this morning to find out if anyone had the place staked out. They don't, so I had her pick up some clothes and other stuff for you. I thought you might like to finally change into something else."

"Thanks," Micha said.

"I think I may have a plan." Sam turned to Cindy. "Where's your ex-husband? Does he still live in Chicago?"

Cindy lifted her eyebrows. "Which one?"

"Kevin Kramer. I'm assuming you took your maiden name back when you got divorced."

"Actually, Preston is the husband after him. What the hell would you want with Kevin?"

How many husbands had she had?

"If you answer my questions with questions," Sam said, "this conversation will never end. Just tell me where he is."

"He works in Wicker Park," Cindy said. "At a bar. He lives not too far from it."

"Do you think he'll be working tonight?"

"I don't know. He might be working day shift. Last I talked to him, he was made bar manager, so he does the opening stuff."

"What time does it open?"

"Eleven, I think?"

"Good. Text or call him, make sure. We have time. You two can order breakfast." Sam nodded to Muse and Cindy.

"Try the veggie bacon," June said. "It's delightful."

"Wait," Cindy said. "You want me to call Kevin? Because trust me, Kevin is not interested in helping the likes of us."

"The likes of us?" June asked.

"Kevin is a normalist sympathizer." Cindy said it again, louder, toward Sam, "A *normalist sympathizer*."

"I know what he is," Sam said. "I don't know why you married him."

"It was...complicated."

Sam looked at June. "I'm taking you with me to see him." He looked at Micha, "You're staying here."

"I'm not gonna argue," June said. "But I want a shower first." She shook her pack of cigarettes. Two left. Maybe the concierge could get her some smokes.

"Good," Sam said. "You reek."

"Eat me."

June took a shower. Showering hadn't been heavy on her mind at Cindy's place, though it was available to her. She had too much distracting her. Getting clean was a glorious experience. She tried not to think about how Jason might not be allowed a shower where he was.

Micha let her borrow a T-shirt from the clothes in his bag. The soft gray fabric smelled like him, and she kept turning her head to the side and sniffing the shoulder. Probably some expensive cologne, something with a pretentious French name. The shirt was also way too big on her.

"Do you have some gel?" She stood in front of the vanity mirror in the bedroom, trying to finger-rake her hair into some sort of order. She'd used the complimentary hair dryer in the bathroom but needed some product to control the frizz.

Micha stood behind her, dressed, digging through the duffel bag on the bed.

"Cindy brought me some mousse," he said. "That's all I use."

"Something." June scowled at her reflection. She looked like a limp black mop.

"I can probably call downstairs and have them bring some up," he said. "I'm not looking forward to hanging out here by myself. Maybe I'll just nap."

"Hopefully we won't be gone long. It's scary out there." She checked the gauges in her ears and stuck her tongue out to check the underside of the bar. Micha was watching her in the mirror, and she closed her mouth.

"I've swallowed the ball twice," she said.

"Excuse me?"

"My tongue piercing." She turned around. "The ball pops off sometimes. Not a big deal. You don't wanna swallow the bar, though. That thing comes out the wrong way on the other end and you could be bleeding for days."

Micha winced. So cute and gullible.

June, Sam, and Cindy left the hotel shortly after eleven. Muse left as well, but when they got downstairs and a car appeared for them, she walked off down the street instead of getting in. Sam made Cindy drive.

"I don't understand how you think Kevin can help us," Cindy said, as they pulled out of the valet area. "He's a huge douche bag, I hope you know."

"Did you call to see if he was there?" Sam asked.

"I texted him. He is. He probably thinks I wanna screw him for old time's sake. Thanks a lot for that."

June was tense on the drive, but she knew better than to ask what they were doing. The "second test," after all. Wicker Park resembled the Mission District in Sacramento: full of shops, galleries, bars, and restaurants designed to draw the young dreamers, the artists and philosophers looking for good coffee, whole foods, and pretentious conversation about ridiculous things like post-modernism. They pulled up in front of a painted-over white brick façade with a black and gold sign that said *Seventh Heaven*. An empty patio encompassed the area in front of the building.

"Are we all going in?" Cindy asked as she turned off the car.

Sam replied by opening the door and getting out.

June followed suit. "I hope they sell cigarettes in here," she muttered.

Inside, the bar sported a mess of brown-and-tan patterned wallpaper, Oriental rugs, and leather couches and glass-topped coffee tables in lieu of tables and chairs. The place looked like a seventies drug den, with subdued eighties rock playing in the background.

As she suspected. Hipster Hell.

They approached a long, gleaming wooden bar on one side of the room, empty of patrons. A man emerged from the back carrying a case of beer. He had dark hair, cut short but long on top, his face narrow and finely-boned. He was tall and waifish. He looked like a model. Cindy waved.

"What's up?" He set the case down. He spoke to Cindy, but stared at Sam.

"Uh," Cindy said. "This is, uh—"

"Hello, Kevin." Sam stepped forward, sliding a hand inside the breast of his coat. He drew out a small white box, set it on the bar, and slid it toward Kevin.

The way Kevin's expression changed intrigued June. His eyes widened; the rest of his face paled and sagged. He took a step back.

"I'm sorry." Sam sounded anything but. "It's time."

"What's going on?" Cindy asked.

Kevin stared at the box for a moment; then he looked up at Sam. His expression changed again, becoming stony and resolved, his pale hazel eyes glittering. "Didn't think it would take this long. Hello, Sam."

"Hello," Sam said.

"Fuck," Kevin replied.

Chapter 6

They moved to a dining room beyond the bar, full of high wooden tables with chairs on them. The walls were brick, covered in beer signs and band flyers. They took the chairs down from one of the tables and sat, Sam and June on one side, Kevin across from Sam. Kevin stared at the box on the table between them. June had never seen a man look so despairing. She expected when he opened the box to see a severed finger inside. Or a cursed amulet. Or a notice from the IRS.

"Someone better tell me what's going on," Cindy said. She stood next to June, rather than sitting.

"Is this what I think it is?" Kevin asked.

"Of course it is," Sam said.

"What is going on?" Cindy demanded again, shrilly.

Kevin opened his mouth.

Sam spoke sharply, "Don't tell her anything." He glared at Cindy. "If you can't shut up, leave. I don't need you for this."

Cindy gaped.

June sat back and impulsively pushed a hand into her jacket pocket but found it empty. "Go get me a pack of smokes," she told Cindy and jerked her head toward the bar. "I saw a machine out there. Nothing menthol."

Cindy clenched her fists.

"Yes, do that," Sam said.

Cindy stormed off.

Sam leaned forward and addressed Kevin. "You will not talk to her about the situation that has led to this conversation."

Kevin scowled. "Of course I won't. I wouldn't even if you didn't tell me not to."

"I'm so curious as to what the hell is going on here," June said.

Kevin snapped his gaze to her. "Who's this?"

She smiled. "Apparently, you don't pay attention, huh? I hear I'm the talk of the town."

"Oh, he doesn't read the Paranormal section of the *Tribune*, trust me," Sam said.

"You're right on that," Kevin retorted.

"This isn't exactly a paranormal friendly place," Sam told June. "In fact, most of Wicker Park isn't paranormal friendly. Of course, it's illegal for businesses to discriminate, but that doesn't change people's attitudes. For that, you usually need to use your fists."

"I can't imagine why we wouldn't want your kind around here," Kevin said. "Manipulation is *so* damn charming."

"This is June Coffin." Sam gestured to her, with a cruel smile at Kevin.

Kevin closed his eyes and pulled in a breath through his teeth. "In *my* bar. This keeps getting better and better."

"You haven't seen anything yet," June said.

Kevin opened his eyes.

"Wait until I get up and take a crap on the table," June said.

Cindy returned. She threw a pack of cigarettes down in front of June. "There."

June snatched them up. "Your offering pleases me."

"I heard you left Chicago," Kevin said to June. "Like that researcher's husband who probably offed her so he could blame it on the normalists."

Cindy gasped. "Kevin, Micha didn't kill Rose!"

June started unraveling the cellophane from the pack of cigarettes. "He didn't, actually. I watched her blood splatter all over the trunk of a car, but he wasn't holding the gun. However, I can appreciate a healthy sense of cynicism." She turned to Cindy. "I need some matches. I left my lighter in the room, I think."

"There's some behind the bar," Kevin said.

Cindy stomped her foot and stormed off again.

"You know she's friendly with Micha Bellevue," Sam said.

"I know," Kevin said. "There's a reason why we're divorced. Many reasons."

"Cindy said you're a 'normalist sympathizer.'" June shook a cigarette out. "Is that like a paranormal Nazi?"

"Killing, no matter who does it, is a terrible thing." Kevin leaned toward June. "But I don't trust your kind anymore, not one of you. The only ones I have any respect for are the militant vampires, because they don't sit around whining about how they're oppressed. But that's only a small respect. They have plenty of other foul qualities."

June held the cigarette between her fingers, noting Kevin's use of the word "anymore." "Go on," she said.

"The vast majority of you are manipulative, dangerous, and demanding. Right now you could twist my mind and make me do whatever you wanted. I think I have a right to be afraid and discriminating. As far as violence goes, if you think the things normals have done to paranormal people is vicious, I could make you a list of the shit I've seen your kind do."

Darkness loomed behind Kevin's eyes. Something haunted him.

June pointed the cigarette at him. "You know where your lines are drawn. I respect that."

Kevin frowned.

Cindy came back and threw the matches at June. They bounced off June's chest, and she caught them in her hand.

"Thanks."

"You're damn right I know where my lines are drawn," Kevin said. "They're drawn where you people can't ruin my life. More than you have."

"Don't tempt me to cross lines, Kevin," Sam spoke ominously.

Kevin stiffened.

June opened the matchbook, peeled out a match, and struck the end.

Kevin glared at her. "This is a non-smoking bar. There's a smoking ban in Illinois."

June shook the match out and took a drag. Sweet nicotine relief rushed in. "Unoriginal." She blew the smoke out the corner of her mouth. "California started that." She plucked the sugar caddy from the middle of the table, dumped the packets out, and flicked her ash in the receptacle.

Kevin clenched his fists, like he might come across the table and throttle her.

"Why are we here, visiting this lousy little smear of a man?" Cindy asked.

June liked Cindy's ability to cut directly to the insults.

"So nice to see you too, Cindy," Kevin said. "I was really hoping that piece of paper we signed two years ago meant I'd never have to listen to your mouth again. But this is what, like the sixth time I've had to look at you since then?"

"Why don't you go get me a whiskey, *bartender*?" She fixed him with a crazy-eyed stare. "You don't want my condition getting riled up, now do you? Or maybe you do."

"Why don't you walk your oversized ass to the bar and get it yourself? Len's back there. He likes fat broads with big mouths."

"I hear he likes working for assholes with tiny peckers, too," she shot back.

June took another drag, enjoying the show.

"Still bartending in Wrigleyville?" Kevin asked, high and imperious. "Won any competitions lately?"

June blew the smoke out. "Competitions?"

"Kevin is a flair bartender." Cindy waved a dismissive hand. "A glorified clown. I don't have to compensate for anything, Kevin. I *know* I don't have a dick."

"We have important business to discuss here," Sam spoke up. "If you two could finish your fucking conversation?"

Cindy snorted. "Important business? Sam, this man is a closet member of the SNC. He would love to see the paranormal wiped from this city. What do you even want with him?"

"The Secular Normalists' objective is to demand ethical behavior from the Institute," Kevin said, "not to wipe the paranormal out."

"So how long *have* you been a member?" Cindy asked. "Were you with them when we were married?"

"I'm not a member. I just do my reading. Knowledge is power, something you wouldn't know anything about."

"Their crazy booklets I'm sure," Cindy said. "Read the Paranormal Alliance's manifesto on the SNC if you want some 'knowledge.'"

"Because that's not a biased piece of literature."

"And theirs isn't biased? We may have a treaty, but that doesn't mean they've changed their ways. They're still killing us."

Sam was rubbing his forehead and gritting his teeth.

June couldn't hold her curiosity in check any longer. "Why did you two get married if you have these wildly differing viewpoints?"

Kevin was glaring at Cindy. "Let's just say I was on the fence about the paranormal when I met her, but she pushed me right off it by the time we got divorced."

"I should have pushed you into traffic," Cindy said.

"That's enough! I want you to leave us," Sam hissed at Cindy. "Go. Now."

Cindy stood steadfast.

"*Go*." he reiterated, more severe. "Or I'm going to have her *make* you go." He indicated June.

"I'm your dog now?" June said.

"Good, you passed the third test."

Looking highly put-upon, Cindy swiveled on her heel and stalked off. June took another drag from her cigarette.

"God, I hate that woman," Kevin muttered, as Cindy left the room.

"Yeah, I can't figure women out, either," June said.

"Back to the matter at hand." Sam focused on Kevin. "You know what I'm asking of you. We just have to find a body."

Kevin sighed, heavy and long-suffering. "Of course we do."

* * * *

Sam ordered Cindy to stay at the bar and wait for Kevin to get off work, perhaps as punishment—though whether he meant to punish Cindy or Kevin, June was unsure. He said he needed someone there to make sure Kevin didn't try to weasel out. Sam and June left, and inexplicably, Sam took her to Navy Pier.

"What are we doing here, exactly?" June asked. The sun was out and glittered on the water, so the lake didn't resemble desolate doom this time. The island-sized patches of ice gleamed like glass.

"This is my territory," Sam said. "I feel a lot safer here. A hell of a lot safer than in Wicker Park, without my bodyguard. I could be killed, or worse, kidnapped."

"This is your territory? Like you own the place?"

"In a manner of speaking, as per the treaty between the Paranormal Alliance and the SNC. We have our territories."

"What about the Institute? Do you have a treaty with them?"

"No, but most of the time they know better than to go on either of our stomping grounds. Incidents have happened."

"Aren't you worried about leaving Cindy at the bar?"

"No one wants to kidnap her."

"You have a point."

They parked in a brightly-lit garage. From one of the exits, they entered the vast mall-like interior of the pier, not terribly crowded but busy enough to make June instantly uneasy. Adults and groups of teenagers drifted by, laughing and talking, texting on phones and carrying shopping bags, involved in their own little microcosms and ignorant of the drama June was experiencing. The air smelled like pretzels and coffee, as if to underline the absurd normalcy of it all.

"Aren't you afraid someone is going to recognize me?" June asked.

"Do you realize how little strangers actually look at each other? And how little they care about what they read in the paper? No one cares about you right now, I'm afraid. They're all looking for Micha. And even if they do recognize you, aren't you an aural captivator?"

"Touché." She frowned. "What about you, though? I'm sure people around here know who you are."

"Unless it's a member of my organization, I don't have fans."

They passed a little jewelry store. She wanted some new body jewelry. She needed her wallet. Her money. Her damn life back.

"If you're hungry, we can eat," Sam said. "I'm sure we have time."

"I don't suppose you're going to tell me what that box was, or why you need a body?"

"You're getting smarter. No, I'm not going to tell you. Trust me, you'll find out soon enough."

A few people *did* look at her as they passed. They weren't looks of recognition, though; she often got such looks. People either thought she looked cool or was a scary criminal.

"I don't suppose you're going to tell me why you had so much power over that angry little bartender, either," June said.

"I barely know you. Why should I tell you my secrets?"

"Maybe because I'm in terrible danger right now and my brother is in even worse danger."

"None of which will be resolved by me answering any of those questions."

"Maybe after you collect your fee from me you'll be a little more talky, huh?"

They were in a food court-type area. Sam stopped.

"I'm not a prostitute," June said. "But in this case, if that's what you're asking in return for saving my brother, I'll close my eyes and think of Kansas or something."

Sam looked to one side and then the other, and then back at her. "You want some coffee?"

"No?"

"You can get booze in it."

"All right."

They got coffee—June ordering hers with a double shot of Jameson—and sat down in a red plastic booth. The place had a Wi-Fi area with computers nearby. June considered e-mailing her mother, to let her know they were all right—or at least she was—since her mother hadn't heard from them all week and had probably started to worry. Unfortunately, contacting her might bring more danger to the people she cared about. She doubted she could lie effectively to her mother.

"I'll tell you something, if you want to know a secret so badly." Sam sat across from her, hands wrapped around a paper cup.

"Is it an interesting secret?"

"I know what's going on at the Institute. I know what they're doing. But proving it, that's another matter."

The light over the table glistened in his eyes and shone on his sleek dark hair. He was an attractive man. Maybe she wouldn't have to think too hard about Kansas.

"I don't think they'll kill your brother," Sam said. "They need him alive."

"They shot at me."

"They only need one of you."

June sat back and draped an arm over the back of the booth. "Go on."

"Your power isn't unique, but it's rare. A little over a year ago, there was a woman, like you, an aural captivator. Her name was Missy Chase. She came here to be studied at the Institute. A sheep to slaughter, just like the two of you. She was the first aural captivator they'd gotten to study, so there was a lot of hype about it. She wasn't staying at the Institute, just at a hotel."

"Did they screw up her life, too?"

"You could say that. She was murdered."

She shouldn't have been surprised, but she still got a little shock. "By the Institute?"

"I doubt it. The Institute was too eager to study her. No one knows. Someone slit her throat and threw her in a dumpster behind her hotel. Of course, everyone points fingers at the SNC. But it wasn't the SNC, trust me. I watch them closely. And Aaron, even though he gets on my nerves, actually means what he says."

"So they made us stay at the Institute so we wouldn't get murdered? Ironic."

"The Institute was founded by a group of wealthy, and normal, Chicagoans who had a special interest in the paranormal long before it was accepted as scientific fact. They also had an interest in exploiting it, and they knew getting scientific credibility would give them what they wanted. The founders of the Institute were the ones who lobbied the hardest to get recognition for the paranormal. They even falsified information to get the government and scientific community to accept them."

"Wait," June said. "Exploit it? What do you mean?"

"Some who don't have our abilities would like to have them. Or if they can't have them, they'd like to be able to use them in other ways. That's the real reason the Institute was founded, a front of scientific advancement, in reality plundering the freaks who spent their lives desperate for answers and were all too eager to flock to their doors when they opened."

She was baffled.

"Unfortunately," Sam said, "shortly after the Institute opened, the SNC was formed. The founder, Aaron's father, Alan Jenkins, really did hate the paranormal."

"Why is that a bad thing? Hating the Institute?"

"There's no better way to get support for something than to create something else that opposes it. The Institute was not created to help the paranormal. It was created to subvert and study them like rats. The new SNC, the one under Aaron, opposes the Institute on those very grounds. But the damage is already done."

"So," she said, "the first dude gave the Institute lots of free publicity. He made people feel sorry for them."

"Yes. He got people up in arms. Sparked this whole activist movement. I don't think it's much of a stretch to say the Institute might not have prospered without the SNC. They might not be here today without their biggest enemy to make them look besieged and tormented."

"Huh. That's an interesting take on it."

"Trust me, nothing makes you look as good as your enemies looking bad." Sam spun his cup between his hands, gazing at her.

In the direct light, his eyes were intensely dark, and she recalled what he'd said about eyes reflecting the level of one's power. Was he powerful too? What was his power, anyway?

"Eric Greerson doesn't know what's really going on," Sam said. "He was put in place to keep up the front. It's the researchers down on the ground who're working with the founders."

Rose couldn't be one of the bad guys; she had helped them, died for two people she had met once. Surely she wasn't crooked. They had to employ a few straight people at the Institute. *A means to their end.* June considered telling Sam the dead lady had visited her, though she still couldn't prove her appearance wasn't a dream.

"It sounds crazy," June said. "How do they think they're going to steal our powers? How is that even possible?"

"Not going to"—Sam's voice dropped a notch—"*have.*"

She stared at him.

"They've made a serum," Sam said.

"A serum?"

"Just like the bacteria that causes vampirism, they've harnessed physical elements of other supernatural abilities and created a serum. But it can't just be injected into a normal person. It'll kill them. The person has to take doses of a prepping agent beforehand for several months to create the proper receptive enzymes. Reams of scientific documentation have been uncovered."

"By whom?" She grew alarmed. Were they stealing Jason's voice?

"By us. The Paranormal Alliance."

"So why don't you go public with it? Expose them?"

"Because documentation isn't proof, especially not when you're dealing with an entity as powerful as the Institute. People would say it was a frame job. People like Micha would cite it as lies and defamation, especially if it's coming from me. We have to either get our hands on the serum or someone it's been used on."

"Sounds like you and I both got a shitload of problems."

"Indeed. But does it make you feel any better? They won't kill your brother. They need him."

"Oh yeah." She dug into her pocket for her cigarettes. "Cutting out his vocal chords won't kill him."

"It won't, if they do it right."

They went outside so June could smoke. Despite the sun, the temperature hovered slightly above "cold as hell." They leaned on the pier railing. Boats cut through the ice in the distance. Sam checked his phone. She smoked and drank her coffee. The booze wasn't even giving her a buzz.

"You like art?" Sam asked.

June squinted against the sun. "Sorta."

"You're covered in it. How do you not like it?"

She flexed her hand. No ink on the back of them yet, but the work on her right arm crept past her wrist. "This isn't exactly the Louvre. Jason's the one who's into sculpture and fine art and all that."

"Whatever. You'll like this. Come with me." He stepped away from the railing.

"Where are we going?" She tossed the remaining stub of her cigarette into the water.

"The stained glass museum."

"The what?"

Sam led her back into and through the interior of the pier, past boutiques and coffee kiosks and gift shops and eventually into a wide quiet corridor.

He spread his arms. "Tah dah."

Panes of colored glass—some huge, some small, and every size in between—shone gently on the walls. Some were classic stained glass, made up of colored panels in various geometric shapes, while others depicted flowers, landscapes, and religious scenes.

"Nice," June said. "Jason would love the hell out of this."

They walked through slowly. June assumed the museum consisted of one short hallway, but soon discovered a vast, sprawling exhibition made up of many corridors. Undoubtedly, something one needed hours to properly appreciate. She liked the use of color. Some of the displays were even ink-worthy; she could see some of the religious scenes as reworked back pieces. Sam eventually led her toward a small gallery tucked off to the side, separated from the rest.

"This is the Richard H. Driehaus gallery," he said, as they stepped into a darkened room. "It's his private collection of stained glass done by Louis Comfort Tiffany. I'm going to show you my favorite piece."

"You know, I think you'd really get along with my brother. I hope you two get to hang out."

"I rarely 'hang out' with people."

Sam's favorite piece hung alone in an alcove, the walls bathed by the amber glow emanating from the glass.

"This is called *Guiding Angel*," he said.

The glass depicted an angel holding the hand of a woman, the woman gazing upward with a benign smile.

"The angel is leading her into death." Sam reached out and placed a hand on the glass. "I think it's beautiful."

June was startled to see such a visceral reaction to a piece of art, especially from him. She bent over to read the illuminated plaque below the glass.

"It's cool," she said.

"It's how I like to think of death." Sam lowered his voice. "Peaceful, meaningful. Makes it easier to contemplate."

The light from the glass shone on his face, making his visage soft and his eyes black.

"You contemplate death often?" June asked.

Sam looked at her, hand still on the glass. For a moment, they held each other's gaze. Then he lowered his hand and a tiny sinister smile quirked his lips.

"Don't we all contemplate death?" he said.

"I prefer to contemplate *not* dying."

Sam turned toward her, the alcove so narrow they were almost touching. He leaned forward, stretching his arm out, and placed his hand beside her head on the wall, towering over her.

"So," he said, the word heavy with implication.

"Yeah." She sighed. "That's what I thought this was coming to."

"You're seducing the man whose memory you just wiped clean of his wife. That's a pretty ballsy move." Sam was so close she could smell him, the same scent from when they first met on the pier, that understated musky cologne.

"It's not like that." She bristled. "He's been coming on to me, too."

"Doesn't seem like you're saying no."

"Just—shut up."

She reached up, gripped Sam's hair, and pulled his face down to hers. His lips were soft and warm. He didn't respond to the kiss at first. She worked his lips open and pushed her tongue in, making her barbell click against his teeth. She figured Sam didn't want any chaste, coy kisses and resigned herself to what needed to happen. His mouth tasted like coffee.

After a moment, he abruptly broke the kiss and stepped back with a harsh laugh. She frowned.

"I don't actually expect you to fuck for my assistance." He sounded darkly amused. He gave her cheek a firm pat. "But thank you for the enthusiasm, little captivator."

June's cheeks heated. "But I thought…"

"I know. I'm irresistible, aren't I?"

A sharp trill emitted from Sam's coat, and he pushed a hand into his pocket. "That's Kevin." He drew his phone out, peered at the screen, and frowned. "That's *not* Kevin. It's Cindy."

"God, don't answer it."

He did anyway. "Cindy? Why are you calling me?" He stepped out of the alcove.

June followed, cheeks still burning. She didn't understand what had just happened.

Cindy's harpy-like voice shouted on the other end. Sam winced, holding the phone away from his ear. He listened, eyes slowly widening. "What?"

"Doesn't sound good," June muttered.

"What the hell do you mean? Are you kidding me? Where are you now?"

No, didn't sound good at all.

"Stay there. I'm coming." He clicked off and spun around, eyes flashing, jaw clenched "Dammit!"

"What happened? Did she get kidnapped after all?"

"Someone shot up the bar."

"Shot it up?"

"With a gun. Come on. We have an issue."

Chapter 7

When they returned to the bar, three police cars were parked out front. A small crowd of hipsters hung out on the sidewalk, gawking. One of the windows had been shattered.

Sam slowed the car but didn't park. "I can't walk in with the police here. I show up at this party and it'll be all over the news. You can't go in, either."

They took a drive, winding their way through narrow traffic-choked streets for a while. Sam called Cindy and told her to call him when the police cleared out. He also called Muse and had a brief conversation with her.

"She's guarding Micha," Sam said. "Otherwise I'd have her come immediately."

"She's really your bodyguard?" June itched for a cigarette. "No offense, but she looks like an albino Pomeranian. What can she do?"

"Powerful things don't have to come in big, swaggering packages. Or be swinging their humongous dicks around to get things done."

"I usually just show my tits. It works the same."

Most of an hour passed before Cindy called Sam back. He and June returned to the bar and parked out front. Yellow police tape blocked off the patio. Sam ducked under the flimsy barricade and they went inside. The place was empty aside from Kevin, looking profoundly disgruntled, and Cindy sitting at the bar, an empty glass in front of her, fisting her hair with both hands. Broken glass littered the floor and cold air poured in through the breach. Kevin and Cindy were both wearing their coats.

"Someone shot out your window." Sam eyed the broken glass. "Like we're in a nineteen twenties gangster movie?"

"It was horrible." Cindy sat up and pointed. "The bullet went right into the bar next to me." A jagged hole had been bored into the bar, the wood splintered around the abrasion. "I could have been taken out!"

Sam walked over to the bar, bent down, and inspected the mark.

"Something tells me," Kevin said, "if you hadn't brought your asses in here today, this wouldn't have happened."

Sam frowned, his brow in a tight, dark line. He stood upright. "Did you see anybody outside?"

"No," Kevin said. "I'd just come back inside from talking to one of our delivery guys and there was nobody out there then."

Sam walked over to the window. June watched him as he reached up and poked at one of the jagged dangling pieces of glass. The shard fell and landed on the floor at his feet but didn't break.

"You see?" Kevin declared. "This is what I get for entertaining the leader of the Paranormal Alliance."

"No one knew I was coming here." Sam peered at the bullet hole again, narrowing his eyes. "No one except people I trust."

"Maybe you can't trust them as much as you thought," Kevin said.

"I think they were trying to kill me." Cindy clutched her chest. "What if I'd died? What would have become of my poor Dipity, at home all by herself without her mommy to take care of her? She would have starved to death."

"Screw that cat," Kevin said. "That bitch used to scratch the hell out of me."

"Hey," June said. "Don't be so harsh on the Dipster!"

Kevin scowled at her.

June shrugged. "I like that cat. She never tore me up."

"My baby." Cindy sniffed. "I was looking for a cat for a friend when I found her. That's why her name is Serendipity."

"Somebody shot up my bar!" Kevin threw his arms open. "And although I'm sure you've done plenty to warrant it, Cindy, I doubt they were specifically targeting you. My guess is someone knew I was letting paranormals in here."

Sam bent and gazed at the bullet hole again. "They take the bullet out of here?"

"No," Kevin said. "They said it's too deep in there. They're gonna send someone to dig it out, at some point, for evidence. You know how fast the police work. I better not have to keep the place closed 'til then."

"Where was your gun?" June asked Cindy. "You can take it out to shoot a hapless funeral director, but you couldn't shoot back at someone shooting at you?"

"I don't have it with me." Cindy huffed. "I don't have a conceal and carry license."

"Because God knows you're such a law-abiding citizen."

"That's it." Kevin made a slashing motion with his hands. "You guys are out of here. I'm getting this mess cleaned up and then I have to call my nighttime bartenders and tell them not to come in. I'm already done with this day."

"No." Sam stood. "I came here for a reason, and you're going to do what I need you to do."

"Somebody shot up my bar!"

"And you're not the only person who can work a broom and make phone calls," Sam said.

"This is a little more important to me right now than your bullshit."

"Is it?" Sam stepped forward. "You've been summoned to repay your debt, and if you don't do it, your world is going to get a lot more complicated than it is now."

Kevin glared at Sam, but his glare lacked conviction. He was clenching and unclenching his hands at his sides.

"Go out the back door." Sam addressed Cindy and June, jerking his head toward the room beyond the bar. "Wait for us outside. I need to have a little discussion with Kevin, alone. Don't let anyone see you out there. Assume at all times we're being watched from here on out."

Cindy obeyed without question, and June followed her through the bar and the room they'd been in earlier and out a door in the back. The door exited onto a patio surrounded by trees. Bare branches hung over white wrought-iron tables and a bar beneath an awning, closed down and empty of bottles. A high brick wall on one side kept them cloistered from the public.

June fished out her cigarettes and lit one up.

Cindy paced in a circle, arms wrapped around herself. "Do you think they were trying to kill Sam?"

"Er"—June flicked her ash onto the concrete—"I dunno. I thought you were more worried they were trying to kill you?"

Cindy stopped pacing. "I know it was probably him they were after, but I didn't want to say that in front of him." Her voice wavered. "I would take a bullet for him, and I almost did. He's done so much for me, more than my family, more than anyone I've ever known. I know he doesn't see it this way, but he's like my best friend."

June didn't know what to say. Her own best friend had a wicked motorcycle and taught her how to smoke weed.

"Damn it." Cindy kicked at the concrete. "Why does this have to be so dangerous? I just want a normal life. That's all I've ever wanted."

"You could always leave the Paranormal Alliance."

Cindy wiped her eyes with the heel of her hand. "I couldn't give up on Sam. He taught me not to fear what's inside of me."

"What the hell are you, exactly?"

Cindy's eyes were bright. "I'm a sex witch."

"A what?"

"A sex witch. That's what we call ourselves. The Institute calls it 'psychic-sexual ability.' I feed on sexual energy."

June took a step away from her. This explained a lot, though.

"Oh, don't flatter yourself." Cindy snorted. "That's why I drink so much, especially when I'm around a bunch of men. It dulls it. I found that out when I was a teenager. Drugs, too."

"That sounds like a healthy alternative."

"Boys were a terrible distraction during puberty. And I did awful things to them."

"I'll read about it in a book or something, all right? Please stop sharing." Shuddering, June imagined the poor teenage boys Cindy molested. "Is that why you've had multiple husbands?"

She nodded. "My ability...charms." She bit her lip. "And too many times, before I wised up, I mistook it for real attraction."

This at least explained Kevin.

"It could be worse," June said.

"Could it?"

"Yeah, trust me, it could."

The door opened. Sam stepped out, his expression blustery, an equally agitated-looking Kevin following him. Kevin wore a leather jacket more tailored than June's—fashion, not punk. June pitched her cigarette on the concrete and ground it out with her boot.

"Cindy," Sam said, "do you know where Robbie is right now?"

"No, but I can text him." She pushed a hand into her coat pocket.

"Do you think he can help us get into a morgue?" Sam asked.

Cindy pulled her phone out. "Is there anywhere Robbie can't help you get into?"

"Let's just hope they have what we're looking for."

"Like what," June asked, "a puppy?"

Cindy got in touch with Robbie. He told her he would meet them there. "There," Sam explained, was the Cook County Morgue, apparently a happening spot, because no one needed directions.

Sam drove them through the neighborhoods of Chicago, past gritty tight-packed urban cluster and alternately lavish blocks of huge beautiful houses. June sat in the back with Kevin, Cindy in the front. They were silent most of the way, Kevin sitting as far away from June as he could physically manage. What the hell were they about to do in a morgue? Maybe she didn't want to know the answer.

They arrived at a two-story catacomb-windowed building with a low wall proclaiming OFFICE OF THE MEDICAL EXAMINER at the entrance to the parking lot. The gloom of evening had descended, turning the world shadowy and sinister. Sam pulled into a spot and killed the engine.

"This is going to be a group effort." Sam turned and looked in the backseat. "Kevin, you know your part. June, you're going to have the most important role."

"As long as I don't have to jack any dead bodies," June said. "I just busted into a funeral home a couple days ago and that was creepy enough."

"You won't be stealing anything. But you're about to get a whole new idea of what 'creepy' is."

"Thanks for the reassurance," she said.

"What am I going to do?" Cindy asked.

"You're going to stay here and keep a lookout," Sam said. "And drive the getaway car, if need be."

"What am I looking out for?" Cindy asked.

"Everything."

They waited for Robbie to arrive. No one spoke, making the tension even worse. Finally, a black car pulled into the parking lot and slid up beside them. Robbie sat in the driver's seat.

"About time," Sam muttered.

They all got out. Cindy walked around to the driver's side. June zipped her jacket and shrugged down into the leather.

"Tell me what I'm supposed to do," she said to Sam.

"We need to get in to where the bodies are." Sam tugged his own coat closed. "You need to convince anyone we come across that's a good idea."

Robbie had a long black coat on, his hair pulled back. In addition to a huge mouth, he had big bulgy eyes as well, like a caricature, and they were luminescent greenish-gray against the dull light. He gazed unflinching at June, strands of loose hair fluttering across his wide forehead. He was creepy, and she couldn't place her finger on exactly why—it wasn't just the mind reading thing. He was skulky and looming and weird.

"There's nothing in my head worth seeing right now," June said to him. "Get lost."

Robbie started toward the building. He also had a strange, slippery way of moving, gliding along as if on roller skates. The rest of them followed him up the concrete walkway to the building, pressing against the frigid wind.

"Is that because of his power?" June asked Sam, walking next to him. "He looks like he's floating."

Sam stared straight ahead. "Yes. My brother was a telekinetic. He could do the same thing."

"Was?"

They stopped outside a set of glass doors, and Robbie pulled one open.

Sam glanced briefly at her. "You're not the only one who's lost a brother."

June stood still for a moment, stunned. Kevin went in. Sam followed.

They entered a foyer dominated by a security desk. A guard with a shiny bald head sat behind the desk. He looked up from writing something.

"Can I help you?" he asked gruffly.

June scrambled for something to say. "We have an appointment." Her power spread through her chest and welled up her throat, warm and prickling. "Let us inside."

The man stared at June for a moment, his gaze going glassy. He pushed his chair back. "Right this way."

They had to pass through a metal detector. June took off her jacket so they wouldn't encounter any unnecessary hassle. After they stepped through, Sam gestured questioningly at her face as she pulled the jacket back on.

"You didn't set it off," he said. "With all those piercings."

"It's a myth body piercings set off metal detectors. Unless you're wearing some huge metal gauge. I can't believe I finally know something you don't."

They entered a lobby with thin blue carpet, the room divided into a small waiting area with chairs and couches and a reception area with a high desk. A woman with long brown hair and glasses sat behind the desk.

"Can I help you?" she asked, with watered-down friendliness.

June readied herself. Cameras peered down from the corners of the room. She had to make her behavior look natural.

"We need to go back to—where you keep the bodies." June leaned on the desk and lowered her voice. "I want you to send someone back with us so we look like we're supposed to be there."

The woman's eyes were unfocused behind her glasses. "One moment." She picked up the phone in front of her.

June watched closely as she punched a button. She silently held the receiver to her ear until a faint voice came on the other end. "Jim, can you come up front and escort some people back to the morgue?" She paused. "No, I'm not sure who they—" She lowered the receiver. "Who are you again?"

Robbie stepped up beside June. Suddenly, the end of the phone cord fell out of the receiver and dropped onto the desk.

"Never mind," June said quickly. "Put the phone down."

She did.

"Why didn't you just snatch the phone off her and talk to Jim?" Kevin asked in an irritated whisper.

"Because my power doesn't work across electronic devices," June said.

"Jim will come out anyway," Sam said. "Keep your poker faces on."

"Stay quiet right now," June told the woman. "Don't say anything when Jim comes out here."

A moment later a door to the right of the desk opened. A tall middle-aged man dressed in a white lab coat emerged.

"Can I help you?" he asked, frowning.

June turned toward him. "Take us back to the morgue."

"We have to hurry this up," Sam muttered. "Before it starts looking weird on the cameras."

Jim held the door for them. June followed the others, trepidatious. Beyond the door stretched a long white hallway. Jim led them silently along the corridor, past various office-like rooms. They saw only one other person, an older man behind a desk who gave them a cursory look as they passed.

When they reached the end of the hallway, they faced a steel door; a security panel was mounted on the wall next to it. Jim swiped a card through the reader. A buzz sounded, and he opened the door.

"I'm afraid everyone's gone home for the day, about a half hour ago." He sounded politely bewildered. "Most of the people who work back here go home at five, unless a special case comes in. You're more likely to get someone early in the morning or just after lunch."

"Stop talking," June said. "Don't wonder why we're here."

They stepped into a short corridor lit by a bare bulb dangling from the ceiling, the air colder than the outer hallway. Two more metal doors loomed in front of them, one labeled MORGUE, the other AUTOPSY ROOM.

"Guess we know our door," Sam said. "June, make him go away."

June turned to Jim. "Go back to what you were doing. Forget we're back here."

Jim promptly turned and walked out. The door closed behind him with a resounding clang.

"Well, that was easy," Sam said.

"For you." June scowled at him.

"Let's get this over with." Sam motioned to the doors.

Robbie stepped up to the morgue door. He tried the knob, but it didn't turn. June hoped they were locked out, but Robbie stepped back, stared at the knob for a moment, and a pop sounded. He tried the knob again. This time it turned, and he pulled the door open.

"Thank you, Robbie," Sam said.

"Yeah, thanks," June added ruefully.

She didn't want to go in. The air streamed out cold, carrying a faintly chemical smell. She tried to find some resolve. She didn't want to look like a scared little kid.

The others filed in ahead of her. She waited until the lights popped on and then cautiously inched through the doorway.

"I don't wanna see any dead bodies all cut up," she whispered. She didn't know why she whispered.

"You're not going to," Kevin said. "They do that in the autopsy room. This is just where they store cadavers."

The morgue consisted of a warehouse-like room with a white tile floor and gray walls, eerily quiet, the atmosphere like a hospital. Along the back wall were square metal doors two rows high. Metal tables with creepy-looking attachments and sinks built into them stood in various places. As they moved deeper into the room, the antiseptic smell gave way to a cold, clean odor with an underlying scent not unlike meat, like the fresh rank odor of a butcher shop.

"To hell with this." The scent made something primal inside of June snap, and she started to backpedal. Before she could get far, Sam grabbed her arm.

"Don't freak out," he said. "There's nothing in here that can hurt you. Unlike out there."

June swallowed and tried to breathe through only her mouth. She reminded herself being in the funeral home had been just as bad and she'd survived that debacle. Sam held on to her arm for a moment and gave it a squeeze before letting go.

"Can we get on with this?" Kevin asked. "Or does your girlfriend need to piss her pants first?"

"Don't test me, Kevin." Sam started toward the metal doors. "Or you might end up in one of these coolers."

June regarded the cooler doors with dread. How many bodies were in them? How did they end up behind those doors? Had they kept Rose in this morgue? Would her brother end up on a slab too? Would she?

"Spread out and start looking," Sam said.

June had no idea what they were looking for, so she stayed in place. Kevin and Robbie walked over to the doors and began perusing the labels below them, while Sam did the same, moving in the opposite direction. After a minute, freaked out standing in the middle of the room alone, June stepped closer.

Sam finally stopped, peering closely at a label beneath an upper door. "I think I found one."

June flinched. "Found what?"

Sam looked over his shoulder at Kevin. "It says she died yesterday. Will that work?"

"As long as it's been less than twenty-four hours, I guess," Kevin said.

"You guess? You know more about this than I do."

"I never asked my grandmother for details. She said it works within a day. I assume that means twenty-four hours."

"All right." Sam stepped back and nodded to Robbie. "I guess we'll try her."

Robbie walked over to Sam and focused on the door. A *clink* sounded. June's heart leapt. The door swung open in a slow arc and ice vapor rolled out, like something from a horror movie. June made a little whiny sound in her throat and backed up.

A metal slab slid out, appearing from the vapor like a magician's trick. On the slab, the unmistakable shape of a human body rested beneath a white sheet. The form didn't jiggle naturally when the slab jerked to a stop, like a living body would. Little tendrils of mist rose from the sheet.

"What is going on?" June summoned every bit of courage to remain standing in place instead of bolting for the door.

Kevin pulled something out of his jacket pocket. The white box.

"June." Sam hurried over to her. He stepped behind her and gripped her arms above the elbows. June widened her eyes. "I know you don't like being here," he said. "I don't blame you one bit."

This couldn't be going anywhere good.

"Something very messed up is about to happen, but I desperately"— Sam shook her—"need you to stay here."

"What are you talking about?" June asked.

"You want to save your brother, don't you?"

"I fail to see the connection."

"You will, momentarily. You need to stay right here. For Jason." Sam looked around at her. "His name is Jason, right?"

Kevin opened the box and dropped the lid on the floor.

"I don't wanna touch the body." June didn't care how pathetic she sounded. "Please don't make me touch it."

"No, you don't have to touch it," Sam said. "I promise."

Kevin, delicately, took something out of the box: a small, glass vial with a black stopper, filled with dark red fluid, like blood.

"I hate this," Kevin said.

"Your debt will be paid," Sam spoke to Kevin over June's shoulder. "For you, at least, the past will be put to rest."

Kevin shook his head subtly, his lips in a tight line. He squared his shoulders and stood up straighter.

"What the *hell* is going on?" June asked.

Sam held her arms tighter. "Please try to trust me. I'm the smartest man you've ever met."

With a screwed-up expression of distaste, Kevin gripped the edge of the sheet and peeled it back. The fabric made a crackling sound.

"Gah." June jerked.

Sam held her in place.

The woman under the sheet was young, slender, and tiny with sharp features and short blond hair. Her skin was unnaturally white, almost gray, and her closed eyes and lips darkly purpled. In delirious horror, June noticed her ears were gauged.

Kevin grimaced. "Can I get a glove or something?"

Robbie walked off and returned briefly with a box of latex gloves. He held the box out to Kevin.

"Thanks." Kevin held the stopper of the vial between his teeth while he pulled out a glove and worked it onto his right hand.

June tried to look away, but her fascination overcame her horror. "Whatever's about to happen isn't going to be cool, is it?"

"I guess it depends on your idea of cool," Sam said.

Kevin pushed a gloved fingertip between the woman's cold-bruised lips and pried them open. June cringed.

After making a gap, he uncorked the vial and tilted the open end over her mouth. The room had gone so quiet June heard a soft gurgle as the liquid dribbled out.

"Be careful," Sam warned. "Don't lose a drop."

"Do you think I'm stupid?" Kevin didn't look up.

Kevin poured the entire vial and then shoved the stopper back in the end. He slipped the vial into his jacket pocket and stepped back. Robbie stepped back as well. June tensed.

"I'm sorry if I seemed offended," Sam whispered, close to her ear. "That kiss was spectacular."

"What?"

June realized a second later Sam wanted to distract her, when the body let out a hiss of air.

When the body fucking *moved*.

June shrieked. She tried to dart away, but Sam held her fast. She struggled.

"Stay here," Sam ordered. "It's the only way to save your brother."

"What the fuck!" June yelped. "What the fucking fuck!"

The dead girl turned her head toward them. A cracking sound like ice breaking rent the air. The girl's eyes were still closed, but she opened her mouth, a dark maw in her ashen face. Kevin averted his gaze to the ceiling. Robbie had somehow managed to widen his eyes even farther.

"Don't panic." Sam fought to hold June in place. "Kevin, cover her up!"

Kevin grabbed the sheet and threw it back over the girl's face. She still moved underneath, turning her head from side to side. Then she spoke.

"Asssssssssk." The sound resembled air escaping a balloon. Not a human voice. Hollow and emotionless. Dead.

"What is this?" June demanded. "What the hell?"

"It's an oracle," Sam said. "The Oracle of the Dead. They know things the living don't."

"An oracle. She's gonna tell the future?"

"Oracles don't tell the future. They give counsel. But you can only ask her one question, and then the spell is broken. You have to act quickly."

"Me?"

"Yes, you. You have to ask her how to get your brother out of the Institute."

The thing under the sheet still twitched. Kevin looked at the walls, the ceiling, at everything but the animated corpse beside him.

"This is some messed up shit," June said. "Fuck!"

"Kevin's grandmother was very powerful," Sam said. "She gave us this particular Oracle. I couldn't do this without him. But I can't do this without you, either. Only a family member can make inquiries about someone."

"You better hurry up," Kevin said. "And also, I think you could do this just fine without me." He sounded bitter.

"June, if you want to save your brother, you have to ask her," Sam said. "Suck it up and do it."

Scarcely a thing in the world could make June get closer to the slab. The movements under the sheet were getting slower, more languid. *Scarcely* a thing, except the thought of Jason under that sheet.

June inched forward, forcing her feet to move, glad Sam stayed at her back and kept pushing her. She reached Kevin, way too close, and couldn't take another step.

"Ask her," Sam urged.

June had no idea what to say. She didn't want to hear that voice again. She drew a shuddering breath and leaned forward a tiny bit.

"How—how do I—" Her words were shaky. "How do I get Jason out of the Institute?"

The body snapped its head toward her. June lurched back. The room seemed to brighten and spin.

"Dooon't gooo insssssiiide," the voice breathed out, every sound elongated in a sigh. "Maaake them briiing hiiim ouuut."

June stared, trembling.

"Puuublic pressssure." The voice seemed to be getting softer, weaker. "Gooo tooo the presssss."

"The press?" Sam asked.

The corpse rolled her head slowly into a supine position. "Ethaaaan Robertssss…" The sound faded with a slow hiss and fell silent.

After a moment, when she didn't speak again, June pulled at Sam's grip. "Let me go."

Sam did. "Don't leave yet," he said. "We need your help to get out." He turned to Robbie. "Put her away."

Through the buzzing in her ears, June heard the slab slide back in and the door clang shut. Her knees had gone weak. Her stomach turned.

Sam grabbed her arm. "Let's go."

June moved mindlessly as they made their way out of the building, down the white hallway, through the reception area, past the security desk. She spoke to people, her power surging warm inside her cold body, but she barely knew her own voice.

Outside, the icy air shocked her back to reality. She stumbled to the back of the car and vomited. Sam slid up beside her and placed a reassuring hand between her shoulder blades as she gagged and retched.

"It's all right," Sam said. "Most people react like this their first time."

After the heaves passed, June remained hunched over, trembling, equal parts stricken and resembling the world's biggest tool, her forehead pressed against the cold metal of the car. Her mouth tasted bitter, and her throat burned. Sam kept his hand on her back.

"Oh, for God sake," Kevin muttered.

"Shut up," Sam said. "Or else."

Cindy had gotten out of the car. She stood a few feet away, nose scrunched up.

"You want some water?" Cindy asked. "I got some in my bag."

Sam removed his hand, but grim understanding glowed in his eyes.

"Well"—June spat into the puddle of puke at her feet—"I guess we better do what the dead body says."

Chapter 8

When June and Sam entered the hotel room, Micha was curled up in a chair asleep, Muse sitting on one of the sofas watching TV. She swiveled around and Sam gazed at her, not speaking. June got the impression he was sharing telepathically what had happened.

Micha stirred and lifted his head. He blinked slowly. "Oh." His voice was thick and he licked his lips. "You guys are back."

"Yeah." June peeled off her jacket.

Micha's eyes were glazed, his face pale.

"You all right?" she asked.

"Yeah." Micha sat up. He raised his eyebrows. "Wow. That's some crazy stuff."

"What is?" June asked.

"What you just saw."

June stepped back, startled and confused.

Sam breezed past, coat over his arm and cell phone in hand. "I'm going to make some calls. Try to get in touch with Ethan."

"Okay." June said absently.

"Ethan's a busy man," Sam said. "I'm not talking to his voicemail."

Micha sat up fully and placed his feet on the floor. "What did you guys get up to today?"

June didn't answer, still too addled to handle anything else. She went out on the balcony to smoke and to bask in the cold air so she could clear her head and get her senses working again. As she finished the cigarette and contemplated another one, Sam stepped outside. She ground the butt out on the railing.

"I'll be in touch with Ethan Roberts shortly," he said. "I don't know why I didn't come up with this myself."

"Why didn't you tell me what you were planning at the morgue?"

"If I had, you wouldn't have gone."

"I would have had a choice."

"There was no choice."

"I would have at least been prepared." She pulled her cigarettes out of her jacket pocket. Her fingers were numb. "You had no right to make me face that without warning."

"I told you how the Oracle of the Dead works. You had to be the one to ask."

"That's not the point." She nearly crumpled the pack in her fist. "You could have told me why we were going there, explained to me what was about to happen."

"And you would have resisted. You know so little about yourself and the people like you. You're a child in the wilderness. That's why you're in this position right now."

She shook a cigarette out and pulled the matches from the bar out of her pocket. "You're a bastard." She cupped a hand around the end of the cigarette and lit it, shaking.

Sam's eyes glittered. "Am I?" He turned and went back into the room.

June smoked the cigarette. Now she had guilt to deal with on top of everything else. When she went back inside, she could barely feel her hands and feet. Sam sat in the bedroom, on the end of the bed. Muse had disappeared, and Micha was slumped in his chair, staring at the TV.

June plodded into the bedroom and sat down stiffly on the end of the bed, next to Sam. He had the TV on as well and was watching the news.

"It'll probably be morning before I hear anything," Sam said flatly. "I was just being optimistic."

"Look. Thank you," she said. "Thank you for everything you've done for me. Everything you're *still* doing for me. I appreciate it. Even if your methods scare the shit out of me."

Sam stared at the TV.

"Sam—"

"It's perfectly reasonable to be disturbed by what you saw today," he said. "Hell, I'd be shocked if you weren't. But there are horrors in this world, and though I don't wish them upon you, you're in a place right now where far more horrifying things may happen. Prepare yourself."

"Yeah, I figured." She rubbed the back of her neck. "I don't scare easy. But I don't like the thought of—mortality, I guess. Corpses and…ghosts."

"Death is not easy to get used to." His voice dropped a notch. "But someday you'll have to accept it."

She pictured the glass at Navy Pier, the angel leading the woman into death.

"I'm sorry I called you a bastard just now," she said. "I didn't mean that."

"I'm sorry I didn't warn you."

They were quiet for a minute. The two televisions blared in stereo. Micha was watching the same thing.

"So," she said, groping for some social grace she knew she must possess. "Your...brother. I take it he's dead? Or disappeared, since you said 'was.'"

"He's dead."

"Older? Younger?" she asked. "Twin?"

"He was older than me."

"When did he die?"

"Some years ago."

"How did he die?"

His expression was unreadable. He didn't speak.

"Sorry," she muttered.

After another minute, Sam got to his feet. "I need to go take care of some things. Muse will be in the hotel tonight, watching over you. If you need anything, simply call out to her. She'll hear."

"So she'll be monitoring our thoughts all night?"

"No, she'll just be listening for you. So you can have some privacy."

June didn't bother denying anything.

After Sam left, they ordered food. Micha got into his pajama pants. June wanted to stay dressed in case Sam returned with some news and they had to leave, even if he did say it would be morning before he heard anything. Morning seemed centuries away.

The food arrived, and while they ate, sitting together on one of the sofas, Micha looked through his phone.

"What are you doing?" June asked around a mouthful of veggie burger. No bun, no cheese. "Should you really have that on? Someone might track it or something."

"Unlikely. You need some pretty sophisticated equipment to track a cell phone. I'm looking through my pictures and my call history. Trying to remember something. About her."

June watched him, chewing.

"The last call I made was eight days ago."

That was when Micha had "disappeared."

"It was to Rose," he said.

June morbidly wondered if Rose's voice was still on his voicemail.

"Look through the photo album." Micha held the phone out. "I remember all those people, except her."

She didn't want to, but she humored him, hoping he'd forgotten he had risqué pictures of himself on there. Most of the pictures were boring, full of people June had never seen before. She stopped on one, obviously self-taken, of Micha grinning like a fool, head tilted against his wife's shoulder. Rose was snuggled up to his side, smiling. She was gorgeous, and they looked gorgeous together. Guilt roiled in her gut, eating up anything peaceful left inside her. She lost her appetite.

"Nice." She set the phone aside.

After they finished, June sat on a lounger in front of the wall of windows. Outside, snow fell, big fluffy flakes swirling past the glass, nearly obscuring the city glittering in the darkness beyond. Micha had gone to the bathroom, and when he returned, he stopped at the room service cart and then walked over and leaned on the back of the lounger, next to her shoulder. His form was reflected in the glass.

"Here." He handed her a white mug. "I poured you some coffee."

She didn't want anything, but she took it. The smell of whiskey wafted up. "Thanks."

"What's on your mind?"

She didn't even know where to begin answering that question. "I gotta get in touch with my mother somehow. Much longer without word, and she'll fly here to find out what's going on. I don't want anything to happen to her." She rubbed her hand, almost unconsciously, along the underside of her right forearm. "I also hope I don't have to tell her Jason's dead."

Micha shifted closer. "Who is it?"

"Huh?"

"The portrait on your arm. I've been wanting to ask, but it didn't seem appropriate."

June bent her arm. A little girl with chubby cheeks and long, curly hair was tattooed on the underside of her forearm, the detail exquisite, all black ink, no color except June's skin.

"It's our little sister," she said.

"You didn't mention you had a sister."

"I don't, technically." She lowered her arm. "She died when she was five and we were eight. Jason killed her."

Micha gasped.

"It wasn't his fault," she said. "Stupid kid stuff. They were picking on each other, like brothers and sisters do. She said something dumb, made him mad. He told her to go jump off the roof. So she did. We lived in a four-story apartment building."

Micha gaped at her in the window. "Oh my God."

"We were just kids. We didn't understand our power. Our parents never found out what really happened. The police told them she must have sneaked up there to play, and the owners were building a rooftop patio at the time. There weren't any railings yet, so they said she must have slipped and fell. Hell, that's what I believed for a long time. Jason didn't tell me the truth until we were teenagers. He stopped using his power after she died, and I didn't understand why until then."

"Christ, that's horrible," Micha whispered. "I'm sorry, June."

"Thanks. But like I said, it wasn't his fault. That was the final straw between our parents, though. They lost their one normal kid, and our dad wanted rid of us." She tapped her fingers against her mug. "When they were making Jason use his power at the Institute, it was like they were torturing him. The whole way here, he was uptight about it. Neither of us wanted to come, but the Institute was so insistent. And they promised us all this money. I was gonna give mine to our mother so she could pay off her house."

Micha placed his hands on her shoulders. He didn't say anything, just started kneading.

"I barely remember Katie. But I found a picture my mom had in a photo album. I didn't get the tattoo in her memory. I got it to remind myself what I'm capable of. What I can do if I'm not careful."

"So many dangers," Micha said softly. "So much to fear. I know I can never understand, not really, but I try. I want to understand, so I can help."

She squeezed her fingers around the mug. "Thanks. I shouldn't have given you a hard time about it. I'm sorry."

"It's all right. I'm used to it."

Quiet swaddled them. June slowly relaxed, the combination of whiskey and Micha's massage softening her muscles. And doing other things.

"So you don't have a boyfriend?" Micha asked, his voice drifting down like the flakes of snow.

June took a sip of the coffee. "No. Relationships make me nervous."

Micha dug his fingers in harder, above her collarbone. "I know the answer."

"The answer?"

"When I said I liked you. You told me I had the wrong answer." He slid his fingers around the base of her throat. "I *do* like you. But you're not interesting. You're a normal person with normal hopes and fears and you just want a normal life. You don't want to be special. You just want to be you. Plain, regular, simple you."

June tilted her head back between Micha's arms. He smiled down at her. She reached up, groped for a handful of silky gold-and-brown hair, and drew him down.

"You know we shouldn't do this," she whispered.

"I know."

Kissing in such an awkward position hurt her neck, and their lips met at a strange angle, so June got up. Standing proved awkward as well, since she had to push up on her tiptoes to even be sort of at face-level with him. She had such a love-hate relationship with being short. She hated her stature, but she loved tall men.

She forgot about the unequal heights, though, when Micha pushed his hands up under her shirt and toyed with the posts through her nipples. Apparently he'd seen them through her shirt the night before, as she suspected. He finished checking them out and slid his hands down her sides, to the top of her pants. She broke away from his mouth and started kissing his neck. He smelled ridiculously good for a man who had been in hiding for a week. She could tell he'd showered while they were gone.

"I like how tiny you are," he murmured. He slid his hands back up her sides, fingers passing over her ribs, making her aware of each one. "Like I could just pick you up and do whatever I wanted with you."

June drew back. Micha's eyes were glimmering. He had such a strong, handsome face; she imagined pushing his chin back and licking all the way from his throat to his jaw.

"A bit on the dominant side, are we?" she said.

"Not really."

"No?"

"I know what I want, but I'm not dominant. A little aggressive, maybe."

June rubbed a hand over her mouth and chin, wet from the kissing. "I'm aggressive too. We might have a power struggle here."

"Kinky." Micha gripped her hands and drew her, while walking backwards, toward the bedroom. "So I take it this won't be romantic?"

"If it's romance you're looking for, you've got the wrong gal."

Micha chuckled. They entered the bedroom, and he let go of her hands. He tugged his T-shirt up and off. He had a broad chest and a tightly-muscled torso. A faint trail of sandy hair stretched downward from his navel on his smooth, flat stomach. June forgot how to talk for a moment. He smiled at her, all come-hither like.

"So"—she managed to untie her tongue—"you sure?"

"Yes."

"I feel like I'm doing something really bad right now."

"Shouldn't that make it more fun?"

"Not bad like, oh no, my mom is gonna find out." She pushed a hand through her hair. "I mean like actual bad, like I'm a bad person."

"You're not a bad person." He backed toward the bed. "Come on."

She turned off the bedside lamp, hoping darkness would somehow make things easier. The glow of the city through the snowfall infused the room. June got in bed with him.

"Don't worry about being aggressive," she said, close to his ear, close enough to his body to do terribly intimate things. "I'm not fragile."

His breath ghosted hot across her jaw. "I'm not either."

She swallowed. "I just don't want you to regret this, if—you know. Your memory comes back."

"Even if it does, I won't hold it against you. I promise."

"I just…" She couldn't believe she was arguing when he was so close, so ready, so willing.

"Just touch me," Micha whispered. "It's all right."

She pulled the waistband of his pajama bottoms out and pushed a hand inside. His groin was warm, his cock hard. He did want this. She pressed against him, equally aroused despite her protests, clenching and liquid inside. She tried not to think of Rose or the terrifying notion she might suddenly appear next to the bed with a knife in her hand.

"Can I check out your piercing?" Micha asked, his voice husky. He slid a hand down her thigh, and she instinctually spread her legs. He wasn't talking about her nipples this time.

"Yeah, go for it." She nuzzled in his hair—soft and smelling of shampoo—like she'd wanted to do for days.

She helped him push her jeans and panties down over her hips. A moment later, she discovered he also wasn't talking about checking it out with his hands, as he slipped down and buried his face between her legs. She tensed. She hadn't shaved in a while. Then she quit giving a damn and started enjoying the hot, wet lapping of his tongue. He swirled the tip of it over the ring and she hissed softly.

Micha lifted his head. "Does it hurt?"

"No. It's just sensitive."

"Did it hurt to have it done?"

"It's a piece of metal shoved through a delicate part. Yes, it hurt."

He chuckled and eased two fingers into her. She gasped and lifted her hips. He made light, sweeping passes over the ring with his thumb. A little stimulation was good, but too much sensation could get overwhelming fast. He seemed to know the balance.

"You like pain?" he asked.

"No. Why would you think that?"

"You're covered in tattoos and you're pierced in places I wouldn't allow a needle anywhere near."

"It only hurts for a second. I'm not into pain, though. Are you?"

"No. But I'm open to anything, really."

"Just keep doing what you're doing. It's great."

His tattoo spanned the space between his shoulder blades. In the dark, she couldn't make out much detail, but it looked like a compass rose.

He dove back in and used his tongue with precision, swirling it over her clit again, flicking the ring, his fingers deep inside her, providing more stimulation. She clenched around his fingers, shuddering, eyes closed tight. He was meticulous in pleasuring her but sloppy in execution—eager and messy but not all over the place. He seemed to be enjoying it too, breathing soft little moans into her. She played with his hair.

After a few minutes, though loathe for him to quit, she urged him to come back up beside her. She took her shirt off so they could be skin to skin. She wanted to get on to the main attraction, now restless and turned on and aching. He squeezed her breasts and played with the piercings again.

"Nice little handfuls," he murmured, and ducked his head down to suck on one of her nipples.

She smiled and stroked her fingers through his hair. "I really don't mind having tiny tits. I don't have to wear a bra. I guess some guys like them bigger though, like Cindy's."

"If they're tits, I'm not complaining. Just putting that out there."

She tugged at his hair and urged him back to her mouth.

Micha possessed all her favorite things about a man: solid everywhere, firm muscles, no soft edges. She slid her tongue along the sharp ridge of his collarbone and inhaled the scent of his skin, warm and sweet like breathing in sunshine, the same scent she'd smelled many nights in a row now. The same scent that had driven her crazy all those nights.

"Pants off," she said. "Make this easier." She rolled away.

Micha took his pajama bottoms off. In the dim light from the window, her eyes having adjusted, she checked out his cock. Not so big it would hurt, but deliciously thick, making the itching need under her skin intensify. She resisted jumping right on it, though. She'd been fantasizing about something for days, her mouth practically watering at the thought now.

She slid down the bed, the sheets smooth and cool against her bare skin. She licked Micha's lower belly, below his navel where the hair started. His stomach drew in sharply at the touch.

"Fair play," he said. "I like you."

"It would be cruel of me to deny you one of my world class blowjobs." She had a persuasive mouth in more ways than one.

She took him in her hand and sank her mouth over his cock. He tried to lift his hips, but she kept him firmly in place with an arm across his stomach. She was in charge of this show.

He scrabbled at and grabbed the back of her hair. His grip was tense and tight. She bobbed slowly, taking as much of him with each pass as she could manage. On the upward stroke, she teased the underside of the head with the ball on her tongue ring.

"So that's what that's for." His voice was shaky. He laughed.

She smiled around him.

After a few minutes, she stopped, not wanting to bring him off too soon—because if he didn't bang the hell out of her like she wanted right now, she was going to scream. She licked her lips.

Micha panted, gazing down at her, hand still on the back of her head. "Wow," he said, sounding dreamy.

"I know. Amazing, aren't I?"

She crawled up his body and settled on top of him. He wrapped his arms around her and swiftly turned her over, so he was on top. He pushed his fingers into her. She emitted a loud "Uh!" of half surprise, half desperation.

"You okay?" he asked, close to her lips.

She trembled, curling and uncurling her fingers against his bicep. "Yes. Except I'm either going to scream or come if you keep that up."

"Why not both?"

"You're so cruel, teasing me."

"I'll stop teasing you, then. Are you ready?"

"So ready." She gripped his arm. "Shit. Fuck. You don't happen to have any condoms, do you?"

"There's some in the bathroom."

"Really?"

"It's a fancy hotel. They have complimentary everything."

She tried to focus on his face in the dark. "How do you know they're in there?"

"I might have been looking."

He slid his fingers out of her. She wanted them back.

"I'll go grab one," she said. She wiggled out from under him and got off the bed. "You better be ready for action when I get back."

"No problem there."

In the bathroom, squinting in the light and obscenely naked in the mirror, June rummaged through the box of complimentary toiletries on the sink. She found a condom and headed back to the bed. She wasn't on any sort of birth control, but even if she were, she didn't know what nasty secrets Micha might be hiding. He might not even know.

She crawled onto the bed and handed him the condom.

"You're really, really sure about this?" she asked. "I mean, I'm horny as hell right now, but the shower head is detachable."

He opened the packet and worked the condom on. He flicked the package aside. "I'm really, really sure about this. And the shower head won't do anything for me."

She crawled on top of him, as he lay back. "I'm going to hell."

"Right there with you." He gripped her hips. "We'll buy condoms for next time."

"Next time?"

She gasped as his cock slid into her, one smooth stroke, no slow penetration. She groaned at the intrusion, her favorite part of sex. He filled her completely, stretched her in a way that was agonizingly good. Nothing better than getting the cock after waiting so long.

"Fuck," she breathed out.

He slid his hands onto her breasts and squeezed. "Goddamn. That's so tight."

"And that's so thick."

She reached above him and splayed her palms flat against the headboard for leverage, and rode him. He jerked his hips, driving up into her, and moved his hands to her thighs while she bounced on him.

His grunts and gasps escalated into full-bodied moans, mingling with the sound of the headboard thumping against the wall and the bedsprings squeaking. She loved how he sounded. Their flesh slapped lewdly, the lovely cacophony of consummation.

"I wanted to fuck you the first day I met you," she said.

"Did you?"

"Yes." She adjusted her hips so he would hit—*yes*. "I wanted you so bad. Even though I knew it was wrong."

"Sometimes it's good to be bad. I jerked off yesterday in Cindy's bathroom, thinking about you."

"Oh, God."

He grabbed her around the waist and, never slipping out of her, flipped her onto her back. She locked her legs around his waist, delirious, gazing toward the window. The snow swirled, glittering in the darkness beyond the glass.

He pounded into her, so good and hard she was soon screaming the walls down. He had his hand between them, working her, playing with the ring, but even without that she would get off. She was near the edge, tense and ready to tumble over. She stiffened and clutched at him.

"Micha," she choked out.

He pushed deep into her, pressing his lips against her ear through her sweaty hair.

"You're so beautiful," he whispered. "That's it. Come for me."

She didn't need to be told twice. She shuddered through a hard, intense orgasm, bucking against him, clawing at his back. Through her delirious haze of pleasure, his sounds in her ear changed, growing more desperate, and he quaked as well. A moment later, he was coming inside her.

"Damn." She nearly purred. "Oh, yes." She raked her nails lightly up and down his sweaty, shivering back.

Neither of them moved for a few minutes. He was twitching inside her and she clenched around him, little tremors still shaking her thighs. Her head spun.

"Fuck," she finally gasped and slumped beneath him.

Micha groaned in response, still pulsing faintly inside her. She shivered.

Quiet fell in the wake of the explosion. Her body was buzzing and slick with sweat. Micha lay on top of her for a few more minutes. Finally, he reached down, gripped the base of the condom, and slid out. He rolled off her.

The cool air was blissful against her hot skin.

"You all right?" she asked.

"Yeah." He rolled toward her. "I'm great, actually."

He caressed a hand over her sweaty, heaving chest. She wanted to cuddle up to him and enjoy the afterglow, despite everything her rational mind told her about getting attached. She gave the room a quick sweep, still paranoid they were being watched. She kept the guilt tucked firmly away in the back of her head so she could enjoy the low thrumming in her limbs for a few minutes.

"That was good," he said. "Even better than I fantasized about." He rested his hand on her stomach. "Are *you* all right?"

"Yeah. For the first time today, I think I am. But I really need a cigarette."

He patted her stomach and chuckled. "I don't even smoke, and I need one."

Chapter 9

Morning light warmed June's eyelids; she opened them and winced. When she'd gone to sleep, the world beyond the windows had been black and glittering with snow. Now the sky was white, sudden and bright like a nuclear flash. She stirred and became aware of her surroundings—the scent of another person, the heat of a body pressed against her side, silken hair on her shoulder—and her stomach sank. She looked down at the top of Micha's head.

"Shit," she muttered. She'd kind of hoped the whole thing had been a wet dream, so she wouldn't need to deal with the eventual fallout.

Micha stirred and lifted his head, his eyes unfocused. "Hey," he grunted.

At some point, they had both put their shirts and underwear back on.

"Damn." June rolled her head on the pillow. "This bed smells like my mouth tastes."

Micha rolled away. "What time is it? Eight twelve," he answered his own question. He flopped back on the pillows. "I don't feel so good."

"You can't tell you're pregnant that fast," she teased. She sat up and discovered immediately she hurt everywhere. Apparently, twenty-nine was too old for sex. Or she'd gotten rusty.

"It's weird." Micha sounded still half-asleep. "I'm just kind of achy. I swear I'm coming down with something. I don't feel right."

"Could just be this insanely cold weather you guys have here."

June rolled out of bed and hobbled to the bathroom. She needed a shower. She needed a smoke. While she peed, and after, washing her hands and splashing water on her face, concerns the previous night's distraction had kept at bay crept back into her head. Jason's face swam before her, and a sick guilt gurgled in the pit of her stomach.

She returned to the bedroom, found her jeans, pulled them on, and sat down on the edge of the bed. Micha rested a hand on her lower back. He started rubbing in slow circles. She sat hunched, staring at the floor.

"I can order up some breakfast," he said. "If you're hungry. I'm not, myself."

June didn't respond. After a moment, Micha stopped rubbing. His hand fell away.

"You regret last night?" he asked.

June lifted her head. "No." She reached over and picked up her cigarettes from the nightstand. "Well, I mean, I do for the obvious reasons. When your memory comes back, you'll regret it too, trust me. I'm more angry at myself." She got to her feet.

"Why?"

She shook a cigarette out, popped the filter into her mouth, and tossed the pack on the stand. "Here I am, getting laid and ordering room service while my brother's a prisoner. Who knows what they've done to him." She snatched up her lighter. "And I'm having the time of my life."

Micha sat up. "It's not like while you're not getting laid and ordering room service, you're sitting around doing nothing. Sam will get him out of there."

June grabbed her jacket and went out on the balcony. The floor of the balcony was covered with snow. The world below had turned white, the streets cutting through the frosted landscape in narrow black stripes. The air was bitter cold. She shivered as she smoked, cursing her habit. When she finished, she went back inside and found Micha dressed, hair tousled and still looking groggy.

"I'll order some food," he said.

June gathered up things so she could take a shower. She'd stay in her jeans, because she was too small to wear Micha's pants, but she had another borrowed shirt from him, a dark green long-sleeve crew neck that would still be too big on her.

"You can use my shampoo if you want," he said. "Instead of the hotel stuff."

"Thanks."

"You really don't regret last night? I mean, other than for the obvious reasons?"

She toed the carpet. "No. It was nice. I just feel bad, you know? 'Cause of Jason."

"I'm sorry if it was an inappropriate time for it to happen."

"Yeah, well. You're right. What's the alternative, lying in bed staring at the ceiling, waiting for a miracle to fall from it?"

Micha smiled faintly. "Thanks for turning my fantasy into reality."

She rubbed the back of her neck. "Likewise. My vagina doesn't regret it at all, trust me. Except for being a little sore."

She took some time in the shower, not because she felt dirty. She needed to be alone. The dull ache between her legs kept drawing her attention back to the previous night's events and away from other things she tried to focus on. She'd picked a terrible time to let lust get the better of her.

As soon as she turned off the water, a knock sounded at the door.

"What?" Panic struck. She slid the shower door open and reached for a towel. Steam filled the room, blanking out the mirror. "Micha?"

"Guess again." Not Micha's voice.

The door opened, a blast of cooler air rushing in and parting the steam. Sam. He grinned lewdly. Luckily, she already had the towel wrapped around herself.

"Good morning," he said.

"Jesus, did I say come in? You never learned any basic manners?"

"I don't believe you're one to stand on propriety." He looked her over. "Washing off your sin?"

She glowered at him.

"I have news."

"Can it wait five minutes while I dry off and put some clothes on?"

"If you insist." Sam leaned casually against the doorframe, arms crossed. He looked fresh and even stunning in tight jeans and a snug black sweater.

"Without you in here." She stepped out of the shower and onto the bathmat.

"I spoke to Ethan Roberts this morning." Sam didn't move. "He wants to meet us at two o'clock."

June gaped at him. A spark of hope ignited in her chest, and she forgot she had nothing but a towel on. "That's good, right?"

"According to the Oracle it is. I didn't tell him I was bringing you. I thought I'd let him be surprised." Sam's gaze lingered on her. Given the good news he'd brought, she was almost tempted to open her towel and give him a free look.

"So you think he can help us?" June asked.

"I don't know." He moved away from the doorframe. "We'll take Micha to Robbie's before we meet with him. I don't want to leave him here alone. I want Muse with me."

"I thought this place was safe."

"It is, when Muse is here. I like to double and even triple my defenses when I can. In this city, paranoia is your best friend, and Robbie is so goddamn paranoid they'd never get inside his house. I might have to bring him over to my place at some point and let him overhaul my security system."

He looked her over again, winked, and left the doorway.

"Creep," she called after him.

Muse sat in the outer room, slumped on one of the sofas, legs drawn up and arms around her knees. Her face kept twitching, the corners of her mouth jerking, little fluttering tics around her eyes.

June ate some of the breakfast Micha had ordered while Micha sipped tea. He was pale and listless, and for the first time, she started to worry. True, her power had never made anyone sick, but then, she had never done to anyone what she had done to Micha.

They left within the hour. Sam drove. They slid through the bustle of downtown, past the businesses and towers and into the narrower streets of tight-packed residential areas. Snow was piled at the edges of the sidewalks and clung thickly to tree branches and rooftops. June caught glimpses of the lake, deep gray under a pale gray sky.

Micha sat with June in the backseat and dozed off during the ride, head reclined against the door. She kept glancing over at him, thoughts bouncing between worry, guilt, and how good he'd felt inside her. She vividly recalled the weight of his body, the taste of his sweat. Every time these dirty thoughts entered her head, she tried to squelch them, lest Muse hear as well.

"Does he live in the city?" June asked, trying to distract herself.

"Yes," Sam said. "I've only been there once, though, when he first joined the Paranormal Alliance." He addressed Muse, "This is the way, right?"

She nodded. She had her phone out and the GPS on. So much for magic.

Eventually, they ended up in a nondescript middle-class neighborhood full of little houses clustered close together, all droll and neat and nearly identical. Sam pulled into the driveway of a one-story with white siding and black-trimmed windows. Two cars were parked in the driveway, one of which was Cindy's.

"Doesn't look like a fortress," June remarked.

"The best defenses are hidden," Sam said.

Sam texted Robbie to let him know they'd arrived, citing in ominous fashion they might be injured if they tried to walk in unannounced. June woke Micha, and they both got out of the car. She walked around to his side, eyeing him as he stood with his hands shoved in his coat pockets, droopy-eyed, wobbling. She slid an arm around him to steady him, her concern deepening.

"You all right?" she asked.

She gripped his waist tighter as he swayed, trying to keep him from face-planting on the concrete—not that she would be able to stop him if he went for it.

"I know what you're thinking." Micha's voice was a languid drawl.

"Huh?"

To her surprise, he gripped her chin and kissed her, forcefully and passionately. She didn't know how to react, and made a sound of surprise into his mouth when he gripped her ass and squeezed hard.

Of course, Sam stepped around the car in time to witness this event. He stopped short. "Is this really the time?"

Micha released her, wobbling as he drew back.

"What the hell, Micha," June admonished him, cheeks burning.

"Come on, you horny bastards," Sam said. "Robbie's waiting." He turned and marched toward the house, and Muse followed.

Micha leaned in to June and whispered, "You want me even more now. Don't feel bad. I want you too. You kept thinking about us fucking in the backseat."

June goggled at him. "What is wrong with you?"

"You two!" Sam barked from the porch.

The inside of Robbie's house was no more impressive than the outside: kind of cluttered, but normal, with beige carpet, white walls, and drab brown furniture. Bookcases lined the walls of the living room, all of them stuffed full. Micha flopped down on the couch, eyes glazed and face slack, like he'd gone into a trance. June remained standing.

"His mind is a mess." Muse stepped up beside June. "I can barely understand it."

"He's acting really weird." June wasn't quite over her embarrassment yet. "Like he can read my mind or something. My power's never made anyone a mind reader."

"He's reading your mind?" Sam sounded alarmed.

"Maybe he's developing late-stage abilities." Robbie bent over and peered at Micha. "Your power could have triggered them."

"I don't know what late-stage abilities are," June said.

Robbie stood up straight. "Late-stage abilities come on later in life, instead of a person being born with them. Sometimes it happens because of an injury or illness that changes brain chemistry. Sometimes it happens for no apparent reason. If you messed up the way his brain works, it's a possibility."

"Awesome." June's mind flew back to what Sam had told her at the pier, about the Institute trying to steal people's abilities. She could save them the trouble of using a serum. Then she realized two mind readers—possibly three—were in the room, and shifted her thoughts to something else in case Sam didn't want her giving the information away. She managed to conjure up an image of Micha's cock. Damn it.

"Hi guys," a female voice said behind them.

June turned as Cindy breezed into the room.

"So what's going on?" Cindy asked.

"A lot," Sam said. "Come with me, Cindy, I need to speak to you."

He turned Cindy around and led her out of the room. Muse followed.

Awkward silence descended, and June looked around to avoid Robbie's "I know everything you're thinking" stare. Several locks graced the door and a keypad for a security system hung on the wall. Nothing odd about that. Then she noticed bars at the tops of the windows, the kind that slid down when triggered.

"Sam says this place is pretty secure," June said. "A real fortress."

"I've had a complex security system installed. You can never be too careful. After all, I may be able to hear your voice in my head, but I *am* deaf and I can't rely on all my senses to keep me safe. I have a special room in the basement, in case someone does get through. I can survive in it for several months."

"Normally I'd call you crazy, but given what I've seen the Institute is capable of, you're probably the sanest person around."

"They'll have a hard time getting their hands on me. I've made sure of that."

She rocked on her heels. "You sure have a lot of books."

"My collection." He made a sweeping gesture. "The Institute would love to get their hands on this, too. Their databases and libraries are woefully lacking." He scoffed. "I've amassed the most comprehensive collection of paranormal documentation in the city. The place that studies it as a science can't even hold a candle." He puffed his narrow chest out. "Ironic."

"You really hate those bastards, don't you?"

"I was studied at the Institute." His voice turned icy. "In the early days, before I knew what I know now. They kept me locked in a room like a prisoner and did bizarre invasive tests on me. I escaped, only because my power is strong and I'm clever."

"So you have good reason to fear they'll come looking for you."

"I'm the most powerful telekinetic in the city, maybe the world." He said this without boast, he seemed to be just stating a fact. "My telepathy is strong because I use it to communicate, but that's not wholly uncommon. The telekinesis is what they're really interested in."

"Oh, yeah?"

"I can move a person." Now pride seeped in. "In theory, living things, even small animals, are too complex for telekinetics to affect. But I can. I can move a person as easily as I can move that paperweight." He looked at the table near June's hip. A glass ball slid smoothly across the surface and stopped at the edge.

"Impressive," she said. "No wonder they wanna get their hands on you."

"But they won't. They get their hands on way too much." His eyes glittered, expression turning sinister, as if he suddenly had murder on his mind. "The old vampires, they don't want anyone poking around in their blood, figuring out what makes them who they are, trying to cure them. Telepaths—real developed telepaths—wouldn't set foot near the Institute because they see the lies. They know behind the gracious posturing there's only a desire to rationalize and subjugate what those bastards don't understand. They want us locked in cages. I won't have that. I won't let it happen. I'll do whatever it takes to make sure our kind aren't used by them."

June rocked on her heels again. "Well. I can certainly get behind kicking the Institute in the dick. Keep fighting the good fight."

"Oh, I'm fighting it."

"I'm sure Sam's happy to hear that."

Robbie sneered, but then turned away so June couldn't see his face. "We're still playing too nice with the Institute. I know some of the things that are going on in there. You have to fight fire with fire. Protests and debates aren't getting us anywhere. The Institute isn't interested in chatting with us and considering our grievances. We have to start speaking their language."

"Hey, you're preaching to the choir here."

Robbie turned back around and his expression had somehow gotten even creepier, more malicious and dark. "The real problem is that some people don't know what's good for them. So you have to show them. There's far too many misinformed fools. If you can't put out the fire, you have to stop feeding it."

June got that weird, uneasy vibe from him again. "What the hell are you talking about?"

Robbie waved a hand. "I'm just angry, that's all. I wish we could actually do something to stop them."

She opened her mouth to speak, but the other three returned.

"June and I are heading out of here," Sam said. "Keep an eye on Micha, you two. I'll be back."

A cat streaked into the room behind Cindy; it stopped at June's feet and gazed up at her with wide yellow eyes.

"Is that…" June bent over. "Dipity!" She squatted.

"Yes," Cindy said. "I brought her over here just in case, you know, something happens to me."

June petted her. The cat rumbled and stretched beneath her touch. "Hey, Dipster. Rough couple of days, huh?"

"I hate cats," Robbie said sourly. "They steal your breath."

June frowned. "I thought that was an old wives' tale?"

"Old wives are wiser than you think," Robbie said. "Not *all* folklore is fabrication."

"It's not cats we should be worrying about putting an end to our breath right now," Sam said. "Come on."

June stood up. Dipity wound around her boots, tail in the air.

"Well, Robbie," June said, "if she steals your breath, come talk to me. I'll put her in time-out."

June said good-bye to Micha as they were leaving. He waved. They left the house, and June got back in the car with Sam and Muse, still worried about Micha. She didn't want to be responsible for screwing up his brain.

"I have a bag back there," Sam said, as they pulled out. "There's a hoodie and a pair of sunglasses. You might want to make yourself unrecognizable. We're not going to be in my territory."

"Where are we meeting him?" June asked.

"At the Tribune building. That's where he works."

The red hoodie June found in the bag wasn't exactly her style. She zipped it up and made an attempt to stuff her hair under the hood, looking over the seat into the rear view mirror. Sam seemed amused.

"I look like a Christmas version of the Unabomber," June complained.

"It's Dolce and Gabbana," Sam said. "Very stylish. I'm sorry I didn't have anything leather for you."

"I don't care if it's Dolce and Kiss My Ass. Red isn't my color."

"Just try to disguise yourself and shut up."

June also found a pair of big dark sunglasses in the bag and slipped them on, scowling. She pulled her jacket on over the hoodie.

"I told Cindy where were going," Sam said, "and that I'd call her within the hour. That way if something happens to us on this outing, she can send people to find us."

"I feel a lot safer now."

They drove back downtown. The Tribune building stood near the bridge Cindy had driven over on Michigan Avenue, the one with the radioactive green ice-chunk water flowing beneath it. The building was a gothic granite tower topped with sharp spires, appearing both ancient and foreboding. Sam parked on the street a short distance away. The clock on the dashboard said 1:45.

"Looks Medieval," June said.

"Wait until you see the inside," Sam said.

The icy air whipped around them as they exited the car, and June and Sam made their way, heads down and hands stuffed into their pockets, across the street. Muse stayed in the car. When they reached the building, they pushed through a revolving door and stepped into a cathedral-like lobby. June peeked over her glasses, impressed. Chandeliers hung on long chains, providing a gentle glow and illuminating inscribed walls reaching up to a coffered wooden ceiling. Across the vast room stood a long desk, an enormous map of the world hanging over it.

"Come on." Sam started across the room.

June followed.

A security guard sat behind the desk, a paunchy man with a thick, gray mustache. "Can I help you?" he asked.

"We have an appointment with Ethan Roberts," Sam said. "At two o'clock."

The guard sat forward and picked up a phone. "Ethan Roberts?"

"Yes. He works for the Paranormal section."

June was amazed by the gigantic room. Chicago, for all the pain she'd suffered during her visit, repeatedly revealed itself grandiose in ways to make her both humbled and awed.

The guard spoke briefly to someone on the phone and hung up. "He'll be right down."

They waited near the desk. Sam kept his head down, June assumed so no one would recognize him. Several people passed through. The ding of an elevator, somewhere beyond the high arched doorways on either side of the desk, sounded intermittently.

Roughly ten minutes passed before a man walked into the lobby, brisk and purposeful, tugging at his suit jacket. He was slender and gangly and had dark hair slicked back from his narrow heart-shaped face. He wore horn-rimmed glasses, like a classic reporter-on-the-beat. June predicted before he even spoke he would be obnoxious.

"Sam Haain." The man extended a hand as he approached.

Sam didn't extend a hand in return. "Ethan Roberts."

"It's a pleasure to see you again." Ethan flashed a wide toothy smile. He had a gold cap on one of his incisors. He lowered his hand, as if he didn't even notice Sam had ignored him.

"Thank you for taking the time to meet with me," Sam said. "I'm sorry I couldn't explain anything on the phone. It's not a secure method of communication."

"Not a problem. And I always have time for you, Sam." Ethan turned to June. "And who is this?"

Sam nodded at her.

She slipped off the sunglasses.

Ethan widened his eyes behind his glasses and dropped his mouth open. "Is this..." He looked at Sam, and then back at June. "You... Are you—"

"I am." June slid the glasses back on.

"I heard you weren't at the Institute anymore, or even in Chicago."

"Oh, we're still in Chicago," she said. "And one of us is still at the Institute."

"You're quite famous around here, you know," Ethan said.

"Famous in Chicago. Just what I always wanted."

"Ethan," Sam said. "I need your help. If you do something for me, I'll do something for you. How would you like a scoop on the biggest damn conspiracy this filth-ridden town has ever seen?"

"You have my interest. Let's go talk."

Instead of hanging out at the Tribune building, they went to a diner down the street.

"Most people at work would recognize both of you on sight," Ethan explained. "Here we can talk without being bothered. I was waiting until you arrived to have lunch anyway."

The diner was empty apart from a few patrons. The place consisted of an open kitchen with a counter around it and a small dining room with lurid orange plastic booths. A grungy white tile floor and garish yellow walls completed the interior design nightmare. They sat in one of the booths closest to the door, June and Sam on one side, Ethan on the other. The waitress brought waters and menus. Despite being hungry, June didn't think she could eat for all the knots in her stomach.

Ethan took off his jacket and draped it over the back of the booth. He set his cell phone on the table in front of him. "What can I do for you Sam?"

"I want June to tell you her story," Sam said. "You need to hear this."

"Oh, awesome." June scowled. "Because I love to talk about it."

They ordered some food first. The menu didn't offer much in the way of delicate-flowers-with-allergies oriented fare, so June requested some vegetable soup. Sam ordered a burger and Ethan a corned beef sandwich. June rehashed what had happened to them at the Institute, finding she hated the story more each time it passed through her lips. Ethan gave her his rapt attention through the entire sordid tale. June considered not mentioning Micha, but Sam told her to go ahead.

She finished the story as the food arrived. They were silent until the waitress walked away again.

"So you have no idea what state your brother is in? If he's even still alive?" Ethan sounded more eager than sympathetic.

June picked up her spoon and stirred the gloopy brown concoction in her bowl. She'd forgotten to ask if the soup was made with beef stock or flour. "I don't. Sam sent a spy, and they saw him in John McKormic's head, but since then... I don't know."

"What's going on at the Institute goes far beyond this latest debacle," Sam said. "I have information that would blow your mind, Ethan."

"Oh, I've heard rumors," Ethan said. "Unethical experiments. Murders. Cover-ups. Trust me, whatever you've heard, I've probably heard it as well."

"I haven't *heard* anything," Sam said. "I *know*."

June attempted a spoonful of soup. As soon as she tasted the stuff, she spit it back in the bowl. Ethan, gathering up half his sandwich, paused and grimaced.

Sam slid his plate over to her. "Have a French fry. You can eat those, right?"

Ethan sat his sandwich down without taking a bite. "So you know where Micha Bellevue is, too. I guess I can stop speculating that the vampires have torn him apart."

"A pity," Sam said.

"Hey." June glowered at him. "Lay off, all right?"

Sam waved her off. "Personal politics aside, Ethan, we came here because we need your help. We need some public pressure to help get her brother out of the Institute."

"Here's the thing," Ethan said. "I would love to help you, Sam. I'd do anything for you. But I'm not sure I'm in a position to influence the Institute. Even if I ran an interview with this Siren, or told her story myself, people would probably think I'm making things up. A lot of normals in this city don't like me. They call me lurid and exploitive. I've been accused of bias. I can try to get the truth out to the people, but they don't listen and neither does the Institute. They're a bigger entity than the papers."

"While all that may be true," Sam said, "I think you can stir up enough trouble to get their attention."

"I highly doubt that. I've been trying to get their attention for years. Thanks to the activists and the SNC, no one gives a shit what the paranormal man on the street thinks. It's just sanctimony spewing from those two sides like never-ending streams of bile."

"You have such charming metaphors," June said.

"If you can do this for me, Ethan," Sam said, "I'll give you some very important, damning information about the Institute. A real story, better than this one."

"I told you, the Institute doesn't give a damn what I print about them." He gathered up his sandwich again. "They think they're above all this. What's it going to matter?" He took a bite.

"Because what I'm going to tell you is the truth. Not a rumor. Not speculation. And it's going to make the Institute incredibly nervous, realizing someone found out what they're up to. What's more, Eric Greerson will be made aware of what's going on. I want him woken up."

Ethan chewed, gazing at Sam, and swallowed. "The Institute isn't shy about replacing their head, if they know too much."

"There are forces willing to stand behind Eric that weren't in place when Michael Paulson was in charge. Hell, I'll back him with the Paranormal Alliance, if it means closing down shop there."

"What exactly do you think I can do to get their attention?"

"Make up something outlandish," Sam said. "Something that will cause a huge fuss."

"Make *up* something?"

"Yes. Something big. Say you got a tip the twins were murdered. Hell, throw Micha in there, too. Maybe the militant vampires took them all out."

Ethan held up a finger. "I don't mess with the militant vampires, Sam. Speculation is one thing. Outright accusation is another."

"Whatever. Just something so outlandish people will pay attention. And it has to be about the twins."

"You can tell them I'm a lesbian," June said.

"It's unethical to make up a news story." Ethan kept his focus on Sam.

"It's unethical to let the Institute get away with this shit," Sam said.

"Even if I make something up and it comes out in the morning edition, so what? How is that going to get her brother out of there?"

"You need to call the Institute out. Demand they hold a press conference with the twins present to prove the rumors are false. And it has to take place outside the Institute. We can't trust any broadcast from inside."

"Not a bad plan," June said, duly impressed.

Sam flashed her a smug smile.

"It won't work," Ethan said. "They still won't give a shit. They won't listen to me. Especially when I'm saying things they know aren't true."

"You have connections at the news stations, right?"

"Of course. I can walk right over to NBC Tower and talk to their top reporters if I want to."

"Can you get the media stirred up by tonight? Get them over in front of the Institute?"

Ethan chortled and pushed up his glasses. "Even if I leaked this false story to the news stations, I doubt you're going to get *that* kind of reaction."

"Oh, I will. If I get the Paranormal Alliance up in arms."

Ethan sat back and draped an arm over the back of his seat. "Perhaps. Depends on the level of belligerence you intend to achieve."

"Ethan, you're talking to me. I fought my way belligerently out of my mother's womb."

June snorted and nibbled on a French fry.

"Okay, say I can pull this off," Ethan said. "Make up a story and help you get their attention. What is this information you're going to give me that'll be the 'real' story?"

"Give me a fax number. One only you will have access to this afternoon. I'll send you some documents. But there's a catch." Sam sat forward. "You can't write a story about what I send you until they bring her brother outside the Institute. Because it's going to stir up so much trouble they won't be worried about anything else after that."

June suddenly started to believe Sam *was* the smartest man in the city.

Ethan was silent a moment, tapping his fingers on the table. "All right. He plucked a pen from his shirt pocket. "I'll be awaiting your fax. And I trust if I do this for you, you'll finally give some consideration to my bid for—"

"We'll talk about that at a later time."

Sam and June left, most of their food uneaten. Plowing through the freezing wind and bustle of Michigan Avenue, Sam tied his scarf.

"This better work." His steaming breath was whisked away on the wind. "I'm about to use my biggest bargaining chip."

After the traffic passed, they started across the street, close together.

"I hope it works, too." June's teeth chattered. "I don't want to talk to any more dead people."

Chapter 10

They drove back to Robbie's house and picked up Micha, who seemed to be his normal self again, aside from acting sluggish, and they returned to the hotel. Sam sent them up to the room with Muse while he faxed some things from the hotel's media center. June was starting to think she ought to give Sam a blowjob or something for all his help.

She smoked a cigarette on the balcony. When she stepped back inside, Sam was just returning, a leather folder under his arm and the duffel bag from the car over his shoulder.

"Now we wait for the shit to hit the fan," Sam said. "From several angles, I have a feeling."

Waiting would be just as agonizing as before. However, they didn't wait long. They ordered room service, and after the food arrived, Sam's phone went off. He looked at the screen, one eyebrow arched.

"That has to be record time." He answered. "Hello, Ethan."

The conversation was brief.

"Consider it done," Sam announced, as he clicked off. "I had a feeling that would get him eating out of my palm."

"Christ, what did you send him?" June asked. "The Institute's blueprints showing their weak spot? Is it like the Death Star?"

"Not far off. I might not have evidence yet, but I have the information."

The serum—the one used to turn normal people paranormal. "You gave him…"

Micha, sitting beside June, raised his eyebrows at them.

"That's a pretty big bargaining chip." June needed to upgrade from a blowjob. She might even let Sam marry her.

"It has to get out sometime." Sam took a drink from the glass of wine he'd ordered. "No time like the present. I can't believe you still doubt my prowess."

"I can't believe you're putting this much on the line for me," June said.

"You shouldn't always think everything is about you. That's my area of expertise."

Afternoon faded into evening as they ate and watched the news. More snow fell, though not as heavily as the night before, swirls of fine glitter in the gloom on the other side of the windows. Sam and Muse left. If Micha was curious about what they'd been discussing, he didn't ask. He seemed to bounce between moments of alertness and a trance-like, listless stupor.

June was horrifically tired, both physically and mentally. The waiting, the expectation, and the fear exhausted her. She lay down on the bed, sprawled on her back, arms flung out as if waiting for something to strike her.

Micha walked in the bedroom and crawled onto the bed next to her. "Do you mind?" he asked softly.

"No."

She listened to the silence. Micha rested in shadow beside her, a long silhouette against the faint glow of the window.

Wordlessly, June sought him out, clutched his wrist, and urged him closer with a gentle tug. He scooted over and pressed against her side. His skin was unnaturally warm, as if he had a fever. She slipped a hand around the nape of his neck and drew him in for a kiss. His lips were hot and soft, as gentle as June's emotions weren't.

They kissed, slow and lingering, and Micha slid his hand down her chest, to her stomach, to the top of her pants. She wasn't in the mood for sex, or anything sexual, but she didn't stop him from undoing the button on her jeans or tugging the zipper down. She recalled Micha's delirious words outside Robbie's house: "You want me even more now." She didn't know what the hell was going on in Micha's head, but he was right, and the wrongness of it all made the whole thing even hotter. She wanted him. She undid his pants as well.

Sometimes, in June's estimation, the best kind of sex didn't involve penetration. She liked a little mutual fondling, and the lesser act seemed perfect just then, so sleepy and close in the quiet darkness. They continued kissing while Micha pushed his fingers into her and started working them, slow and deep. His hand, like the rest of him, was over-warm.

June tried to get her senses about her enough to return the favor. Micha's cock, once she got it out, was thick and hard. As she stroked him and was stimulated in return, she grew more alert, less tired, and more aroused. A nap could wait until after her orgasm.

Micha toyed with her ring with the pad of his thumb, working it in firm circles. The sensation was almost too sharp, too intense to be pleasurable. She wanted to come though, so she tried to focus on Micha's cock and keep her senses from being overloaded. She bit into his lower lip. He moaned, and his hot breath gusted against her nose and cheeks. Then suddenly, he pushed her onto her back and got on top of her.

"Micha," she gasped.

He fingered her harder and faster, and the abrupt change of speed and pressure, coupled with his aggressiveness, sent her shooting straight for her peak. She barely had time to think before she was clenching around his fingers and shuddering.

"Fuck," she gritted out through clenched teeth. She rode out the tremors as he continued working his fingers and his thumb, drawing it out. "Micha, Jesus Christ." She didn't think she had ever actually *writhed* during an orgasm, but she was totally up for new experiences.

Micha didn't stop until she pushed his hand away, the stimulation overwhelming in the wake of her orgasm. She gripped his cock in both hands, her palms slick with sweat, and stroked him with the same aggression. He pressed his forehead to hers, hot, sweaty. He went tense and silent above her, not breathing. Then he let out a low, deep groan, and his cock pulsed in her hands. His release splattered her stomach and she was glad her shirt—his shirt—had gotten hiked up. The wetness trickled down her side and over her hip.

June slowed her strokes, her fingers slippery. Her lips tasted like sweat and Micha's mouth.

After Micha rolled off her, she went to the bathroom to clean up. Though the majority of the mess had gotten on her, she brought a towel back for Micha as well.

"I was gonna take a nap," she said. "But since you convinced me otherwise…"

"A nap sounds good." He hadn't bothered to tuck his cock away yet.

June tossed him the towel and crawled back on the bed.

"Thanks," Micha said.

After righting their clothes and settling down, he rested his head on her shoulder, an arm slung across her stomach, holding her, not possessively, but a gesture of comfort. This helped ease the tension under her skin enough to allow her to fully relax.

"Thanks," she murmured. "I didn't even know I needed that."

"I did," Micha whispered.

The words were eerie and weighted with meaning, but she couldn't keep her eyes open any longer to worry what he meant, or why he knew what she was thinking when she was unaware herself. Sated and exhausted, she slipped into much-needed sleep.

* * * *

June was dreaming. Or she thought she was. She opened her eyes to the darkened room and the air around her was distinctly cool, in sharp contrast to Micha's warm body pressed against her side. Her heart leapt into her throat. She knew what the chill meant before she even turned her head.

Rose stood between the open French doors, a silhouette in the darkness.

Despite being little more than a shadow, June could make out her pale, blank face and her dead, staring eyes. They caught the light from the window and glistened, as if they were corporeal instead of an illusion from beyond the grave. Rose stared fixedly at June on the bed with her husband. June tried to speak, to cry out, to move, but all her muscles were frozen. She could only lie still and vulnerable, heart pounding, trembling. Micha didn't stir.

"Nothing is what it seems," Rose whispered, though her voice carried in the silence, as loud as a scream. "Both sides have secrets."

June tried to respond, fighting the urge to cry like a scared little kid. She didn't want Rose to come any closer to the bed. When the apparition took a few slow, stiff steps into the room, June was on the verge of passing out from fear. Or pissing herself. The mounting dread in her chest swelled like a black bubble about to burst.

"You will find the truth," Rose said.

Though Rose's voice lacked inflection, June could easily decipher what the statement meant. Rose didn't speak to bestow hope—she was making a demand. June *would* find out the truth, or else Rose would curse her with her presence forever.

"The truth," Rose whispered. "Find it."

June's paralysis broke. Rose disappeared in a flicker, as if someone had turned off a movie projector. June jerked against the mattress, letting out a gasp, the only release of a pent-up scream.

Something thumped out in the main part of the room.

Micha jerked up his head. June's shoulder was hot where he'd been resting. He looked up at her in sudden wide-awake fear, his eyes glittering.

"Someone's in the room," June whispered. This intruder was flesh-and-blood and much more dangerous than a ghost, though. Probably.

Micha quickly rolled away. June sat up, heart pounding. The air in the room was still chilly. The darkness left her on edge, as if something might be lurking in the shadows near the bed. She scrambled off the bed and to her feet, looking around for a weapon. She'd rip the TV off the wall and use it as a bludgeon if she had to.

Like an idiot, Micha called out, "Who's there?" He hadn't even grabbed something to defend himself with.

A familiar voice replied, making June jump.

"It's just me, don't panic. Where the hell are the lights?"

An immediate rush of relief spread through June's chest, followed by a quick, burning anger. "For God's sake," she snarled and marched across the room. "Cindy, what the hell are you doing, coming in here and scaring the shit out of us like that?"

"Sam sent me over." A light popped on in the outer room.

June hesitated to pass by the spot where Rose had stood, but she made herself do so. She stepped through the doorway and squinted at Cindy in the light. Cindy stood between the sofas, wearing a fuzzy brown coat and matching boots.

"He sent me to watch over you," Cindy said. "Muse is—busy."

June ruffled her hair, scowling. "Great. Did you bring your gun?"

Cindy patted her bag at her hip. "Yes."

June lowered her arm. Micha walked out of the bedroom behind her.

"Good." June wanted to ask if ghosts could be shot.

"You need to turn on the TV." Cindy took her bag off her shoulder, tossed it on one of the sofas, and grabbed up the TV remote. "You gotta see what's going on."

"What channel?" Micha turned and went back in the bedroom.

"All of them," Cindy said.

As the screen between the sofas blazed to life, a female reporter stood in front of the Institute courtyard. People were huddled behind her, bundled up in coats and scarves and hats, livid faces caught by the camera lights. On the bottom of the screen were the words, "Nancy Cleary, live from the Chicago Institute for Supernatural Research."

"What the hell?" Micha asked from the bedroom.

He had turned on the TV too, and the woman's voice was in stereo.

Nancy was about to interview Sam, who stood beside her, looking the angriest of all. At the bottom of the screen, they flashed, "Sam Haain, leader of the Paranormal Alliance," as Nancy thrust the microphone in his direction. She didn't look happy to be given the task.

"We refuse to stand aside and be silent." Sam glowered at the camera. "We've put up with enough of the Institute's lies. Now they try to orchestrate a cover-up? If I don't get some answers, I'll have every single member of my group down here on their doorstep, twenty-four hours a day, and Eric Greerson will not rest until he comes out and answers my questions."

Nancy pulled the microphone back. "Mr. Haain, this still begs the question: where is the information coming from that has your group so upset? We're trying to substantiate these claims about the Coffin twins, and there doesn't seem to be any—"

Sam grabbed the microphone and jerked it back to him. He had a huge hand compared to Nancy. She now looked more frightened than angry.

"I have sources your ineffectual reporters couldn't begin to tap." Bile dripped from Sam's words. "We're tired of normals thinking they have a better grasp of our kind than we do. That you know so much more about us than we know about ourselves. That the only place reliable information comes from is this unholy edifice of lies and sanctimony." He pointed damningly at the Institute.

The people behind him shouted in agreement.

Nancy forcefully pulled the microphone back. "Mr. Haain, we're simply trying to confirm the claims that have been made. For the sake of your own validation, some proof—"

"You want proof?" Sam yelled, loud enough the microphone still picked him up. "Ask the vampires. Ask those who have been scarred by the Institute's research! The Institute is run by normals, for normals, for the express purpose of—"

"Mr. Haain!" Nancy backed away. "Most people believe the twins went home after Rose Bellevue's death."

"Why hasn't the Institute released a statement?" Sam got in her face. "Why haven't the twins talked to the press? This is a cover-up. I want someone to come out here right now and prove me wrong!" He seemed on the verge of pounding the wide-eyed woman into the pavement. A couple of large men became involved. Nancy swiveled toward the camera, eyes glittering with irritation as the men forced Sam away. The scene switched to a studio, where a somber-looking, white-haired man sat behind a desk. He perked up at the camera.

"Well, things certainly seem volatile there, Nancy," he said, with no particular emotion. "Folks, if you're just tuning in: unrest tonight at the Chicago Institute for Supernatural Research. Nothing new in that vein, but tonight we have Sam Haain, leader of the Paranormal Alliance, along with members of his group outside the facility, reacting to a rumor that the Coffin twins—who came to Chicago for the purpose of research earlier in the week—have been *murdered*," he nearly chuckled, "and that the Institute is covering it up." He looked to his right. The camera panned over to take in a younger dark-haired man with eyebrows arched in mild, affected surprise.

"Well, Dennis," the younger man said, "as you know, this isn't the first time Mr. Haain has organized a protest or reacted passionately to an unsubstantiated rumor. It's believed the Coffin twins went home in the wake of Rose Bellevue's murder, though this hasn't been confirmed." He turned fully toward the camera. "We hope to get a statement from the Institute, and we'll keep you informed of any further developments at the scene."

"Holy shit." June started pacing. "He wasn't just blowing smoke. He can put on one hell of a show." Hope finally burned inside of her, but something else, cold and bitter, warned her not to get too excited yet. A million things could still go wrong.

Micha walked out of the bedroom. By the look on his face, he thought the same thing. "This is too much," he said. "Just because Sam's throwing a fit doesn't mean anything will happen. He's like a comic book character as far as the media is concerned. It's hard to take him seriously."

"Well, they did film Batman here," Cindy said, as if this were some sort of defense. June frowned at her.

"I'm not going to stop holding my breath until he actually gets the Institute to respond," Micha said. "And you shouldn't either, June."

"I haven't been able to breathe for days," she said. "No problem there."

Cindy stayed, and they left the TVs on tuned to the news station. Sam kept the protestors lively all evening, even getting them to accost a heavily-guarded Eric Greerson on the way to his car. June finally couldn't handle the sound of the reporter's voices. She fell asleep as a means of blocking further anxiety.

She awoke to morning light and Cindy sitting on the edge of the bed with a coffee cup in hand and a newspaper thrust in June's face.

June lifted her head and squinted at her with one eye.

"Read," Cindy said. "Ethan ran the story."

June tried to find the clock. Micha was asleep on the other side of the bed. "What time is it?"

"A little before seven."

"You have the paper already?"

"The concierge delivers it at six thirty."

June sat up. She rubbed her face, pushed a hand through her hair, and took the coffee and newspaper from Cindy. Cindy made a sound of protest when June grabbed the cup. The paper was folded over to the front page of the Paranormal section.

"There's more coffee out in the room," Cindy said pointedly.

June took a sip. Even though the coffee had sugar in it and tasted like sweetened crap as a result, she needed caffeine, stat.

"Yeah, so go get yourself some." June gazed at the paper.

Cindy huffed, but didn't move.

The headline at the top of the page screamed COVER-UPS AND CONSPIRACY AT THE INSTITUTE. Below the headline was a picture of Sam outside the Institute, surrounded by a small group of belligerent-looking people. None of them looked as belligerent as he did, though. He stared crazy-eyed at the camera, as if trying to set the morning's readership on fire with his mind.

"I see they got his good side," June said.

"They're still at the Institute," Cindy said. The TV behind her was still on, volume turned down low. "I don't think Sam sleeps. He's like the Devil, always watching."

June took another sip of coffee and skimmed the article. Farther down was a picture of Rose, and June's skin crawled. The caption said, "Unsolved tragedy: the late Rose Bellevue, lead Vampire Studies researcher, responsible for isolating the bacteria causing vampirism." Below that was another picture, this one of June and Jason on the day they'd arrived at the Institute. The photograph looked like a paparazzi picture, taken in the lobby while they stood near the reception desk, bags over their shoulders. Below, the caption said, "Jason and June Coffin: victims as well?"

"Yeah, we're victims," June muttered.

"Read the article," Cindy said. "It's interesting."

June started reading, blinking to focus through the sleep-blur over her eyes. The article described the scene outside the Institute in much more breathtaking terms than June recalled seeing on television. According to Ethan, the Institute was bombarded by "a tumultuous and raucous mob" that was "exploding upon any reporter who would entertain their cries of conspiracy." He described Sam as "militant and vivacious, an avid and steadfast denouncer of injustice and a champion of paranormal truth."

"Is he in love with Sam by any chance?" June asked.

Ethan speculated extensively and, of course, luridly, on June and Jason's fate, and demanded a press conference revealing them, if they were in fact still alive, "outside the secretive walls of the Institute, in a neutral venue." June choked on the coffee when she read herself described as "a primal-visaged, intriguingly raw individual, evoking the mysterious, mythical creature her power is named for." June tried to imagine herself as the iconic siren on the rocks, luring sailors to their deaths. She would more likely use a harpoon gun than her voice.

"I can't stomach his writing." June tossed the paper on the bed. "I've read less lurid shit in *Penthouse*. Apparently the *Tribune* doesn't care about unbiased reporting in their Paranormal section."

"Of course they don't. Then no one has to take it seriously." Cindy slid off the bed. "But Sam likes him. He's right up Sam's alley."

"Sounds like he's up Sam's alley, all right."

Micha woke up a short time later, and June showed him the paper while Cindy went to take a nap on one of the sofas. Cindy had apparently been awake all night as well. Micha took a while to fully wake up and behave as if he were coherent. He still felt feverish.

"I'm worried about you," June finally admitted.

"I don't feel well." His voice was gravelly. "Maybe they can send up some cold medicine."

She refrained from pointing out colds didn't usually make a person able to read minds.

June tried to make herself presentable while Micha read the paper. She hoped Sam would take her on an outing later. Micha told her to get in the duffel bag for some clothes, and June pulled out a fresh shirt: a long sleeve black Henley. The shirt had to be formfitting on Micha because it actually fit her rather well. As she stood at the vanity trying to finger-rake her hair into order, she noticed Micha on the bed behind her, not reading the paper but gazing at her.

"Don't get all dreamy-eyed," she said.

"Let's order some breakfast."

She gave up on her hair, pulled it into a ponytail, and fetched the room service menu. The whole thing was written in flourished script and bore a notable lack of prices. "Just as I suspected," she said. "I can't pronounce half of what's on here."

"I'll tell you what ingredients are in things. Should we order some Mimosas?"

June snorted. "No. Are we at brunch after our yoga class?"

She picked the gluten-free fruit crepes because at least she knew what those were and they didn't sound like they would kill her. "And Cabernet Sauvignon."

She meant it as a joke, to mock Sam, but Micha wrote the wine down on the pad he was recording their order on.

"God, no." She stopped him. "I was kidding. You don't drink Cabernet Sauvignon with fruit crepes. Get me a Chenin Blanc."

Micha scratched it out. "I can't believe you just made a cultured joke after complaining you can't pronounce anything on the menu. You're such a dichotomy."

"My mother taught me about wine. She's far more cultured than I am. Beyond that, I don't know much. Except cigars. I know a little about them. My uncle smokes them."

"You adore your mother, don't you? I can tell."

"I do. And I don't want her to suffer. Anymore."

After Micha ordered breakfast, he switched off the TV and grabbed something from the bedside stand. "Look, I had Cindy go downstairs and get this for me last night, after you fell asleep." He held up a small blue book titled *The Pocket Guide to Chicago.*

"What's that for?" she asked.

Micha turned the book around. "They have these behind the concierge's desk downstairs. It's for visitors who want to go sightseeing."

"What good's it going to do me?"

Micha settled back on the pillows and opened the book. "Since you didn't get to go sightseeing, I'll read you some facts."

June grunted and lay back too. "Facts. As long as you're not gonna test me later."

Micha read to her about the Chicago River, which sounded like a polluted mess and periodically flooded everything downtown. Parts of it were apparently so nasty organisms couldn't live in it, and at one point it had to be redirected so as not to fill Lake Michigan with shit and kill everyone. Micha was obviously trying to distract her and give her something to focus on besides her own mental anguish, but it wasn't working.

"Your river is depressing me." She stretched her arms above her head. "Tell me about something else."

Micha flipped through the book. "Ah. The Cloud Gate. You said your brother likes stuff like that."

June didn't answer.

Micha started reading about the sculpture. They were facts she already knew, thanks to Jason's enthusiasm, but she let him read. Maybe it was distracting him, too.

"Jason would take a million pictures of it," June finally said. She closed her eyes and tried to picture the silver blob she'd caught a glimpse of when they passed the park. Yes, Jason would take pictures and get posters printed from them.

"There's other things in Millennium Park," Micha said. "Jay Pritzker Pavilion, Crown Fountain, Wrigley Square. You want me to read about those?"

"Nah." She opened her eyes. "I'm gonna go see them with Jason."

Micha closed the book and rested it on his chest. He leaned in close and said softly, "Yes, you are."

"Thanks." She stole a quick kiss. His lips were intensely hot. "And thanks for the tour."

"See, Chicago isn't all bad."

June shrugged. "Are you feeling any better?"

"Not really."

Breakfast arrived. Micha didn't eat much. They weren't far into the meal when a cell phone rang in the other room, followed by Cindy grumbling. June took a bite of her crepe and chewed, listening closely as Cindy answered.

Cindy didn't say much except, "All right. All right. Yes. Okay."

"What is it?" June called out, after Cindy stopped talking. June needed more wine if bad news was on the way.

"Eric Greerson announced he'll give Sam his press conference." Cindy sounded tired and unenthusiastic. "With you and your brother there to show everyone you guys are still alive."

June dropped her fork on her plate. "He'll be kind of shocked when I'm not there."

"Sam's on his way. I'm sure he has a plan."

Chapter 11

Sam arrived with both Muse and Robbie in tow. Sam was humming. Dark circles under his eyes proved he was human and capable of being tired. He had, after all, been up all night having a fit.

Robbie, when he walked in, plunked an animal carrier in Cindy's lap, and she yelped.

"I'm not leaving this cat at my house," he told her. "Find someone else to babysit it."

"Poor Dipity." Cindy set the carrier aside on the sofa and opened the wire door on one end. "Has he been manhandling you?"

Dipity slid out and climbed onto her lap. The cat looked around and, seeing June, jumped down and rushed over to her. She slid around June's calves.

"Dipster," June said.

The cat hopped up on the back of the sofa next to June with a pleased rumble.

June petted her. "Don't worry, you can come live with me. I'll smuggle you back to Sacramento."

Sam tugged off his scarf and wheeled around to June, all puffed up. "I told you I can get attention."

"So you're really getting the press conference?" June asked.

"Yes, Eric assures me both you and your brother will be there. Safe and sound."

Muse sat down beside Cindy, and Robbie sat on the opposite sofa. Micha stumbled out of the bedroom, still in his T-shirt and pajama pants. His eyes were glassy, his cheeks flushed. June had so many things on her mind, her worry for Micha had to go down a few notches on her priority list.

"How the hell can he assure you I'm going to be there?" June asked Sam.

"My guess is because his people haven't told him you're not at the Institute."

"This is gonna be interesting."

"Yes, it is. I'm going to order some coffee. God knows I need an entire pot right now. Everyone sit tight for a moment."

Micha wobbled on his feet, eyes drooping.

"Go back to bed," June said gently. She took him by the arm and guided him back into the bedroom. Dipity jumped down and followed. "You need rest."

Micha got back in bed. Once again, he didn't seem wholly present.

"Rose's older sister got turned into a vampire," he said, as June covered him up. "When Rose was a teenager."

June froze.

"This was before the Institute." His speech was lazy and slurred. "Before people knew the truth about vampires. Her sister had a boyfriend. He was a vampire. They were in love, so he turned her. After he did it, he was so overcome with guilt he ran away. They never saw or heard from him again."

June opened her mouth and closed it. Dipity sat next to her feet, purring.

"Things were harder back then." Micha languidly rolled his head on the pillow. "We didn't understand their natures... Not the way we do now. Rose's family didn't believe their daughter was a vampire. They thought she was crazy. They thought she was psychotic when she started attacking people because she couldn't control her urges. So they put her in a mental institution..." He paused for a beat. "She died three weeks later, because the bacteria infecting her blood depleted it without a fresh supply."

"That's...horrible," June said. "But—you remember this?"

"Rose didn't know exactly what happened, until she isolated the bacteria. That was a rough week..." He slumped against the pillows. "She was a good woman." His eyelids slid shut. "Just wanted you to know."

He went still, as though he'd suddenly fallen asleep or passed out. June watched closely to make sure he was still breathing. She looked down at Dipity. The cat gazed up at her, yellow eyes complacent.

"What the hell?" June whispered.

She joined the others in the outer room. Dipity sat on her lap, and June petted her absently, glancing anxiously now and then toward the bedroom. She wished they could take Micha to a hospital, or at least find a doctor to look at him.

"Eric wants to know where I wish him to fellate me." Sam stood between the sofas, mug in hand. "So do you have a plan, June?"

"A plan?" she asked.

"When your brother is paraded out at this press conference. What should we do?"

"I—"

The others all stared at her. Muse's mouth twitched.

"Don't know?" June said.

"You haven't been thinking about it?" Sam asked.

"This has been your plan from the start!"

"All right." Sam took a quick drink of his coffee. "I was just trying to be a gentleman actually, seeing if you had any input. I do have a plan. Simplicity is the best recourse. The Institute wants to bring you and your brother out to show me how much of a big persecuting jerk I am. So you need to be there."

June narrowed her eyes.

"You come out," Sam said, "show everyone you're there, and walk out. With your brother."

"Gee, why didn't I think of that? Just walk right up in public and take Jason away."

"The public thinks you're there. So what is the Institute going to do when you show up where everyone thinks you are?"

"That's not a half-bad idea," Cindy said.

"It's an amazing idea," Sam corrected her. "The Institute can't take you down in front of everyone."

"What about when we're not in front of everyone?" June asked. "Yeah, I show up, they can't do anything in front of people. But once we're not in public—"

"That's what I'm here for," Sam said.

"You can get Jason and me safely away from them?"

"I can get you into a car, which I can't guarantee won't be shot at. Is that good enough?"

"It's better than anything I have."

"That's why I'm a leader. You'll be helping us," Sam said to Robbie. "Your skills will be useful. Yours won't," he said to Cindy. "You can drive the car."

Cindy made a displeased sound.

"This is a huge risk," June said. "Not just for me. For you, too."

"By next week the Institute will be crumbling," Sam said. "When Ethan goes to press with his story, all hell will break loose. I'd like to get my knife in before they completely bleed out."

"I think we should take Micha with us," June said, trying not to sound anxious.

"Why? He's not going to be useful."

"He's not well. He's acting even stranger than he was before. We can't leave him here alone. We can just put him in the car or something."

"We might be able to use him actually," Cindy said. "Let Eric Greerson see him. Make him aware of what's going on. The more people we have on our side the better, especially if that person happens to be the head of the Institute."

Sam was silent a moment, and then he said, "You're starting to think like me. I like it."

Cindy smiled.

"If he's ill, though," Robbie spoke up, "he might encumber us."

"You're a big-time telekinetic," Sam said. "You can move his carcass."

Robbie frowned. His expression darkened, and it reminded June of when he'd went off on the weird rant at his house.

Muse was still twitching—only one side of her face now. "I'm trying to read Micha and his mind is such a jumble I can't sort it out."

June tensed. "This can't be my power affecting him. It doesn't work that way. I told you guys, my power doesn't make people sick."

"Maybe he's just more pathetic than normals usually are." Sam turned and walked over to the windows. "I know where we can have this press conference. But before I throw myself on the fire for you one more time, June, I want to ask you a question."

"What's that?" she asked.

"Are you willing to die for your brother?"

"Of course I am."

"Noble," Sam said, "and easy. So next question." He fixed her with a glittering gaze. "Are you willing to kill for him?"

* * * *

Sam made some phone calls. June went out on the balcony and smoked one cigarette, and then another. She paced in the cold, filled with an anxiety even nicotine couldn't assuage. Afterward, she checked on Micha and found him still asleep and feverish. Sam quickly received word Eric had accepted his choice of venue. Planning began.

"Promontory Point," Sam said. He had pulled a small table in between the sofas, and they all huddled around it. "The field house. Three p.m." He looked at his watch. "We've got roughly three hours."

"Promontory Point?" Cindy gaped at Sam. "That's Paranormal Alliance territory."

"No kidding? I was there when the treaty doled it out to us. Why do you think I chose it? They'll be on my turf. Everyone at the Institute who isn't an idiot knows that place is mine and they'll be on their best behavior."

June didn't know what "Promontory Point" denoted, but she didn't bother asking. Sam started hashing out his plan. Cindy peered over his shoulder; Robbie seemed edgy; Muse sat at Sam's side, silent and twitching.

"This is pretty straightforward." Sam had drawn a picture on a piece of notebook paper, more inexplicable than "straightforward." In the middle he'd made a square, some squiggly lines on one side, and a big rectangle on the other.

"When we get to the park, Robbie, you'll take June down to the revetment, so no one knows she's there." Sam tapped the squiggly lines. "*And* you can take Micha down there with you. I'm not leaving him in the car for someone to see and blow our game. Robbie will act as a lookout and go-between." He tapped the square in the middle. "I have to be at the press conference in the field house. Ethan will be there too. He'll signal Robbie when it's time, and Robbie, you tell June to come up. June, you'll meet up with Ethan at the field house and go inside."

"And then what?" June asked.

"You walk your ass into the press conference. Step up to the mic, say something witty. For my entertainment, at least. You owe me that much."

"And I get Jason out of there?" June asked. "If he's there."

"If he's not, there's going to be hell to pay anyway." Sam tapped the square again. "No one's going to stop you walking out of there, not in front of all those cameras. Robbie, you bring Micha up from the revetment when the conference is over and everyone comes outside."

"That could ruin the whole plan," Robbie said. "If Eric walks out, do you think others won't be behind him? Micha's presence will start a riot."

"It'll create a diversion," Sam said.

This was the first time June had heard Robbie argue with him.

"June will have a better chance of getting out of there if everyone is distracted," Sam said. "If I can't tell Eric the truth, I can't. But June and Jason will still escape, so it won't be for nothing."

June clenched her fists in her lap.

"June," Sam said. "You and your brother will run like hell for the parking lot where Cindy will be waiting with the car." Sam turned to Cindy. "Get them out of there. Don't wait for the rest of us. Take them to the airport. There will be tickets and a flight itinerary in the glove box."

"Tickets?" June said. "Back to California?"

"When you get home," Sam said, "I want you to tell the police, tell the press, tell everyone you know what happened to you here. That, combined with Ethan printing the story I gave him, will have shit raining down on them from everywhere. At the very least, they'll be forced to close their doors pending investigation."

"It all sounds so easy," June said.

"Trust me, it won't be."

Sam sent Muse, Cindy, and Robbie to arrange the details. Before Cindy left, she turned to June and delved into her huge purse.

"Take this." Cindy pulled her gun out and held it out to June, butt first. June stared at it.

Cindy jerked it at her. "You might need it. It's the least I can do."

"You'll be driving the getaway car," June said. "I think that's quite a lot."

"You might need to shoot someone."

June took the gun, delicately. The weapon was lighter than she expected, and she held it out at arm's length, fearing she would accidentally pull the trigger. Cindy hurried out the door after the other two.

"Thanks," June said after her.

Sam produced a duffel bag full of clothes and toiletries from one of the closets. "I keep stuff in here in case I ever need to make a getaway. I have bags all over the city, actually. I'm going to give you this one in case you can't get back to California right away."

"I haven't brushed my teeth in over a week," June said. "I'm not too concerned with hygiene right now. I'm more focused on living."

"Still," Sam said. "It'll make me feel like a Good Samaritan. Take it."

"Thanks." She placed the gun gingerly on one of the sofas. "We need to get Micha ready too."

June went into the bedroom and fished a blue cable-knit sweater out of Micha's bag and, with Sam's help, got it on him. She wanted to keep him from freezing to death when they hauled him out in the cold. He barely woke up during the procedure.

"He's burning up," Sam said. "Jesus Christ."

"He needs a doctor, I think. He was also talking about Rose earlier."

"He remembers?"

"I don't know. It was strange. Like, he seemed to remember, but there wasn't any emotion attached to it."

"Something is definitely going on with him. As soon as we get you and your brother out of here, I'll try to get a doctor to look at him. I have several private ones."

"Thanks."

When they returned to the main room, June spied a furry form slipping into the duffel bag on the floor.

"Dipster," she said sternly.

The cat gazed out at her, eyes reflecting the light.

"I was only kidding about taking you with me. You don't wanna go where I'm going, trust me."

She sat down on the sofa. "I've never fired a gun," she said. "This thing is useless in my hands."

Sam sat next to her and picked the gun up. He turned it over in his hands. "It's a Glock twenty-six," He pushed something, and a narrow cylinder slid out the bottom. "Fully loaded, you've got ten shots."

"Is the safety on?" June eyed the gun cautiously.

"Glocks don't have safeties." He pushed the cylinder back in. "The safety is in the trigger. They don't fire unless you squeeze it. You can shake it."

He did, and June winced.

"You can drop it," he said. "Throw it against a wall, it won't fire. You have to actually pull the trigger. It's accurate. Very little recoil, so it won't jerk your arm out of the socket. The only thing that scares me is Cindy totes it around."

"I'm not sure I have the guts to use it." June hadn't been able to answer Sam's question earlier, about killing for her brother.

Sam motioned for her to stand up. She did, wary, and watched, cringing inwardly, as Sam stood up as well and reached around her side.

"We'll tuck it in your pants." Sam stood so close she could smell him. Apparently he was still making showers a priority, as well as that interesting cologne he wore.

"You promise it won't go off?" June said.

"Not unless you reach down and squeeze the trigger." He made a space between her jeans and body. "You don't have to be afraid. You can handle this gun." He worked the muzzle into her pants.

"Why are you still helping me?" she asked. "Is this really benefiting you?"

"I hate the Institute. I'd do anything to make them pay." He drew back.

The gun pressed against her hip, heavy and menacing. "It has to be more than that. You sound like you've got enough evidence to back them into a corner. You don't need my plight to help you accomplish anything."

"Do you want me to say I care about you? That I've taken some kind of liking to you?" He shrugged. "Maybe I have."

"You don't care about me. You don't know me. You don't know anything about me."

"I know you're willing to risk your life to save your brother."

"I ran when they took my brother."

"If you hadn't, you wouldn't be able to save him now. Things happen the way they do for a reason. I know what's inside you."

"You don't." She tensed, on the defensive. "You see me in this situation, fighting because I have to. I'm not like you, Sam. I'm not proud of this thing I have. I grew up ashamed of what I am, when I saw it ruin lives and break up my parents. I never embraced it, and I never *will*. I'm an artist. I tattoo people. I hang out with my friends in shitty bars. I like whiskey and wine and I've never figured out how to have a boyfriend longer than six months. I'm a mess, but it's my life. It's normal, compared to all this. I just want a normal life."

"I know what you want." His eyes were intensely dark. "I know why you act the way you do, why you look the way you do. You draw attention to everything else so no one notices the one thing you want to hide."

She took a step back, an instinctive wall going up. "I'm not this thing inside me. I don't give a damn about the paranormal community, and activists, and science. This world just wants to make me a lab rat. You don't know me, Sam, because you've only seen me trying to escape my inevitable persecution."

"June." He spoke as though addressing a temperamental child.

"Listen to me." She held up a hand. "Everything you've done for me is phenomenal. I will be indebted to you until the day I die, which hopefully won't be any time soon. But please, don't think I have some emotional connection to you or anyone else here, not even Micha. I just want to get my brother and go home, and after that, I never want to see this city again."

"I can understand that, trust me."

"No you can't. You love this city, and these people. You love your followers. You're kinda crazy, but you're a good person. I can see that. But we don't want the same things."

He snorted. "You think I'm a good person?"

"I think you're a great person."

"As great as your darling Micha?" He motioned toward the bedroom.

"I told you, I have no emotional connection to him."

"You feel more than you think you do."

"We could all die today." She raised her voice. "The only thing I'm feeling right now is terrified."

He reached out, grabbed the back of her head, and jerked her in close; he was surprisingly strong. June widened her eyes.

"Just shut up and kiss me good-bye," he whispered, close to her mouth. "I'll regret it if you don't."

June stared into his eyes, so close. "Who do you think you are?" The words didn't come out as severe as she wanted them to.

"I know who I am, but you don't know me. You mistake me for a selfless person. I'm not, and it's better that you're leaving. Now do as I say, like you've been doing all along."

June did, though she wasn't sure if the kiss was of her own volition. Sam's lips felt the way they had at the pier, soft and smooth but much more yielding this time. She liked it, found herself willing and sinking into it. When he broke the kiss and drew back, her cheeks were burning. Sam turned away.

"Don't get yourself confused with someone else." He snatched his mug from the table. "You'll realize who you are, who you really are, before this is over."

June patted her hip and the gun under her waistband, awkward and searching for something intelligent to say in return. She didn't know how to react, if she even should react, if she needed to. She licked her lips and tasted Sam's mouth, the taste of coffee and something dark and dangerous and thrilling. Her stomach sank. His words foretold the end of her life as she knew it. She couldn't turn back now.

"You're awful pushy." She tried to sound belligerent. She didn't so much.

"Someone has to be."

Chapter 12

The others returned with two cars, and they left for Promontory Point a half hour before the press conference. Sam, June, and Muse rode in one car, while Robbie, Cindy, and Micha followed in the other.

June sat in the passenger seat, Sam driving, entombed in tense silence. They took a freeway, speeding over pavement washed white by the winter's punishments. The lake loomed to their left, choppy and dark under a low bleak sky. They seemed to be driving to the end of the world, and June figured they probably were. Sam's earlier, prophetic words still rang in her ears. His knuckles were white on the steering wheel, his skin pale in the stark light. He glanced at her.

"What did you mean?" she asked, voice low. "Not to get myself confused with someone else?" She didn't care if Muse heard, but speaking too loudly seemed wrong.

"Most people like to think they're someone they're not." He flexed his fingers on the wheel. "It's a symptom of being alive in this world, in this day and age. It's worse for us, for people like us."

She gazed past Sam, at the water. "What if I don't like the person I might actually be?"

"Of course you don't like the person you actually are. That's why you don't try to be her."

"What will happen to you after today?"

"What will happen to any of us? Let's throw the dice and find out."

When they exited the freeway, the clock on the dashboard said 2:56. They entered a parking lot situated below an overpass, the lot packed with cars and news vans. They parked at the back of the lot, and Cindy pulled in beside them. A tunnel opened beneath the overpass, gaping like a mouth, complete with an arch of granite teeth waiting to chew them up.

"Looks like the whole damn circus is here," Sam said.

June wanted to get out, and at the same time, she wanted to stay in. Her brother might be close, but untold dangers stood between them. She slid her hand over her left hip, over the bump under her jacket.

Everyone started getting out. June opened her door.

Cindy's face was scrunched up as she got out of the other car, her cell phone in hand. Robbie got out of the backseat and pulled Micha out after him. Micha was sagging, limbs flopping. Even though Robbie was slightly shorter, he didn't seem to exert any great physical effort in maneuvering Micha upright.

"This is perfect," Sam said. "Everyone's here by now. I can make an entrance."

"Sam," Cindy said, "I just got a call from Kevin."

"How unfortunate." Sam grabbed the duffel bag out of the back of the car and held it out to June. "Put that in the other car."

June took the bag with a mumbled "thank you." She opened the back door of Cindy's car and set the bag on the floor of the backseat. When she turned around, Muse was watching her, one eye twitching rhythmically. Muse had her fluffy furry white coat wrapped around her, like the day June met her. She still looked like a snowball with legs.

"Kevin said the police came by to dig the bullet out of the bar," Cindy said. "Except…they didn't find one."

Sam went still. Cindy withered under his gaze.

"What?" Sam asked.

"He said there wasn't a bullet in the bar when they went to take it out."

Sam was unmoving except his hair being tugged by the wind. Muse, standing beside him, was also completely still, her face blank and no longer twitching.

"How could there be no bullet in the bar?" June asked. "We saw the hole."

"I knew it." Sam glanced sideways at Muse.

"What the hell is going on?" June asked.

"We should go," Robbie said, from the other side of the car. "We can't wait much longer. The conference is about to start."

Sam nodded at Muse. Muse looked around the parking lot. June tensed, and her heart pounded even harder.

"He's right." Sam snapped to attention. "We need to get in there. Muse and I will go in first. Then June, you and Robbie follow exactly two minutes after. We don't want anyone to see us together. Remember the plan."

Cindy frowned at her cell phone and got back in the car.

"Good luck," Sam said. "You'll need it. We all will."

"Be careful." June gazed at him. "If this is the last time we see each other—"

"We already said good-bye."

He turned and strode toward the tunnel, coat billowing, scarf flapping. Muse followed. June shivered as they went, unsure if fear or cold was making her shake as much as she did.

When they disappeared through the tunnel, Robbie looked at his watch. Micha sagged against Robbie's side, head hanging. The whole world seemed to stop, poised on the brink.

"What the hell is going on? With the bullet thing?" June's question was more to the air than Robbie.

Robbie didn't respond.

Two minutes seemed to take forever. Then Robbie said, "Time to go," and the wait didn't seem long enough.

They crossed the lot, pressing against the frigid wind. Robbie appeared to glide, pulling Micha along. Passing into the tunnel did indeed feel like being swallowed up; stepping out on the other side proved worse. Suddenly they were in the wide vulnerable open. No turning back.

Straight ahead stood a fountain comprised of a basin and a short black pillar, a sculpted sleeping fawn curled on top. A rather subdued greeting for Hell's lobby. Paved paths wound through snow-caked lawns and snaked under the bare black branches of trees. No one was walking or biking. Aside from the sound of cars on the freeway above, all was still.

"This way," Robbie said.

She followed him along one of the paths. The sight of him nearly floating unnerved her, so she stopped watching him and kept an eye out. In short time, a building rose into view: a one-story white stone structure with a red brick roof and a turret in the middle. People stood outside.

"That's the field house," Robbie said. "This way, we can't walk past it."

They veered onto another path.

They didn't stay on the path for long, leaving the pavement and crossing the lawn instead. June crunched through the snow, while Robbie and Micha didn't even leave tracks except for faint lines on the top layer. After a few minutes, they reached the edge of a revetment bordering the lake. Wide slabs of rock provided uneven steps down to a concrete promenade. In the distance, beyond a flat, pale beach, the looming buildings of Chicago extended out into the water, ominous against the dismal sky.

"Let's go down," Robbie said. "We're too exposed up here."

The rocks were icy, and June carefully picked her way down. Robbie, despite his passenger, descended easily and deposited Micha on a stone bench near the water. Micha slumped over, head hanging, arms limp in his lap. The wind off the water was the coldest June had ever experienced in her life, like they'd accidentally stumbled into Antarctica. When she reached the bottom, she pushed her hands deep into her jacket pockets and ducked her head.

"Damn this *sucks*," she said through chattering teeth.

"I'll go back up and watch." Robbie dragged a hood up out of his coat and over his head. He bounded swiftly back up the revetment.

"So creepy," June muttered.

"It's his power," Micha said.

She turned. He was sitting upright.

"Gives him a sort of force field. He slides around on it." He sounded lucid again.

June walked over and sat down next to him. The seat was like a slab of ice. Micha wobbled, and June steadied him. His hands and face were bright red. She worked his hands into the pockets of his coat for him. Despite the cold, his skin still felt unnaturally warm.

"You gotta be all right," June said. "I can't live with the guilt if you kick the bucket."

Micha's eyes were heavy-lidded but focused. "I met Rose when I was passing out fliers in front of the Institute." His voice fell softer. "She mistook me for a normalist, spreading propaganda. Then she took me to lunch."

Micha's eyes were vivid blue against the dull light, but everything behind them had gone black.

"You remember her, don't you?" June asked.

The wind whipped around them, ruffling Micha's hair, revealing layers of gold and brown. He nodded and looked out at the water. "She's dead," he whispered, and the anguish in his voice, more than his words, confirmed his memory had returned. "And I soon will be."

"Don't say that."

"I had faith," His voice was hollow, the way Rose's was. "Faith in the Institute. She had her vampires. I had my cause."

June was afraid to speak, fearing if she said the wrong thing, agitated him, or caused a burst of emotion, he might topple over dead.

Micha closed his eyes and slumped against June's side. She slipped an arm around him. A certainty blossomed inside her, huge and terrible.

"It's not my power doing this." She looked out over the water, as if she could find an answer there. "There's no way it can be. But what the hell is it?"

"I wanted to prove I could be just as good a crusader as she was." His anguish intensified. "I wanted to make an impact, the way she did."

"Judging from the things I've heard about you, you did."

"I wanted to help people, show the normalists that paranormal people really have worth, like my mother did."

"It was noble. It's not your fault the Institute betrayed everyone. It's not your fault at all."

"I shouldn't have been trying to compete with her." His voice remained strained. "I shouldn't have let envy cloud my judgment. She was brilliant, and I loved her for it. She wasn't trying to be a better person than me. But I was trying to outdo her with my stupid crusade."

June recalled the picture on Micha's phone, the one where they were both smiling. Maybe more tension existed between them than attraction. June had judged their entire relationship based on one image, filled herself with guilt over some imagined love story that might not have been so glamorous after all.

"Micha." She fumbled for words. She'd never been good at consoling. "This isn't because of you being envious. It isn't your fault any of this happened. Those bastards are way beyond any of our control."

"This is my fault." His voice broke. He clamped a hand over his eyes. "If I had stopped being jealous of her, none of this would have happened. I would have seen what they were doing a long time ago."

June gripped his hand and pried it from his face. Her fingers were numb. "You're not any more to blame for this than I am for my sister's death or my parents' divorce."

Saying those words caused something disgusting and slimy to come loose inside her, something that crawled up her throat, and she now needed to spit it out.

Micha's eyes were wet. Glistening trails were frozen on his cheeks.

"I hope you and your brother get back home," he whispered. "I hope you make it."

She stroked his cheek. "I'll keep in touch with Cindy." Her voice caught. "I want to know what happens to you. And I'll find you again someday. Maybe you can come to California. Maybe you'll be safer there."

"I'm not angry at you for what happened between us. I promised you I wouldn't be. Thank you for looking out for me."

Megan Morgan

June pressed her lips to his and they were cold, but behind them, the furnace-like heat inside his body still raged, burning him up. Tears slipped from her own eyes and were quickly dried, as if for once, the city was trying to help her by hiding her weakness. June pressed her forehead to Micha's and closed her eyes.

"You're not going to die," June whispered.

Micha clutched her arm and whispered back, "Neither are you."

Minutes passed, not slowly, but faster, and faster, building to a terrifying crescendo. June considered her last cigarette in her jacket pocket, but she was actually too cold, too scared, too heartbroken to want it.

The tension snapped when a voice from above called out, "Hey!"

June jerked her head up. Micha lifted his as well. Robbie stood at the top of the revetment, a black figure against the gray sky, his coat whipping around him. June's pulse raced, sending heat into her frozen limbs.

Robbie bounded down the steps. "Let's go."

June couldn't move for the fear in her, a solid mass holding her in place.

Robbie reached the promenade, his pale face peering out from his hood. "Your brother's here."

Chapter 13

A stillness filled June's chest, her heart seeming to have stopped. For a moment she was on the verge of doing something melodramatic, like bursting into tears, a lot of them, so many the wind couldn't dry them.

Instead she whispered, her voice shaky, "Thank God."

"You have to go." Robbie jerked his head toward the revetment. "Ethan is waiting at the field house."

Micha was sitting up now. His lips were dark from the cold. June understood of course, for better or worse, no matter her promises, she might never see him again.

"You stay strong." She clasped his cold hands. "None of this is your fault."

"It's not your fault, either."

June was cemented to the cold bench, push-pinned in place by Micha's beautiful blue eyes, the last beautiful thing she might ever know. Robbie moved into the corner of her vision.

"You have to go," he said. "Ethan is waiting."

Somehow, she managed to stand, cold and stiff, not ready, but fully aware the time had come to act regardless. She looked up the revetment, four steps into the unknown, her brother seconds away. Uncertainty, danger, and possible disaster were also seconds away.

"Good-bye, June," Micha said.

"Good-bye," she whispered.

She squared her shoulders, took a deep breath to numb her aching lungs, and plunged forward.

The lonely vulnerable walk to the field house terrified her. She kept looking around. She didn't see anyone, but the back of her neck crawled, like someone was watching her. She focused on the building, driven by the knowledge Jason was inside. Alive. Waiting to be rescued. Through tall latticed windows, she could see lights and people.

A man stood at the back of the building, near a doorway. June slowed, cautious. Ethan.

"Eric Greerson just started talking," he said, when June reached him. He huddled into the fur trim of his long tan coat, an errant lock of hair dangling in front of his forehead, glasses reflecting the light. "Sam is trying to keep him busy, but you need to get in there."

"Jason's in there?" She needed to hear it confirmed.

Ethan nodded. "He doesn't look good, but he's there."

Alarm bells went off in her head. What did "doesn't look good" mean?

"Come on," Ethan said. "Time to tantalize the masses."

They went inside, entering a short hallway with a plank floor and stone walls. The warmth was glorious, but she had no time to bask. Light shone from a doorway to the right, casting shadows from the room beyond. A man spoke, his voice amplified, and it sounded like Eric Greerson.

"I have to get in there," she said.

"Wait for a good spot to come in. The stage is to the right." Ethan turned and disappeared through the doorway.

June swallowed thickly, wide-eyed and terrified. She wanted to run back outside, but she couldn't flee. Jason needed her.

Eric was currently extolling the virtues and moral standards of the Institute. June leaned against the wall, trying to hear over her pounding heart. She had no idea what a "good spot" might be, or what she should say when she entered. The only things she could come up with were asinine exclamations like, "Say hello to my little friend!" followed by whipping out Cindy's gun. But she couldn't shoot up the place, no matter how much she wanted to. That wouldn't ensure their safe escape at all.

Then she heard Sam's voice.

Even without a P.A., he was loud and clear. He didn't keep his offense bottled. "You treat us like guinea pigs! The paranormal community is an intelligent, prolific, well-organized entity. No matter what crap you try to spoon-feed the public to make them believe we need their help, we don't. How *dare* you, Mr. Greerson, come here and spew your holier-than-thou rhetoric. How *dare* you."

"Mr. Haain." Eric sounded less reticent than before. "When our founders brought the Institute of Supernatural Research to fruition over a decade ago, their intent was not to study anyone like guinea pigs. The paranormal is a vast and revered subject. Study and advancement in the field will only benefit all human kind. We only seek to—"

"You seek to oppress us!" Sam overrode him. "Your lies and immorality will be the end of—"

"Mr. Haain, if you cannot control yourself, I will have security remove you from this conference."

"*Remove me?*" Sam barked out a laugh. "Do you know where you are right now?"

"I know where I am. I'm well aware of the treaty between your organization and the SNC. However, I belong to neither."

"Where is the other twin?" Sam demanded. "Why do I only see one of them? Where is June Coffin?"

This was her cue.

A murmur rose. June touched the gun under her jacket. Before she could lose her nerve, she lurched away from the wall and walked through the doorway.

"June Coffin is—" Eric began.

"Right here," June said, startled by the power and clarity of her own voice.

The murmurs hushed as all eyes turned to her.

Her bravado was embarrassingly short lived. She froze, cemented in place with terror. Oh. Fuck.

The long, wide room looked like a banquet hall, with the same stone walls and plank floor as the hallway. Intensely bright light from an array of TV cameras left no inch in shadow. A huge crowd was packed into the room, all looking at June with eager, curious expressions. Sam stood in the front row of the crowd. To June's right, a raised platform held Eric Greerson standing before a podium and dressed in a charcoal gray suit, his silver hair perfectly upswept. Behind him, sitting on folding chairs, were John McKormic and a few other researchers. All of them stared at June in thinly-veiled horror.

At the end of the row and farthest from her, sat Jason.

He wore black jeans, a white T-shirt, and blue Chuck Taylors—the last outfit she had seen him in. He didn't look good, his skin ashen and dark circles under his eyes. He didn't look like June's twin, either. His face was rugged and square, his eyes brown, and his shaggy hair sandy blond, though that was also the natural color of her hair. When he saw June, he sat up straight, eyes wide, mouth falling open.

June swallowed back a fierce surge of emotion—rage, relief, anguish—and strode toward the stage. This was the hardest walk of her life, but it was the only direction she could move in.

"I'm sorry I'm late." She ascended a short flight of steps up to the stage. "I was on the phone with our mother in California." She walked up to the podium, up to Eric.

Eric gave her a small but kind smile. "It's all right." He clearly didn't know what the nervous group behind him did. "Would you like to say something?"

"Sir." John McKormic leapt to his feet. "I think we should conclude this conference. I believe we've said—"

"Let her speak!" Sam yelled. "Have you got something to hide?"

Two hard-eyed security guards hovered near Sam, watching him. Muse stood next to him. Flashes went off. Voices rose.

"Of course she may speak," Eric said. "Both of you may, if you like." He looked around at Jason. "We have nothing to hide."

John McKormic's eyes were huge behind his glasses. June glowered at the scared little man. For the first time in over a week, she had the upper hand. This fact gave her courage.

"I *would* like to say something," she said.

Jason sat stiff in his chair, his throat working. He had his hands clenched in his lap. Red marks marred his wrists. She wanted to plunge her fist into John McKormic's face. *What have they done to him?*

"Go right ahead." Eric stepped back, gesturing to the podium.

June turned toward the microphone and looked out at the sea of keen faces and waiting cameras. Shouts erupted, hands waving, microphones thrust forward. Everyone wanted to ask a question.

"I just wanna—" she said into the microphone.

The crowd barely quieted.

"I just wanna say something," she said louder.

The commotion died to a murmur.

Sam looked around, glaring, before focusing on June.

"As you can see," June said, "we're both alive." She still had no idea what to say, but she realized, looking out at the attentive crowd, what she *couldn't* say. In her anger, she could easily rattle off a litany of wrongs and horrors they'd been subjected to. But if she did, the chance of walking out peacefully would be minimal.

"However." She cleared her throat.

Everyone stood quiet and listening now.

"Jason and I have decided to go home, back to California. This afternoon, in fact. We hate having to cut our stay here short. But given the…controversy, we feel it's better if we leave."

A cacophony of voices rose.

Sam shouted above them, "June Coffin!"

The other voices withdrew. June stared at him.

"Don't you believe the Institute is doing you, and the paranormal community, a great scientific service?" he asked. "Don't you want to stay here and let them learn all they can about your ability? Help them advance their knowledge, and all of human kind's knowledge, despite the danger?"

June stared at him in panic and confusion. Was he messing with her? Then after a drawn-out, tense silence, she recognized the sarcasm and found the answer. The words he wanted her to say, the ones he wanted to hear and the ones that, maybe, she believed now.

She tilted her face down to the microphone.

"I think," June said, "there are some things that should remain ours."

A slow smile spread across Sam's face, an unnerving sight. Like a triumphant warrior, winning his long-fought battle at last. Or a serial killer.

Eric stepped up beside June. "Ms. Coffin…"

She ignored Eric and turned to Jason. "We're leaving. Let's go."

Before Jason could stand, before anyone could react, a sharp bang sounded from the back of the room. Everyone looked around. Someone had slammed a door open. Two figures skirted the crowd, making their way toward the stage: Robbie, pulling Micha along beside him.

"What the hell?" June said.

Micha swayed on his feet, limp and unaware. Robbie glowered at Eric. He held a narrow curved blade, like the blade of a scythe but smaller, to Micha's throat.

"You're going to listen to me!" Robbie shouted. "Or he's going to be my next victim, followed by them." Robbie thrust the blade at June and at Jason behind her.

"My God," Eric said. "Is that Micha Bellevue?"

June gaped at Robbie. This definitely wasn't part of the plan.

"Focus those cameras on me." Robbie reached the area in front of the stage and stopped. Sam's eyeballs looked like they were about to shoot out of his head.

Robbie placed the curved blade back to Micha's throat, and a collective more-excited-than-horrified gasp went up. *Reporters.*

"I'm doing this for the benefit of all our kind," Robbie announced. "Before it's too late. I'm doing this for the Paranormal Alliance, Sam."

"Mr. Haain," Eric said. "Is this man part of your organization? Is this some sort of stunt for publicity?"

"He *was* part of my organization," Sam said. "Until about ten seconds ago."

"I'm doing this for us Sam, for *you*," Robbie said. "While you've had your hands tied with politics and bureaucracy, I've been doing the dirty work. Someone had to."

"I never told you to do anything."

"I never needed you to." Robbie stood tall and confident. "I did what you couldn't do, Sam. I'm a soldier, and a soldier does what must be done for the good of the army. I know what you want, and I'm willing to act it out for you."

"I never wanted to hold an activist hostage in front of a crowd of reporters." Sam paused. "All right, I admit it's a nice fantasy, but I would never do it."

"Mr. Haain!" Eric stepped forward.

Robbie jerked around. The cameras followed his every move. "You stay right where you are," Robbie told Eric.

"You do realize," Eric said calmly, "you have a knife, and these security guards currently surrounding you have guns."

Indeed, the guards previously looming over Sam had drawn their weapons and trained them on Robbie. Robbie didn't react. Suddenly, the guns flew from the guards' hands, as if attached to strings someone had jerked. Gasps and excited yelps went up. A group of guards in the back of the room rushed forward and were abruptly, violently thrown backward, into walls, onto the floor, right into the crowd. The yelps became screams. People scattered.

"Go ahead!" Robbie yelled over the commotion. "Try to stop me again."

"Robbie," Sam said. "Why are you doing this?"

Muse stayed behind Sam, focused on Robbie.

Eric lifted his hands. "What is it you want? Talk to me. Don't hurt anyone else." He shot a sideways pleading look at June.

"I can't do anything," June said. "He's deaf."

"What do I want?" Robbie said. "What we all want. For paranormal people to be left alone. For corrupt normal-run, 'scientific' organizations to stop exploiting us. I can't stop you myself, no matter how powerful my abilities are. But I can stop you from getting your hands on our secrets. That's what I've been doing." He seethed at Sam. "What I've been doing for you!"

"What are you talking about?" Sam asked.

Robbie smiled, with the perverse delight of a cruel, mentally twisted child. "I've been keeping their lab rats from them, Sam. Unfortunately, I couldn't stop them from collecting the twins. Too much security. They've gotten smart to what I'm doing."

Cold horror swept over her, at the same moment Sam appeared to get the gist as well.

"You've been killing paranormal people," Sam said. "Killing us."

"So they couldn't use us!" Robbie said. "All this time they've blamed the SNC. It was the perfect cover. But I'm not letting them take my glory anymore. I want the world to know what I've accomplished. What I *will* accomplish."

June thought of the story Sam told her at the pier about Missy Chase, the Siren who was murdered and thrown in a Dumpster. Apparently, her mysterious killer had been found. Sam looked miserably horrified.

"I knew it," Sam said. "It was you at Kevin's bar. I knew that wasn't a bullet hole when I saw it. It was damage from a telekinetic blast. You were trying to kill June, but June wasn't there."

"I knew you'd figure it out eventually," Robbie said. "I thought I saw June through the window."

June flinched. She remembered something. "You saw Kevin."

Robbie jerked his head around. June pictured Kevin wearing his leather jacket and recalled him saying he'd been outside right before the shooting took place, taking a delivery. Kevin would have had his jacket on if he was outside.

"You asshole," June said. "You were trying to kill me?"

"I'm sorry," Robbie said. "But believe me, it's better that way."

"Screw you!"

"The paranormal community does not belong to the normals." Robbie swiveled back around to face the crowd. "We don't want exposure. We don't want what the Institute has to offer."

"Not every paranormal person feels that way," Eric said. "We've helped many."

"Oh really?" Robbie snarled. "How are you helping them? By keeping them locked up? Doing terrible things to them? Science hurts, doesn't it? Well it's going to hurt you a lot more than it does us, very soon."

"You crazy bastard." Sam's voice was tight with the strain of self-control. "Even if the Institute isn't right, even if I hate them, there's a whole spectrum of right and wrong and you can't sit on one end and ride it like a fucking teeter-totter. I would never order violence against our kind as a means of thwarting the Institute!"

"This is our world, not theirs," Robbie said. "We have to live by *our* rules."

"Our rules don't mandate cutting off your nose to spite your face."

Robbie stared at him, eyes burning. He seemed stunned that Sam didn't agree with him. Then his incredulity morphed into rage.

"You're weak and spineless, Sam." Robbie whirled around to face Eric, Micha wobbling at his side.

The movement seemed to shake Micha out of his stupor, and he tried to pull away.

"I have your activist, your dearest, most decorated supporter," Robbie said. "And I'll take more. I'll take everyone who supports you! I'll kill them all. If you want me to stop, you're going to open your files to the public. The world is going to see what's been going on inside your walls."

"We have nothing to hide." Eric remained calm. "You don't have to kill anyone. We'll give you whatever information you want."

"Oh really?" Robbie sneered. He jerked his head at June. "Were you so kind to them? When you tried to kill them when they attempted to escape?"

"You're delusional," Eric said. "We've never harmed anyone."

Micha continued trying to pull away from Robbie. Robbie let go of him, and he collapsed in a heap at Robbie's feet.

"You lied to me," Micha slurred. He swiped at Robbie's legs, but Robbie sidestepped him.

"You're going to be exposed." Robbie pointed his blade at Eric. "Everything you've done, every sin you've committed against us. And then I'm going to bleed you dry, in front of the whole city."

Sam took a tentative step forward. "Robbie…"

Without looking at him, Robbie swung the blade around and pointed it at Sam. "You've proven yourself unworthy of my cause. I don't need you anymore."

"What the hell are you talking about?" Sam said. "*Your* cause?"

John McKormic had his head lowered, murmuring into a cell phone. Sam looked up at June.

What the fuck should I do? June asked in her head, hoping Muse could hear her.

As if he had been the one to catch the question, Sam mouthed a single word: *RUN*.

In the next instant, Muse shot forward, a white streak, and snatched the blade from Robbie's hand still extended toward Sam. As Robbie spun toward her, she swung the knife in an upward arc. A *shink* sounded and a shower of blood sprayed the floorboards like grisly rain. Robbie reeled and stumbled away, hands to his face, shrieking.

Screams erupted. People bolted for the doors. June dashed across the stage to Jason, grabbed his arm, and hauled him up. Jason lurched on his feet. The researchers were already in motion to try to stop them.

"Sit down and don't move until we're gone!" Her power rushed up her throat and made the air vibrate.

They all slammed back down in their seats.

She dragged Jason off the stage and made for the door to the hallway, trying to reach safety before the rush of panicked reporters hindered their escape. Jason was taller and weighed more than she, but June was determined—and pants-shittingly terrified—enough to pull him along as if he were a small child.

Most of the reporters didn't possess the sense to get away from the building and were still trying to film and report outside. June wanted to run for the parking lot, but Jason was in no state to move fast.

"What did they do to you?" she asked him.

Before Jason could answer, an explosion erupted to their left. June lurched to the side, grabbing Jason and jerking him out of the way. People around them yelped as broken glass scattered on the snow. One of the security guards had been launched through a window and now lay quivering on the concrete walkway, covered in blood. Clearly, Robbie was still alive and on a rampage.

"Jesus Christ," June gasped.

Muse appeared at June's side and clutched her arm.

"Don't just stand there," Muse said. "Run!"

The three of them took off toward the parking lot. As June suspected, Jason couldn't move fast, but thankfully no one seemed to be chasing them. June kept looking over her shoulder to make sure, holding Jason's arm as they loped through the snow.

"Where are we going?" Jason asked, his voice hoarse.

"There's a car waiting for us," June said. "People we can trust are getting us out of here."

"Oh my God." Jason huffed for breath. "I can't believe you're here. I can't believe you're alive."

She fought back tears. "I can't believe you're alive either."

Muse was a couple steps ahead of them. "Save the sweet reunions for later. We're not out of harm's way yet."

June clutched Jason's arm, keeping him upright with all her strength.

They reached the fountain at the entrance of the park. The tunnel to the parking lot loomed ahead of them. June started to think they were actually going to escape. Her heart climbed into her throat.

As they passed the fountain, her exaltation was quickly, violently dashed.

A tall man dressed in black stepped abruptly into their path. A black rod protruded from his balled fist as he shot his arm out. He hit Jason square in the chest.

Jason crumpled, collapsing onto the pavement with an agonized scream. The attack was so sudden, June couldn't react. She was nearly pulled to the ground as well, still holding on to his arm.

"You bastard!" June railed at the man.

June let go of Jason and lunged at the man, but as if they were falling from the sky, another one appeared and leapt on her.

The second man pushed her to the ground, slamming her down hard on her knees. Pain rattled up her thighs, and before she could yell, one of them jammed something into her mouth. She gagged as the hard object pushed past her teeth, hurting as the post of her tongue ring was crushed into the bottom of her mouth. She tried to scrabble for the gun at her hip, but her arms were jerked behind her. Jason was choking and sobbing and Muse was screaming. Someone had her, too.

They reached the parking lot, but not the way June hoped. She struggled as they dragged her through the tunnel, until one of the men gave her a subduing punch to the ribs. They moved across the lot, toward a black van where several more men stood. Jason coughed and groaned behind her. She didn't hear Muse and assumed they had gagged her as well.

The back doors of the van opened. They hauled Jason inside first.

"Quit your fighting," one of the men who had June restrained growled in her ear. "I ain't afraid to kick your ass if you keep it up."

June bit the gag, snarling. They *would* need to kick her ass if they wanted cooperation.

"Here he comes," one of the men said.

June wrenched her head around to see whom they were talking about. A group of people crossed the lot toward them, fast and with purpose.

"Make sure you put them out," a man's voice called. "We don't need any more incidents."

Eric Greerson arrived at the van, followed by his researchers. He must have left the field house as fast as they did. June screamed around the gag and bucked against the men holding her, pain in her ribs be damned.

She recalled Rose's words then, echoing in her head. Nothing is what it seems. Both sides have secrets.

"You know," Eric said, hands tucked into the pockets of the long gray coat he now wore. He also wore sunglasses and a wide-brimmed fedora.

"I figured when Sam started having his little tantrum, he knew where you were. That's why I agreed to the press conference. I suspected he knew where Micha Bellevue was as well, and that was of even greater interest to me." He turned away from June. "But you...you're a big, brilliant bonus."

June jerked her head around. Muse, indeed gagged, struggled against the tall, burly man who held her. Eric walked over, gripped her hair, and jerked her face back to look at him. She seethed around the gag.

"Aaron Jenkins' daughter," Eric said. "Yes, I know who you are. Sam Haain can't keep secrets from me."

June forgot to struggle. She tried to process this surprising revelation. Then Eric turned his attention back to her, releasing Muse's hair, and June started fighting in earnest. The smugness in Eric's expression foretold bad things.

"Put her out now," Eric said. "She won't be slipping off again."

A man walked from the direction of the van. He had a syringe in his hand. June kicked at him as he approached.

"Stick her in the throat," Eric said. "Don't fool around."

Someone grabbed June's hair and wrenched her head painfully to the side. She could no longer struggle, so many people were holding her. The needle went in with a sharp stick. She screamed against the gag.

The men kept their grip. She was going to die, along with Jason and Muse. Eric looked on while his researchers dispersed behind him. June wanted to call him a bastard, a liar, but she couldn't speak even if the gag hadn't been in her mouth. Her body sagged and her vision blurred. Her mind went foggy. They heaved her into the van, before she slipped into darkness.

Chapter 14

June awoke with an aching body and a thick head. For a moment, in her confused state, she thought she had a hangover. Then memories trickled in: the press conference; the guard flying through the window; Jason, Robbie, Eric Greerson. She opened her eyes.

She was lying on her back on a cold tile floor. Everything around her was silent, aside from a buzzing fluorescent light overhead. Her jacket had been removed, the chill from the floor seeping through her shirt—Micha's shirt—and the gag, thankfully, had been removed. She reached down. Her gun had been taken away, but she wasn't surprised.

After a moment of getting her wits about her, she lifted her head. The room spun. She squeezed her eyes shut, took a few deep breaths, and slowly opened them again and looked around.

She was in a small bare featureless room. A camera hung in one corner, up by the ceiling. Muse was propped against an adjacent wall to June's left. She sat slumped, head hanging, hands limp in her lap. She had also been stripped of her coat. About ten feet away, Jason was on the floor, lying on his side, knees drawn up and arms crossed over his chest. His eyes were closed, but even in sleep—if he was asleep—he winced. The marks on his wrists were dark mottled red and purple rings.

"Where are we?" June's voice was hoarse and her jaw hurt. She propped herself up on one elbow, the ache in her ribs making the movement painful. The room spun again. She closed her eyes and waited for the vertigo to pass. Her hands were shaky and clammy from lack of nicotine, adding to her total unpleasant physical state. When her head stopped spinning, she opened her eyes again.

"Jason," she whispered. Her mouth was dry and tasted metallic.

Jason didn't stir.

"Jason!"

He opened his eyes, expression still pained, his brow knitted. He blinked a few times, shifted, and grimaced.

"Are you all right?" she asked. "Do you know where we are?"

"No." His voice was small and weak.

She wasn't sure which question he'd answered. Maybe both.

June tried to scoot toward him, but her strength was diminished. "What did they do to you, Jason? What happened to you?"

"They're watching us," Muse murmured.

June had to close her eyes again.

"Don't get feisty," Muse warned. "They probably won't like it."

June flopped back down on the tile. She opened her eyes. Muse still sat slumped, but her eyes were open.

"Assholes," June snarled. "Taking him down like that. He was already weak. Why'd they have to hit him?"

"Because they knew it would stop you," Muse said.

A surge of rage helped June struggle into a sitting position. Her vision swam and her stomach lurched. She felt top-heavy. "Where the hell are we?"

"I'm guessing the Institute." Muse lifted her head. The corner of her mouth twitched. "I'm sorry I failed you at the park."

"You didn't fail us. How were you supposed to hold all those guys off?"

"I should have known they were lying in wait. But I was reaching out to Sam, trying to make sure he was all right. I wasn't paying attention."

"I think even if you'd known, it wouldn't have mattered." June looked around, trying to find a way out, a vent, anything. "Even if we went another way, they would have chased us. They were determined."

"It's a very bad thing that I've been captured," Muse said. "Sam is alone now, and vulnerable. And Robbie got away. Sam won't know what's coming at him without me there."

"I'm not too happy they got us, either."

With uncoordinated, graceless effort, June got to her feet, but once she did she almost didn't stay upright. Despite the weakness and vertigo, and the pain in her knees from being slammed down on the asphalt, she loped over to the door, the room moving with her. Her movements were like swimming through thick water. She tried the knob and found the door locked.

"I don't think we're getting out of here until they take us out," Muse said.

June dropped her head against the door, clutching the knob with both hands. She wanted a smoke so her head would clear and her thoughts would focus.

She turned around and slumped against the door. One corner of Muse's mouth pushed up, as if the muscles on that side of her face had frozen. Jason rolled onto his back, eyes closed, hands still clasped over his chest.

"So you're Aaron Jenkins's daughter?" June figured they had plenty of time for conversation now.

"Yes." Muse looked up at the camera. "No point trying to hide it now. They clearly know everything already. Sam has been protecting me."

"I thought you were *his* bodyguard."

"I've spent my entire life hiding who I am. I'm sure you can understand that."

"Why have you been hiding?"

"Because of my father, because of who he is. His group might depose him if they knew his daughter was paranormal. My grandfather would have killed me if he knew. My father kept me away from him. Now he has to keep me away from the SNC." She took a deep, rattling breath. "My name isn't Muse Sagan. It's Mary Ellen Jenkins. Sagan was my mother's maiden name. Muse is—kind of a long story."

June marveled. This was the most she had ever heard Muse speak. "That sucks. But there's protection for you, if they find out. Isn't there? The activists, the organizations—"

"Protection." Muse thumped her head back against the wall. "Would you like to hear why Sam is harboring me? The more complicated reasons?" Her voice seemed to be getting raspier as she spoke.

"Yes. We don't have anything else to do."

"There's some things I think you should know. Things I told Sam he should tell you. And since—not all of us might make it out of here, I'm going to tell you now."

June didn't like good-bye speeches.

A tic made one of Muse's eyelids flutter. "Sam had a brother, named Thomas. Kevin, Cindy's ex-husband, was Thomas's best friend. Thomas was murdered by paranormal extremists. Four of them, or so a couple witnesses said. They restrained him, and one of them burnt him alive with pyrokinesis. My father had just taken control of the SNC and he was working out a treaty with Sam. Everyone assumed the killers were rogue Paranormal Alliance members who opposed the union."

June stared across the room, mouth open, and tried to absorb this story in her already spinning head.

"Neither Sam nor my father knew how to handle the situation," Muse said. "And Kevin lost his mind. He went to Old Town and hired some militant vampires to track down the killers and punish them. Vampires are smart, you see. They know things. They hear things. Two days later, three of the four murderers turned up bloodless in a drainage ditch near Jackson Park Beach."

"Wow." June slipped down the door and sat, legs out in front of her. So here, at last, was the story of Sam's brother.

"The problem with militant vampires is they don't care about discretion. They would have given Kevin up for enlisting them, but Sam offered my father a deal. He took me into his protection in exchange for my father paying off the vampires to keep their mouths shut. My father has a lot more money and a lot more to offer than Sam does, or did at the time. As a consequence of all this, Kevin then owed Sam a favor."

"The Oracle of the Dead," June said.

"Yes. Kevin's fear and hatred of the paranormal has grown since then, but he tried to alleviate it by getting into a relationship with Cindy. Big mistake. And Kevin couldn't handle being involved with someone in the Paranormal Alliance. I think it reminds him too much of Thomas."

June sagged against the door. "I guess we shouldn't be so quick to think someone's a jerk until we know his story."

"Trust me, you can have a tragic story and still be a jerk."

June would have laughed, if she were capable of any humor at that moment.

"Sam intended to use Kevin's favor for himself eventually," Muse said, "but he's always believed the needs of the many outweigh the needs of the few."

"What was he going to use it for?" June wasn't sure she wanted to know.

"To find out where his brother's fourth killer is. They still haven't caught them."

Horror swept over June. "What the hell? Why would he waste it? What am I to him? I'm nothing, nobody. Why would he waste an opportunity like that on me?"

"Because you're the future." Muse's mouth twisted, and the movement looked painful. She even winced. "Sam needs an icon. Someone to use as an example of what the people in this city are doing to us. He wants what happened to his brother to never happen to anyone else ever again. He's just been waiting for the right person to come along."

"He wants me to be an icon?"

"He said there would be a price for him helping you. That's it. He needs a pariah. I wanted it to be me, for so long. I wanted to do it for him, damn my father's organization, but I can't. I'm dying."

"What?"

"My power is killing me. It happens to some of us. It's destroying my nervous system. It's happening to Robbie, too. That's why he's deaf. He's losing his vision, too. Probably why he mistook Kevin for you."

"Holy shit."

"For a while I was able to control it with medicine. But now." She huffed. "Suffering makes you pure, they say. In some holy text. Maybe I'll end up a saint."

A cold weight settled on June's chest. "Does this happen to everyone?"

"No. But if it does happen to you, you'll know."

June swallowed. "Damn. I'm sorry, Muse."

Muse tilted her chin up at the camera, eyelids fluttering. "It doesn't matter what the Institute does to me now. I'm almost gone anyway."

"Muse." June tried to sit up straighter. "Don't flake out on me. I need you."

"I know. I won't. Sam wants me to save you, and I will, if it's the last thing I do."

Muse dropped her hand on the floor beside her hip and started signaling. Signing. June watched as she repeated four movements. She lifted her pinky finger. Jerked her open palm toward herself. Pointed at June. Made her hand in the shape of a gun. June didn't understand sign language, but she got the gist.

I. Have. Your. Gun. June widened her eyes.

Sounds came from outside the door, footsteps and voices. As quickly as her body would allow, June pushed away from the door. A moment later a *click* sounded, the knob turned, and the door opened.

Eric Greerson slid into the room, smooth as a snake. He quickly closed the door behind him.

"My little rats in a cage." His smile was cruel. "How gleeful and blind, you all stumbled into your trap. It's good to see you all awake and ready for some fun."

If June had had her gun right then, he would have paid.

"I almost feel like I have no right to be proud of myself," Eric said. "Since you did all the work. I could only be happier if Sam Haain were rattling around in here with you." He chuckled as Jason tried to sit up. "Oh, he doesn't look good at all."

"You asshole," June said. "Let us go."

"Don't try to use your voice on me, Ms. Coffin. It won't work, and you'll just look foolish."

"How could you do this?" Muse asked. "You're supposed to be our champion, or some shit."

"It was easy, actually. My predecessor was a great help. People like your father and Sam Haain believe I was put in place to serve as an ignorant figurehead. It's highly beneficial to me."

"Michael Paulson knew what was going on," Muse said. "He wouldn't go along with it, would he?" Sam had said Michael Paulson was the first, mysteriously vanished, head of the Institute.

"Oh, he did, at first," Eric said. "But the more he learned, the more his conscience took over. Then he had a fit of morality and had to be displaced."

"You mean killed," Muse said.

"I'm afraid that's a top secret matter. I could have stepped in here just now and shot every one of you, by the way." He clapped his hands together. "But I'd rather you bear witness to the reason you've been so bedeviled by me and my organization. I know what intelligence Sam has gathered. Why don't you come see the final proof, the one thing he's been trying so hard to get his hands on?"

June slid forward. "Screw you. Slam your head in the door you ruthless bastard!" Her power rose unbidden, flowing out with the words. She had never used her ability to inflict harm on another person, and even as she said it, knowing it was deserved, she felt bad for it.

Eric threw his head back and laughed.

"What the hell?" June ground out. Maybe he was wearing fancy earplugs or something.

Eric's eyes glittered with malevolence. "Get him on his feet." He jerked his head toward Jason. "Or I'll get him up myself, and he won't like it." He turned and opened the door. "Now. Time's wasting."

June, still weak and dizzy, could barely stand on her own, let alone help anyone else stand, but she didn't want Eric touching her brother. She crawled over to him.

Muse crawled over as well and tried to help her, despite her being as short and weak as June.

"This isn't going to be good," Muse whispered.

"You're telling me," June muttered.

Somehow, together, they managed to get Jason on his feet. He was like a dead weight across June's back and she nearly collapsed after moving only the several feet to the door. What awaited them outside the room *wasn't* good at all.

Chapter 15

In the hallway, two men holding guns stood on either side of Eric, one a heavily-muscled, stocky black man, the other a tall white man with close-shaved hair. Both were dressed as security guards and wore headphones. They were the same headphones the researchers had worn while doing experiments with Jason and June.

The white man stepped forward, gun trained on June, and pulled out of his shirt pocket a black ball with straps attached. June had seen the gag once already, at the park. She shrank back, making Jason wobble. Her withdrawal didn't deter the bastard. He stuffed the ball into her mouth and pulled the straps around her head. June snarled behind the gag, but didn't fight, afraid they'd shoot her to make a point.

"You're such an asshole," Muse spat at Eric.

"The other Siren, too." Eric motioned to Jason. "I know you're hardly a threat, but let's make you look like your twin sister, hmm?"

The black man produced a second gag and affixed it on Jason. He didn't fight, either. He just sagged and allowed them to do it. June wanted to punish them all. She wanted to punish herself.

The guards took off the headphones.

"Cuff them as well," Eric said.

June raged some more as her hands were secured behind her. The black man cuffed Jason and started leading him, weaving and stumbling, down the hallway.

"Where are you taking us?" Muse demanded, as she and June were goaded after them. "They're purposely blocking their thoughts so I can't read anything," she said to June.

"Don't be so eager to see the end of this," Eric said. "If I were you, I'd be hoping for as much time as I'll allow you."

They walked down the hallway and passed by a bank of windows. Outside, night had fallen, the skyscrapers of downtown glittering in the distance. The hallway was empty and eerily quiet, the buzz of the overhead lights mingling with their collective footsteps. A clock hanging over a desk said 8:12.

After several minutes of walking, they reached a set of double doors and the guards led them through. They stepped into a narrow green tile room with a row of metal sinks along one wall and another set of double doors on the other side. The place looked like a surgery prep room.

"What's going on?" Muse asked. "Where are we?" Clearly, once provoked to anger she wasn't so demure and quiet anymore.

"Are you ready to witness what your beloved's intelligence-gathering has been leading to?" Eric asked her.

"What are you talking about?" Muse asked.

"Right this way."

Eric went through the doors first. The guards forced the three of them after him.

The room beyond was bigger and brighter, full of medical equipment, the walls the same green tile as the outer room. The room looked like an operating theatre, but more sinister, like a mad scientist's laboratory. The assessment probably wasn't far off. A group of people—four men and two women, all wearing white lab coats—stood in the middle of the room. Someone else stood in the room, too.

"Micha!" Muse gasped.

June stumbled and almost fell.

Micha stood in the midst of the group, wearing the jeans and T-shirt he'd had on earlier, the sweater June and Sam put on him gone. He looked disheveled but alert.

"You should be happy to see him," Eric said. "He's the only reason I'm letting you live right now." He turned to Micha. "Feeling a bit more lively? Withdrawal from that stuff was an unforeseen consequence. If we'd gotten to you sooner we could have given you something to take the edge off."

"What the hell is going on?" Muse demanded.

June jerked at her cuffs, making wet, seething sounds behind the gag. Saliva dripped down her chin, but she didn't care how undignified her current state had rendered her. Her jaws hurt. Her head hurt. The pain made her angrier.

Eric stepped up to the group. The brilliant overhead light shone on his hair, turning the silver strands translucent and showing the pink of his scalp. "Mr. Bellevue is going to make history."

"How could you do this?" Micha sounded perfectly lucid. "How could you betray everyone? All your lies about wanting to protect the community, all that bullshit about making the Institute a safe haven for the paranormal."

"I do want to protect paranormal people," Eric said, with affected affront. "They're no good to me dead. Haain's crazy disciple has been a thorn in my side for quite some time."

"Robbie didn't do anything under Sam's command," Muse said.

"Whether he's Haain's charge or not, it doesn't matter. He almost took out my first test subject, and for that I would have been greatly vexed."

"You're going to give Micha the serum?" Muse asked. Apparently, she knew everything Sam knew. "Why? He's not the only one campaigning for paranormal rights. Is this supposed to be his punishment?"

"Punishment?" Eric put a hand to his heart. "This is an *honor*. But you're right, there's nothing particularly special about him." He gave Micha a patronizing pat on the shoulder. "You were just convenient, Mr. Bellevue. Easy to get to and prep. But you *will* be special. Very special."

"What do you mean, prep?" Micha asked.

"You need special enzymes for the serum to work," Muse said. "There's an agent you have to take to build them. That's what we found out. We just couldn't figure out what the agent was."

"I haven't taken anything," Micha said.

"You have, actually." Eric tilted his chin up. "You were convenient because of your association with—formerly—top members of this facility."

Dread stole across Micha's features. "Oh God. Rose…"

June widened her eyes. *A means to their end.*

Eric chuckled. "Yes. It was a terrible inconvenience for me, but maybe my men did you a favor when they accidentally shot her."

"How was she giving it to me?" Micha asked.

"I never asked her. It's a tasteless, odorless powder, so I'm sure in anything she had access to that you were drinking. Really quite easy."

"Drinking…" Micha said.

June recalled Micha talking about Rose's coffee. He didn't have late-stage abilities. Rose had been feeding him the serum.

"Allow me to offer my condolences on your wife, by the way," Eric said. "Know that she was not meant to be eradicated. She was a vital and treasured researcher, and I'm sorry to have lost her."

"What is this prepping agent?" Micha asked. "What's it supposed to do?"

"It's a special compound we created." Eric clasped his hands, sounding pleased Micha had asked. "It creates special receptors in your cells. We've found these receptors in almost all classifications of paranormal people, and also, specific hormones that bind with the receptors, unlike anything normal people produce. It's fascinating science. You can read all about it once you've experienced it. Now that we've built the receptors, we'll give you the hormones."

"How do you know it won't harm him?" Muse asked. "Have you tested it on anyone else?"

"We did some animal experimentation," Eric said. "It's perfectly safe."

June pictured a bunch of paranormal rats and monkeys running around.

"Animals aren't humans," Muse said. "What if the receptors didn't form? You don't know what the hormones might do to him."

"Experiments suggest formation of the receptors can spark bouts of paranormal ability even before the hormones are introduced." Eric looked at Micha. "Have you been experiencing abilities?"

Micha didn't answer, but he glanced at June. He *had* been reading her mind. Under the light, Micha's face appeared sunken and sallow, like the face of a man sick for a long time, but his eyes were full of healthy rage.

"I'll take that as a yes," Eric said. "Unfortunately, when you got cut off from the prepping agent upon your wife's death, it affected your health. But you won't have to worry about that anymore. We'll take good care of you."

"You can't do this!" Muse lurched forward. "I won't watch you destroy him for your sick notion of science."

"Enough of this," Eric snapped. "Shut that little bitch up."

The white guard grappled with her.

Muse bucked against him. "No! You can't—"

He clapped a hand over her mouth.

"Here." Eric grabbed a roll of surgical tape from a cart and tossed it over.

The black guard helped hold Muse down on the floor. For being so little, she gave them a hell of a fight. They placed the tape over her mouth and wrapped several layers around her head, over her hair. She made desperate muffled sounds against the tape, breathing fast through her nose. They yanked her arms behind her, bound her wrists as well, and hauled her up on her knees.

June and Jason were pushed to the floor. June growled behind her gag.

"All right then," Eric addressed the group of researchers. "Let's begin this." He strode across the room.

The researchers dispersed, save for one man and one woman. The two led Micha to a bed in the center of the room, and the man told him to take off his shirt.

"You're going to pay for this," Micha said after Eric. "You won't get away with it. And if I survive it, I'll never jump through your hoops and pretend I gave my consent."

"We have ways of keeping you from talking, don't worry about that." Eric added ominously, "And you don't necessarily have to survive it for us to release the results."

The three of them probably wouldn't be around to call bullshit, either.

Micha was told again to remove his shirt. He pulled it up and over his head, not resisting, but still obviously furious.

When they turned him around, the tattoo on his back was visible in the bright light, spanning the space between his shoulder blades. The tattoo was, as she thought before, a nautical compass rose, colored gold and rust, the letters at each point in black calligraphy. She wasn't close enough to take in all the detail, but each degree had been marked and the sunburst in the middle painstakingly textured. Something so intricate took several sittings. Nobody got a tattoo so complex done on a whim; the design clearly had deep, personal meaning. He wanted to be a guide, to provide direction.

The sight of the tattoo made it all the more poignant when he lay silent, while the two researchers affixed restraints to his ankles and wrists. Tears slipped from her eyes.

"Don't be nervous," Eric said from across the room. "If anything goes wrong, these people are trained medical professionals. This is going to be exciting."

June wished she could wipe the tears from her cheeks. Instead she wept harder, silently, behind her gag. Micha gave her a faint smile, as if to assure her everything would be all right. But it wouldn't be, and she couldn't trick herself into believing it would.

The woman started prepping Micha's arm for an injection. The man placed sensors attached to wires on his chest. Nothing could stop the awful forward momentum of the moment.

"We're going to inject you with a small dose of hormones first," Eric said. "We'll be watching your vital signs closely. If there doesn't seem to be any distress, we'll give you another larger dose. Once we know you're physically stable, we'll give you an MRI, so we can see what's going on inside you. We'll be documenting this. You'll be in the history books.

Or at least the scientific journals." He chuckled wryly. "The first blank human to receive paranormal powers. Think of the adulation."

No doubt the adulation would all be Eric's.

They wrapped a blood pressure cuff around Micha's right arm and wheeled a crash cart over to the bed. The sight of it made things scarier. One of the men brought a tray over; a syringe rested on it, filled with pale blue fluid. The woman picked up the syringe. Micha was unflinching.

"This is a cocktail of various hormones," Eric said from his vantage point. "It represents several different paranormal classifications. We'll see if any of them stick."

Muse's eyes were wide above the tape. Jason looked about to topple over. June wanted to scream behind the gag, but she couldn't make a sound.

The room was deathly quiet as the needle slid into Micha's arm.

Chapter 16

June sat slumped against one of the green tile walls. The awkward position, arms behind her back and legs folded beneath her, had long since pushed her body past discomfort to pain, and then to numbness. Muse sat beside her in a similar pose, head hanging, the occasional jerk or tremor of her muscles making her quake. Jason sat on the other side of Muse, slumped and gazing across the room in a daze. They had probably tortured him in a similar room, tied him down and done terrible things to him like they were doing to Micha.

In the immeasurable amount of time they'd been watching, Micha experienced a wide range of physical reactions June considered bad, but Eric didn't seem overly concerned. She suspected even if Micha burst into flames, Eric probably wouldn't be concerned; he'd turn a fire extinguisher on him and give him another dose.

Micha turned frighteningly pale within the first few minutes after the shot, as if all the blood had run out of him, as if he were dead. Then he became flushed, his skin reddening and glistening with sweat. He shook for a while, and then he was deathly still. June had seen people detox in the same manner. He didn't cry out or look anywhere but above him, into the lights.

Eric went back and forth between a bank of monitors and the bed. The room, aside from the blip of machines and the occasional murmur of the researchers, remained agonizingly quiet. The tension grew so heavy June thought the weight would snap her neck.

Eric approached the bed again. The woman researcher was checking Micha's blood pressure. She started talking to Eric, and June strained to hear.

"His blood pressure and heart rate are elevated," she said. "His temperature keeps fluctuating."

Eric lifted his arm and looked at his watch. "It's nearly nine thirty. I have an important meeting at ten."

June narrowed her eyes. Who the hell had important meetings at ten o'clock at night?

Eric placed his hands on the bed and leaned over. "Mr. Bellevue, can you hear me? Do you understand me?"

Micha's eyes were glazed and unfocused, the way he'd been for the past couple days.

"You've been very cooperative," Eric said. "So, I'm going to let your friends go. I'll see them out myself."

Muse snapped her head up. June tensed.

"I think we can give him the second dose," Eric said to the woman. He patted Micha's arm. "We're going to give you the next round. I'll come back and check on you in a bit."

"I thought we were waiting until he processed the first one?" the woman said, with some concern.

"There's no need. He's doing fine." Eric motioned to his men.

June's heart raced as they hauled her, stiffly and painfully, to her feet. They weren't being let go, she would put a lot of money on that.

Eric followed them out. In the hallway, he spoke to the guards. "Take them down to Special Projects. I think there's still a few things we can learn before we dispose of them. No need to waste good research material."

Eric turned and walked briskly down the hallway. June wanted to lunge after him, but she was pushed in a different direction.

"Move it," the black guard said gruffly.

The guards ushered them through the empty hallways, Jason still unsteady, the white guard gripping his arm. With every step, June's fear increased, mind racing to figure out a way to escape. They turned a corner and faced a bank of elevators. The black guard pressed the down button next to one.

June prayed Micha wouldn't die. She couldn't dwell too much on it or grief would overwhelm her and she wouldn't be able to focus on getting out.

A *ding* sounded, and the doors on one of the elevators slid open.

The elevator was wide and deep, as though made for transporting beds. They were herded in, and the white guard hit the button for the twentieth floor.

"Don't you worry," he said. "They'll take good care of you down there. Eric doesn't like his monkeys bruised."

The doors slid shut.

June looked at the numbers. They were on the thirty-third floor. The elevator started to move, and each number after their floor lit in succession, counting down. Thirty-two...thirty-one...thirty... Her stomach dropped. She could barely breathe around the gag.

"You know," the black guard laughed, mockingly, "you just got to witness history, how about that? Something to take with you to the other side."

Twenty-seven...twenty-six...twenty-five...

"You're both awful pretty though," the white guard said. "I'm sure you can probably bargain your way out of being treated too badly." He swept June with a slow, disgustingly appraising look. June wanted a sharp object and her hands free, so she could stick him in his eye.

At the twenty-second floor, the elevator lurched to a stop, settling beneath them. June stared at the strip of numbers, the changing light frozen. She looked at Muse. Muse looked back at her. They both looked at the doors.

"What the hell?" The white guard jabbed the "twenty" button several times, but the elevator remained still.

"Someone called for the elevator on this floor," the black guard said. "There's not supposed to be anyone down here, is there?"

They both drew their guns and took a step back. June braced herself. After a tense physics-defying moment, the doors slid open. The appearance of the two men on the other side shocked everyone in the elevator, except for probably Jason, as he wouldn't know either of their faces.

"Drop those toy pistols," Sam said.

June knew little about guns, but she knew Sam had a shotgun. A sawed off one, with two barrels.

"I guarantee I have better aim," Sam said. "And mine will take out an entire internal organ."

The two guards didn't drop their guns, but they didn't fire, either.

"You heard him," the other man said. He too held an impressive-looking gun, but his looked like something out of a gangster movie. He was tall, older, handsome.

Muse looked a lot like her father. That's why June had recognized him on TV.

"We'll drop you both before you can pull the triggers," Aaron said. "They'll be cleaning bits of you out of the elevator shaft for weeks."

"We have orders from Eric Greerson," the black guard said. "We're not letting you near these prisoners."

Aaron stepped forward and jerked a hand out to stop the elevator doors from closing. Both guards aimed their guns at him. Aaron remained calm.

"Drop your guns," Aaron said firmly, "or I'll shoot you right between the eyes, which will probably blow both of them out of the sockets. I'm guessing you wouldn't have the skill to shoot my balls if they were hanging out, while I, on the other hand, know exactly what I'm doing. Do you really want to die for Eric Greerson?"

June suddenly understood why, though they had differing views, Sam and Aaron had a treaty.

The guards seemed to consider Aaron's words. Sam looked impatient.

Finally, the guards dropped their guns and put their hands up, stony-faced and glaring.

"Good lackeys." Aaron stuck his leg out, hooked one of the guns under the heel of his leather loafer, and drew the weapon toward him. He toed the gun out of the elevator and kicked it away.

Sam stepped in and picked up the other one.

"We're not the only ones in the building," the white guard said. "You're gonna be in trouble, real soon."

"Why don't you come out of there now?" Aaron said.

The men hesitated but, after a moment, cautiously stepped out, hands still up.

"You won't get away with this," the black guard said. "This whole place is on lockdown right now. You won't get anywhere."

"How'd we get in, then?" Sam asked.

June flinched as Sam and Aaron swiftly stepped around them and brought the butts of their guns down on the back of the guard's necks, nearly in tandem. Both men dropped to the floor in a heap, the white one twitching. Aaron slid forward and stopped the doors from closing again.

"Why don't I ever get to shoot anyone?" Sam grumped.

"Killing is the Institute's job." Aaron moved into the elevator and hit a button. The doors stayed open. He set his gun down and started pulling the tape off Muse's mouth.

Sam strolled in behind Aaron, gun on his shoulder, and stopped in front of June.

"That's a good look for you." Sam poked the ball of the gag.

June frothed at him.

"Hold on, hold on." He smiled lasciviously. "I need to capture this moment."

June snarled behind the gag and jerked at her cuffs.

"Sam, get her out of her restraints." Aaron unwound the tape from Muse's hair.

"I knew coming here with you was going to be no fun." Sam set his gun down, propping the weapon against the wall of the elevator, and started undoing the gag behind June's head. When the ball popped out, a gush of saliva followed and plopped quite satisfactorily on Sam's shoe.

June worked her jaw. "Holy *deus ex machina*." Her words were slurred. "Where the hell did you two come from?"

Sam turned her around. The sound of metal on metal, like a knife being removed from a sheath, and Sam slipped something under the chain of the cuffs and started jerking.

"Don't call me God yet," he said. "Save that for later."

"I don't know how much I'm enjoying being rescued by the pervert squad," June said.

"Would you like us to leave so you can take care of your own fate?" Aaron asked. He'd gotten the tape off Muse's mouth.

Muse's lips were swollen and red. She stared at her father. "Where *did* you come from?" she asked.

The chain on the cuffs broke. June brought her arms around in front of her, teeth gritted. Her shoulders and biceps burned, and her fingers were numb. She turned around and glowered at Sam. He was holding a huge serrated hunting knife. He twirled it, and walked over to free Jason.

"I got a phone call a couple hours ago," Aaron said. "Who knew baiting Eric Greerson into a press conference was a bad idea?"

"I've always overlooked that bastard." Sam started taking off Jason's gag.

"I haven't." Aaron turned Muse around and undid the tape on her hands. "I always suspected he was shady. I wouldn't have cared that the Paranormal Alliance got themselves in a bind except"—Muse turned back around—"Sam told me they took you."

"Nothing went as planned," Muse said.

"Obviously," Aaron replied.

"Cindy saw them throw you guys in the van," Sam said. "So I called up Aaron, we got some guns"—he turned Jason around to cut off the cuffs—"and boom. We came on over."

"You just walked into the Institute?" June asked. "I almost died trying to get away from here, and you're telling me you strolled in the front door?"

"Yes," Aaron said.

June looked between them, baffled.

The chain broke on Jason's cuffs. Sam stepped back and slid the knife into a sheath on his hip. Aaron gestured to him, as if expecting him to answer June's question.

Sam sighed dramatically and tilted his head back. "There's this rumor going around that I don't actually have paranormal powers." He lifted his hands. "That I'm a false king."

Aaron rolled his eyes.

"The reason people think I don't have abilities," Sam said, "is because they've never seen me use them. I'm a shapeshifter."

"A shapeshifter?" June asked.

"A glamour generator," Aaron said.

"*Shapeshifter*," Sam said. "I can make people see me as something else, some*one* else."

"Using a glamour," Aaron pointed out.

"I can extend it"—Sam raised his voice—"to someone else, as long as I have physical contact with them."

"So we looked like security guards," Aaron said. "A couple of really close, glued-at-the-hip security guards, but regardless, it got us in. The goon was right. The place is on lockdown. Eric is paranoid."

"We did some eavesdropping and found out where they were keeping you," Sam said. "We were on our way up when we were told they were bringing you down and to report to the Special Projects Department. Figured we'd head them off at the pass."

"There's a little problem, though," Aaron said. "I'm sure by now they've realized you're not on your way anymore."

"Which means we've got a very fast-closing window to get out of here," Sam said.

"Jesus." June was trying to wrap her head around everything. "This day has definitely been a lesson in not taking things at face value."

Aaron and Sam picked up their guns.

"Hang on kids," Aaron said. "This is about to get ugly."

Aaron pressed a button and the doors closed.

June stepped forward. "Wait!"

Aaron looked around at her, hand poised to press the button that would set them in motion.

"We can't leave yet." Adrenaline surged through her limbs. "We have to go back up."

"Up is not out," Aaron said.

"They have Micha Bellevue," she said. "On the thirty-third floor."

Muse swallowed and stepped toward her father, the corner of her eye twitching.

"The serum Sam and I have been telling you about is real," Muse said. "They injected Micha with it. Eric is doing the experiment."

Sam widened his eyes at her.

"We don't have time to—" Aaron began.

"We can't leave him." June looked at Sam. "He's an innocent victim. He doesn't deserve this, he doesn't deserve to die at their hands. We have to help him. I thought you wanted to crush the Institute? Stop them. Stop what they're doing."

Silence fell. June's heart thudded in her ears. If Aaron wouldn't go up, she'd go by herself.

"I thought you didn't care about this war?" Sam said, gazing at her.

June tried to gather her courage. "That's when I thought it had nothing to do with me."

Sam tilted his chin up, his face smooth but stony. "Eric doesn't care if they get away," he said to Aaron. "But if we leave Micha here, he wins for sure. We may have different ideals, Aaron, but we have a common enemy. And this is our chance to cripple him."

They were all staring at Aaron, Jason too. Aaron drew a breath through his nose.

"Well"—his expression was grim—"I hope this is a good day to die. You're always itching for a fight, Sam. Something tells me you're about to get it." He turned to the buttons, lifted a hand, and after a moment's hesitation, hit thirty-three.

The elevator lurched into motion. June stepped back, next to Muse, and sought out her hand between them. June squeezed her fingers, and Muse clutched her hand in return.

"Don't worry," June said. "No more innocent people are going to suffer."

"I don't know about that," Sam murmured.

Chapter 17

When the doors opened on the thirty-third floor, Sam and Aaron had their guns raised, shielding the rest of them. The hallway beyond was empty. The two quickly exited the elevator and checked the surrounding area.

June turned to Jason.

"Stay here," she told him. "Engage the emergency stop. Keep the doors closed. You're too weak to go with us."

"June," he said hoarsely.

"Who has a watch, a cell phone, anything that tells the time?" June asked.

Sam and Aaron were standing outside the doors, Sam keeping them open with his foot.

"I do." Aaron lifted his arm. A silver watch with a round black face gleamed on his wrist.

"Give it to me," June said.

Aaron took the watch off without hesitation, despite the fact it probably cost more than all the ink on June's body. He gave it to her, and she pressed the watch into Jason's hands; they were cold and trembling.

"Fifteen minutes," she said. "If we're not back, get out of here, any way you can. Get out of this place and run."

Jason gazed at her. June held her brother's hands tightly, noting the marks on his wrists again.

"I'm sorry." She lowered her voice. "I'm sorry I left you. I'm sorry I failed you. If I don't come back, make sure Mom knows I love her."

"This is not your fault," Jason said. "June, don't—"

"Fifteen minutes." She let go of his hands. "Promise me."

"Come on," Sam demanded. "We can't stand here forever."

"*Promise me*," June whispered fiercely.

Jason nodded, clutching the watch, his eyes bright. June turned and stepped out of the elevator, followed by Muse. June looked back. Jason lurched forward and hit a button. The doors slid shut with a soft thump.

"Where's he at?" Aaron asked.

"This way," June said.

They started down the hallway, retracing the route the guards had brought them to the elevators.

"Was I getting that earlier?" June asked Muse. "You have my gun?"

Muse perked. Still walking, she pushed a hand down the front of her white leggings. "I took it in the van. They thought I was out. Luckily, they just patted us down and didn't check our crotches. That's the one shortcoming of most of these idiots. They're always avoiding the crotch. It's the first place I go for."

Muse's underwear were white silk with little pink hearts, absurd to notice in that moment but impossible not to. She produced the gun with a flourish and held it out to June. The metal was warm. And a little slippery.

"Tell me this wasn't in your pussy." If they were in any other situation June would have refused to touch it.

Muse shrugged. "I learned a long time ago how to hide a gun on your body. You do what you gotta do. Would you rather I didn't take it and hide it?"

"So you've been walking around with my gun tucked up your vag this whole time?"

"Just the grip. It hasn't been fun."

"And they didn't knock you out?"

"I've never been rendered unconscious, by chemical or physical means. I don't know why. Something to do with my physiology. It comes in handy."

"They probably used sodium thiopental on you," Sam said. "Knocks a person out quickly. Muse has been injected with it several times and it has no effect on her."

June wasn't sure she wanted to know why Muse had been repeatedly injected with sodium thiopental. Or why Sam had such an intricate knowledge of knockout drugs. Or how Muse learned to hide a gun in her vagina. Maybe it was all some sex game they played.

They passed the bank of windows. The night pressed thick against the glass. Up ahead loomed the doors to the surgery room.

"There's a bunch of researchers in there," June said. "I don't know if any of them have guns."

"We'll take care of them if they do," Aaron said.

June pushed through the doors first and went right for the second, inner doors, raising the gun, hand steady, determination driving every step. She felt a bit like the hero rushing in to save the damsel in distress. For once, it was nice not to be the damsel.

When they burst into the room, they moved as though they had everything planned, confidence outweighing good sense. The researchers, most of them gathered around Micha's bed, scattered.

"Get back! Get back!" June didn't need to use her power yet.

Aaron and Sam approached the bed, guns raised. Micha was convulsing in his restraints, white foam oozing from his lips.

"Get those off him!" June yelled at the woman researcher who had injected him. She stood a few feet from the bed with her hands up.

Muse hurried over to the bed and jerked at the restraint on Micha's left ankle.

June pointed her gun at the woman researcher. "Take them *off*."

Aaron swept the room with his gun, and the researchers still standing nearby backed away. June rushed to the bed.

"Get in that room, over there." Aaron jerked his gun at a door on the other side of the room. "All of you!"

The woman researcher worked frantically at one of Micha's wrist restraints. Micha jerked against the mattress, his skin bright red and shiny with sweat. His eyes were rolled back in his head.

"What's wrong with him?" June asked. "What's happening?"

"He's having a reaction to the hormones," the woman said.

The restraint popped off, and Micha's hand jerked wildly as it sprung free.

"I need to give him a shot of epinephrine to stop the seizing," the woman said.

"Then do it!" June placed her gun on the bed and started working on the other wrist restraint. The woman hurried over to a nearby cart.

Aaron continued forcing everyone into the other room with Sam at his back. Muse undid the restraints on Micha's ankles. He was making hideous wet choking sounds, as if asphyxiating on his own saliva.

"Hurry the fuck up!" June yelled at the woman.

She rushed back to the bed with a syringe, her hand shaking. "I need to get this in his arm. Hold him down."

June flung herself over Micha's quaking body and grabbed his arm. His skin was hot, and the sweat made him hard to hold. Muse helped, both of them forcing down his arm.

"Do it," June said.

The woman, despite her shaking hands and Micha's uncontrolled jerking, got the needle in after two attempts. She pushed the plunger. "It'll take a moment." She looked up at the wildly beeping monitors above the bed.

For a hellish minute they continued holding him down. Then his tremors tapered, and his bucking body gradually stilled. June let go of his arm and slid off. Micha took huge gasping breaths that sounded much better than what he had been doing. The woman grabbed an oxygen mask.

"Is he all right?" June asked.

Micha's eyes were rolling, his lips tinted blue. He was still shuddering, though not as badly as before.

"I don't know." The woman pulled the mask over his mouth and nose.

Aaron had herded all the researchers into the other room and blocked the door with a chair under the knob.

"Please don't hurt me," the woman begged.

June picked up her gun. "We're taking him out of here. Don't try to stop us and we won't."

"He's not stable." She looked at the monitors again. "You can't move him."

June leaned over. "Micha, can you hear me?"

Micha's eyes rolled and focused on June, or somewhere in her proximity. He reached up and grabbed clumsily at the mask and pulled the plastic dome from his mouth. "June?" he wheezed out.

"Yes." Relief sped through her. "We have to get you up. We have to get out of here." They couldn't wait, stable or not. "Help me get him up, Sam!" June looked around at the doors to make sure no one had arrived yet to stop them. When she did, she got a rude surprise.

Rose, in all her ghostly glory, stood a few feet from the end of the bed. She stared at June. This time, she definitely wasn't a dream. June almost yelped, but managed to stifle herself.

Aaron and Sam walked toward the bed and both passed Rose without noticing her presence. June tried to ignore her. She had no time for the dead when she was trying to keep someone alive. But Rose spoke.

"Don't leave without the truth," she said.

June almost couldn't hear her over the noise of the monitors.

"The worst is yet to come," Rose said.

"Awesome," June muttered. She started pulling the sensors off Micha's chest, making the monitors scream. She tried to sit him up, but he was limp and heavy, and June's muscles were still the consistency of warm gelatin. Sam slipped an arm under Micha's shoulders.

"Let me do it," he said.

June looked back at the foot of the bed. Rose had disappeared.

Sam got Micha on his feet and hauled him across the room, Aaron leading the way, June and Muse following Sam. Before they reached the doors, voices came from outside.

They were too late.

"Shit," Sam said. "They're coming. Take him!" He turned and heaved Micha off on June.

June stumbled under the full weight of Micha's body, but filled with both desperation and adrenaline, she managed to drag him back to the bed. The woman researcher screamed and scurried into a corner.

After depositing Micha on the bed, June turned and pointed her gun at the doors, trying to get ready for whatever burst through them.

When the doors flew open, Eric strode through—clearly, positively, fear-inspiringly livid. Huffing with rage, he focused immediately on Aaron. Four security guards poured in behind him. June didn't know where to aim. She didn't even know if she could hit anything.

"I should have known it would come to this," Eric said. "The SNC and the Paranormal Alliance, breaking into the Institute. Taking our research subjects hostage!"

"Oh, please, Eric," Aaron said. "Cut the theatrics."

"Take them down!" Eric bellowed at the guards.

The guards didn't decide whom to shoot first fast enough. The second of hesitation cost them.

"Get down on the floor!" June yelled. "Throw away your guns!"

The air vibrated and rushed around her like a hot wind. The security guards dropped, sprawling face down on the tile as if a weight had landed on their backs. All four guns were flung away and skidded toward them. June had to step aside to avoid being hit by one.

Eric's self-righteousness morphed into incredulous fury. "Filthy Siren. I should have killed you at the park."

"Why did you only target the guards?" Aaron asked June.

"My power doesn't affect him for some reason."

Eric strode boldly toward them. "You are not leaving this place alive."

"Oh yes, we are." Sam aimed his shotgun.

And fired.

The blast echoed through the room, huge and startling, and immediately sent June's ears ringing. Eric's chin flew back, and blood burst from his throat like a grisly water balloon. The woman researcher screamed. June screamed. Eric fell to the floor, hands at his throat. June went numb with horror.

"Don't kill him!" Aaron yelled, his voice muffled in June's ears.

"We can end this right now," Sam said.

"No one knows as much as he does! His secrets need to be spilled."

"His blood needs to be spilled!" Sam said.

Aaron grabbed Sam's arm and directed his gun away from Eric "If we kill him, we'll only be murderers. Get Micha up. We have to get out of here before more guards come."

Sam growled. "Dammit, Aaron." He jammed his gun under his arm and marched toward the bed. "You better not make me regret this."

Eric was bleeding and writhing on the floor, a bright red puddle spreading around his head. June couldn't look away.

Aaron spoke to June. "Don't take this as pity, just prudence. We *can't* kill him. But we can take him hostage and make getting out of here a hell of a lot easier."

"Oh God," June said. "This is some messed up shit."

"Just lead the way out of here," Aaron told her. "Get us back to the elevators."

June was too far in shock to think, so she was glad for the order. She moved past the guards, all still face-down on the floor. Aaron grabbed Eric by the lapel of his jacket and hauled him to his knees. More blood gushed from his neck, spilling down his front and saturating his shirt.

"Let's go, Eric. Make yourself useful." Aaron let go of Eric's jacket, grabbed his wrist, and dragged his body.

June went first through the doors, through the outer room, and into the hallway, gun raised. She expected a battalion, but found the hallway empty. Sam followed with Micha, Muse hurrying after them. Aaron walked out last, dragging his twitching, choking, bleeding load.

"You should have brought more guards with you, Eric," Aaron said. "Afraid of letting too many people find out what you've been up to?"

Every time they went around a corner or past an open door, June tensed, expecting someone to spring out at them. When they got to the elevator, she pounded on the door.

"Jason!" She looked over her shoulder. A bright red trail marked their progress. She was glad she was too focused on survival at the moment to process the horror going on around her. She'd surely have nightmares about it later.

The elevator doors slid open, and June was ecstatic to see Jason still inside. Alive. As whole as she'd left him.

The worst is yet to come.

A man suffering such massive blood loss as Eric Greerson shouldn't have been able to get to his feet, let alone as fast as he did, and in the same blinding, startling instant take Aaron's gun. He placed the muzzle to the back of Micha's head and wrenched him away from Sam. Eric then stumbled backwards, reeling away from them and holding Micha upright, with what looked like little effort.

"Come near me and I'll blow his brains out," Eric snarled, bloody spittle flying from his lips. His chest heaved. The ragged hole on the right side of his neck gaped with each breath, oozing fresh blood. His clothes were soaked black.

Micha was alert and wide-eyed.

"Eric," Aaron said. "What the hell…"

"You're not taking this from me," Eric said. "What I've accomplished here is the greatest scientific achievement the world has ever known." Pink saliva dribbled down his chin. "You'll thank me for what I've done," he said to Micha, almost tenderly. "When you see what you become. It'll be glorious."

"Fuck me." Sam groaned. "He's a fucking vampire."

Eric laughed, wet and gurgling. A bubble of blood formed between his lips and popped. "I'm sorry, Micha," he slurred. "I lied to you. I did the first experiment on myself." He lowered his bloody mouth to Micha's ear and whispered, "But I won't tell anyone you're not the prototype. I promise."

"Get off me," Micha growled, squirming.

"Are you serious, Eric?" Aaron said. "You gave yourself the vampire virus?"

"It's never quite worked right," Eric said. "Not the way it does when it's transferred right from the source. But it works well enough."

"That's why your voice didn't affect him," Sam said to June.

"And why he's having meetings at ten o'clock at night," June said. "And why he was wearing that ridiculous fedora at the park."

"You'll regret what you've done here," Eric said. "You'll never get out of here alive. All exits are blocked by my security force. And even if you do, all of Chicago will know the SNC and the Paranormal Alliance launched an attack on the Institute and tried to kill me. They'll hunt you down. The whole city will condemn you. I'll tell them how the two of you tried to assassinate me."

"The city will know the truth," Aaron said. "We'll make sure of it."

Eric jerked his head toward Aaron, the wound making a squelching sound. June had to look away, her stomach turning.

"Your father would be ashamed of you," Eric said. "Making treaties with the Paranormal Alliance, working with Sam Haain. Your father never would have stood for such things. He was a worthy opponent. He understood hate."

"My father was a close-minded, bitter, twisted man," Aaron said. "And he was ashamed of me in life, so I have no doubt he carried that sentiment into death."

"Eric, let him go," Sam said. "If he's that precious to you, you won't kill him."

"I will kill him." Eric renewed his grip on Micha. "To keep you from taking him."

"Please!" June stepped forward, fighting down her nausea. "You have to let him go. He's an innocent man. There have to be people working with you on this who would gladly take his place. Why can't you experiment on them?"

Eric gave a slurred laugh. "Little girl, you are so very naïve. You were right to run away like you did. The things we were going to do to you. But you're so far in over your head now, you don't even know it." He nodded at Sam and Aaron. "These two men, they're monsters, figuratively and literally. *Monsters*. Oh, Aaron is human, but he keeps company with monsters, and that makes him one too. Make no mistake. They are evil and their agendas are evil."

"If you think we're monsters," June said, "why do you want to be like us?"

He laughed again. "So we can destroy you, silly girl. The only way to stop you is to become like you."

"And you'll be such fine replacements," June said. "Micha supported you, and you betrayed him. In the worst ways possible. He wasn't a monster. He was innocent."

"There are no innocents, girl. Not you, not me. Not anyone."

"My brother was innocent," Sam spoke up. "Did you have a hand in what happened to him? Were you trying to stop our treaty?"

Eric rolled his eyes, though it seemed more a physical symptom of his condition than a gesture of disgust. "Your kind is far better at taking care of things like that than I am. Like I said, monsters."

"Let me go!" Micha struggled again.

"I've heard enough of this," Aaron said.

"You know how to kill a vampire," Sam said. "Right?"

"Destroy a vital organ," Muse replied calmly, behind Sam.

"Idiots," Eric raged, droplets of blood flying from his mouth and showering Micha's cheek. "You can't do anything to me. Go ahead and try."

"You killed Micha's wife and everything he believed in," Sam said. "But you're not going to kill him."

Sam lifted his gun and fired, as unceremoniously as before.

June jerked, still not recovered from the first blast. Eric flew backward, the top of his head bursting in a red, chunky shower. Micha spilled onto the floor as Eric's body slammed against the wall behind him. Eric slid down the white surface, dragging blood and gray-pink goop.

"Oh, fuck!" June shouted. "Fucking fuck, I hate Chicago!" She reeled backward, toward the open elevator. How she didn't throw up was a small miracle. Maybe her body knew she was about to need every ounce of nourishment she had to convert into energy.

"Why did you wait so long to do that?" Aaron admonished Sam. "The idiot left us a clear shot the entire time."

"You wanted a hostage!"

Aaron grabbed Micha by the arm and pulled him up. "Get in the elevator."

June stumbled into the car. "I really, truly hate this place."

"Wait around." Sam got in. "You might get to hate it even more."

Aaron hauled Micha into the elevator. "Let's get out of here for real this time." He pushed Micha toward one of the walls and he slumped against it.

Jason stood in the middle of the elevator, still clutching Aaron's watch, clearly shell-shocked.

"You okay?" June asked, gripping Jason's arm with a shaking hand.

"No," he squeaked out.

"Yeah, me neither."

Chapter 18

June tried to block out what she had seen. Nightmares could be dealt with later. Nothing felt real. The haunting silence underlined everything.

Aaron and Sam stared grimly at the strip of numbers above the doors. Micha remained slumped against the wall, breathing heavy. Aaron's shirt cuff was stained red and Micha's bare torso had been splattered with blood.

"We can't just walk out of here," Muse said, standing next to Sam.

"No," Sam agreed. "I don't guess we will. But we just did the world a huge favor."

"If he's dead," Aaron said.

"I blew his brains out."

"If you didn't blow enough of them out, we may still have a problem."

June studied the buttons on the control panel. The violence she had witnessed oddly made her think clearer, as if the horror of Eric's exploding head had cleansed her of all other horrors and sharpened her focus.

"We have to get off at the fourteenth floor." June reached over and jabbed the button.

"Why?" Aaron asked. "We're not doing this again."

"It's the vampire floor. Not all of us. Just three."

"Splitting up," Sam said. "Now there's a great idea."

"Can you use your power on more than one person?" June asked him.

"Yes. Anyone I'm touching."

"So you can get the three of you out. Make it look like you're carrying a wounded guard. But there's no way in hell, even if you could figure out a way to touch all five of us, it wouldn't look weird. We'll take the elevator down to the underground garage and get out the way I did before." She gripped Jason's arm. "But this time, you're coming with me."

Jason nodded. The hope in his eyes was all the motivation she needed.

"I'm assuming you have a getaway?" June asked Sam.

"Cindy is waiting."

"Pick us up at the exit ramp."

"I have a feeling quite a few guards are waiting at the bottom of this elevator shaft," Aaron said. "We'll tell them you attacked us and went back up. It'll buy you some time. I hope you know what you're doing."

"I don't," June said.

When the doors opened on the fourteenth floor, June stepped over to Micha. His face was still flushed, his cheek dotted with Eric's blood. His eyes were wide and clear, the blue irises glimmering in the fluorescent light. June gripped his chin, stretched up on her tiptoes, and gave him a firm kiss. His lips were salty.

"You're gonna be okay," she whispered. As she dropped back flat on her feet, she gestured to Sam. "Trust this man. He's the smartest man in the city. He'll get you out of here."

Micha looked up at Sam, and Sam nodded.

June turned toward the doors.

"I don't get a kiss for luck?" Sam asked.

"You're lucky I don't punch you in the nuts."

June stepped out of the elevator, gun raised. The hallway beyond was empty. Jason, and then Muse, walked out behind her. The doors slid shut.

"Don't be afraid," June told the other two. "We're going to get out of here."

Unlike the rest of the floors, the windows on the vampire floor were all blacked out or covered. The lighting was dimmer and the temperature cooler, and everything was quiet, unnervingly so. June's skin crawled with déjà vu as she led them down the corridors, around corners, and finally toward another elevator. They hadn't emerged from the same elevator as the night they ran into Rose, but things looked familiar. They passed a set of glass doors with the words "Vampire Research and Science" emblazoned across them. As PC as the paranormal community attempted to be, they'd never coined another term for vampire. The classics died hard.

"Hopefully they're so busy elsewhere they won't be watching this exit." June pushed the down button next to the elevator. "But let's not count on it."

The doors opened. They got inside. One more elevator ride, to freedom or death.

June punched a button marked P on the control panel. The doors slid shut.

As they descended in silence, June took in the two on either side of her: Jason on her left, fear in his eyes, and Muse on her right, little tremors jerking the corners of her mouth. June spread her arms, placed her hands on their shoulders—her free hand on Muse's, the gun on Jason's—and pulled them in for one final, will-strengthening embrace. Jason rested his chin below her ear. Muse dropped her head on June's shoulder, snaking an arm around June's waist. They were both trembling.

"Whatever happens when these doors open," June's voice shook, "we'll face it together."

"It can't be any worse than what we faced before," Jason said, his voice muffled against her cheek.

June closed her eyes, felt the drop beneath her feet, squeezed the grip on the gun. For one brief moment, chaos held no sway. She opened her eyes

"Do you love Sam?" June asked Muse.

"More than I can speak it."

"Would you kill for him?"

She nodded, once, silent.

"Then we've all got reasons to fight our way out of here," June said.

"For Mom," Jason murmured.

"For each other," June said.

"For giving those bastards a huge slap in the face," Muse said.

The doors opened.

Chapter 19

June steeled her courage. The parking garage gaped vast and dark beyond the doors, a blast of cold air rushing in. She untangled herself from the last comfort she might ever know, raised her gun, and stepped out.

The garage was shadowy and echoing, full of dark spaces, and she couldn't tell if anyone else was around. Row upon row of cars stretched away from them; plenty of hiding places, for them, but unfortunately for the enemy as well. June turned in a swift circle with the gun held out in front of her, clutched in both hands; like she'd seen in cop shows on TV.

Silence. Nothing moved.

"That way." Muse pointed.

The exit was on the other side of the garage, at least a hundred yards away. The sodium lights above the ramp shone like beacons of hope. They moved quickly, their footsteps loud in the quiet. Jason lagged behind, and June slowed down.

"Don't worry," June said. "You're not getting left behind this time."

They passed one row of cars, another, and another. Moving as swiftly as they could with Jason, they made it to the second row from the ramp. Escape opened up promising and glorious ahead of them. June's hopes were starting to lift when a voice rang out.

"Hey! You there!"

"Shit!" June yelped.

They scrambled in front of a red car at the end of the second row. A blast rang out. Car alarms shrieked.

"They're shooting at us," Jason gasped. "Just like before."

"Dammit." June flattened herself on the cold pavement, trying to see under the car.

Footsteps, voices. Coming toward them, from the direction of the ramp.

"They're over there!" a voice called.

June scrambled up. "Go," she ordered, pushing at Muse.

Crouching low, they moved between the cars in the row they were in and the adjacent ones in the facing row. June feared Jason wouldn't be able to keep up, but he managed to stay behind them, probably functioning purely on fear. They froze at the front of a white car when footsteps sounded close by. Peeking around, June saw several security guards dart past the back of the car.

"They had to have come down this way," a man said.

June slunk around the passenger side of the car. The ramp was farther away now, and they still had to cross over to the last row of cars before they could get to it. Doing so would leave them in the open for a moment. She crept to the back of the car and peeked around. The guards were at the other end of the row, next to a wall. They seemed to be discussing something. June counted five of them.

"What are they doing?" Jason whispered.

June watched as two guards broke away and headed toward the ramp. One of them pulled out a radio. The other two started back up the row.

"They're coming this way," June whispered. She stole back to the front of the car where the other two were crouched. "Soon as they pass, start going down the row, toward the wall."

The guards advanced only a short distance in their direction, before walking between cars, looking around and underneath them. This meant an abrupt change of plans. June had to lead everyone back the way they'd come. When they reached the top of the row again, they'd be faced with the dilemma of where to go next. They were running out of options.

They went a few cars back up the row and crouched behind a big black truck. June inched to the rear of the truck and peeked out again, toward the exit ramp. Her heart dropped when she saw the two guards who had broken away were standing at the bottom.

"Goddamn it." She drew back and sat down hard, her back against the tire of the truck. "They're guarding the exit ramp."

Muse knelt next to her, Jason crouched and shivering on the other side of Muse.

"We're trapped?" Jason asked hoarsely. He sounded on the verge of hysteria.

"Just stay calm." June closed her eyes, trying to think.

Unfortunately, the wretched, bleak truth presented itself all too obviously: they had only one hope for escape. June opened her eyes.

"The only way to get out of here is if one of us distracts them," June said. She peeked around the back of the truck again, to see where the searching guards were.

"I'll do it," Muse said.

"No, you won't."

Muse's eyes glistened in the dim light, the corner of one fluttering. "I said I'd kill for Sam. I'd die for him, too." Her voice was strained. "I've always wanted to be the icon he needed."

"You'll be a martyr. There's a difference."

"There really isn't. I'm not afraid." Her tone didn't match her words though, not even close.

"I'm not letting you die for Sam," June said. "Not yet. Not here."

"You have to," Muse whispered. "June, that's the only way for you two to get out of here. I'll distract them. They'll kill me. But you and Jason will escape. I'm dying anyway."

"You're not dead yet."

"What's the alternative? Then we all die. Make the choice. Me, or all of us."

"That's not a choice I'm comfortable with."

Muse gripped her shoulder. "We don't have much time. They're coming this way. They're going to take any choice away from us."

June closed her eyes. Sam's words echoed in her head. *You'll realize who you are, who you really are, before this is over.*

"Maybe my angel of death will be benevolent," Muse said, her voice tight. "The way Sam hopes it was for his brother."

June opened her eyes. Muse stood up.

"Muse!" June scrambled to her feet as well, but kept crouched so they wouldn't see her.

"You'll make it," Muse said. "I *know* you'll make it."

Jason got up as well, hunched over.

"No," June said. "Don't confuse me with someone else, Muse."

Muse's eyes glimmered. June stood up straight and gripped her arms.

"Take my brother," June said. "Get him out of here. Don't stop until you get to safety." She shook her. "You can do it."

"June!"

June squeezed her tighter. "Do what Sam needs you to do. He doesn't need you to die." June let go of her. "Go down between the cars, all the way to the end by the wall, and cut across. Fast as you can."

"June, you can't—"

June raised her gun, turned, and walked out into the open.

"Hey!" Her voice echoed. So did her footsteps as she marched down the wide lane between the rows of cars. "Come on you assholes. I'm right here."

The two guards at the exit ramp darted from their spot and ran toward her, as she hoped. Two others popped out from between the cars farther down the row, and the third, at the end near the wall, broke and hurried in her direction.

"Stand down!" one of them yelled. "Drop your weapon or we'll shoot."

"Wouldn't be the first time." June stood her ground.

All five of them entered the lane, stalking toward her from opposite directions, guns raised. She pointed her gun at the two coming from the ramp and made them slowly circle her, until all their backs were toward the wall and they wouldn't see Muse and Jason pass. She could have used her voice on them at that point, floored them like the guards upstairs. But she wanted this. She wanted this moment. She wanted them to be afraid of her, afraid of what would happen, the way they'd made her afraid.

"Drop your weapon," a guard said. "Or we will take you down."

June kept them focused on her.

"You're outnumbered here, young lady," another one said.

Their faces were now visible under the lights. She recognized one of them.

"You shot Rose Bellevue." June aimed at him.

"Drop it!" he roared back.

"You took my brother down after you killed her. You should have killed me then, when you had the chance."

Against the wall at the end of the row, two hunched shadows darted from one side to the other. She stood in the middle of the lane with the guards. Their guns were all leveled on her, but she wasn't afraid.

"You won't be so lucky this time," one of them said, "unless you drop that gun. You've got five barrels on you right now, not good odds."

"You weren't afraid to shoot me before." Their lack of fire bolstered her confidence. "You have to bring one of us back alive, don't you? And you don't know where my brother is right now."

From the corner of her eye, June saw two figures streak up the ramp. She jerked her gun at the guards to keep their attention, so they wouldn't notice.

"Just drop the weapon," one of the guards said. "We know plenty of places to shoot you that won't kill you."

June didn't budge. "Then shoot me."

"You're playing with fire here."

"So are you." She focused on the man who shot Rose. "Don't you know who I am?"

"You got three seconds," another one said. "One. Two…"

June closed her eyes. She reached deep down inside herself, down into dark, cold depths, to a place she knew but refused to visit; it lay deeper than the voice of her conscience, deeper than the inner voices of the people she loved, deeper than her sanity.

She opened her eyes. Opened her mouth. A sound ripped out of her, vast and inhuman and horrible. The sound made the very shadows recoil, a scream that cut across cars, cracked concrete, burst windows, shorted out lights. The power behind the sound burned her chest and seared her throat, opened her up like a knife from navel to sternum. Four of the men fell instantly, writhing, blood spurting from their ears, noses, mouths. The fifth remained, horrified, blanched, wide-eyed, but unaffected.

The man who had shot Rose.

A vampire.

June aimed her gun and pulled the trigger. So did the vampire. Everything seemed to happen in slow motion.

Her gun jerked and sent a jolt up her arm, the discharge hardly a pop in the wake of her scream. The vampire lurched and reeled away. She had hit him. But in the same instant, a violent shock struck her body, and the sensation seemed to fling her right out of reality.

She lost her feet and fell hard on the concrete, though she didn't feel the impact. Her whole body went instantly numb, her surroundings flying away. Her breath caught like a solid mass in her chest. She jerked her hand to her side and wetness spilled over her fingers. Her vision brightened and blurred at the edges, as if someone were shining a light into her eyes.

The vampire ran away. This was the last thing she saw that she could actually process.

Nothing made sense. She wasn't in pain; the world had stopped, nothing to feel. But in the back of her mind, she knew she'd been shot in the right side of her chest. She wasn't afraid, but a sense of urgency commanded that she hold on and not give in to the rushing white gathering around her, roaring in her ears like building static.

Perhaps she would die. This thought didn't particularly alarm her, either.

Through the buzzing in her ears, some undetermined amount of time later, a sound pervaded. Wheels on concrete. An engine. More light filled her vision, and she tasted copper behind her teeth. Footsteps approached, and she tried to lift her head, but her body was too stiff and heavy. She coughed, struggled for breath, and found little. Something squeezed inside of her, deep under her ribs.

A figure, larger than life, blotted out the light around her.

"June!" A familiar, female voice. Someone lifted her head off the concrete and touched her face. "They shot her. Sam, get over here. Help me!"

Micha entered her mind with a twinge of remorse, and a vague detached resentment sparked inside her, that she might be forced to leave him.

"What did she do to them?" Sam's voice, sounding awed. "Let's get her in the car. This crazy bitch is not dying on my watch."

The white light around her shimmered. For the first time, she experienced pain, in the form of a hot, spreading ache deep in her chest. She was aware of movement, but she seemed to be floating, like she'd been lifted up in the arms of Sam's angel. Someone put her into a car.

"Oh God!" A man's voice, rough and afraid. Jason. "She's been shot?"

"I think it's in her lung." Sam's voice was like a pulsing black light over June's head. "I can hear sucking. I need something plastic to cover it. We got a bag in here or something?"

"Drive, Cindy." Muse's voice. "Follow my father."

Despite the accumulating pain, June still floated outside her body, observing rather than experiencing. The car moved, the sound of the engine filling her ears again. The squeezing in her chest increased, and her ability to breathe diminished. She couldn't find the strength to panic.

Someone had her hand. A weight pressed against her shoulder. She smelled a familiar shampoo.

"You can't leave me," Micha whispered, close to her ear. "You saved me. You have to make it too."

June lifted her hand, distantly aware she had done so, her fingers seeming insubstantial. She barely felt the silky, elusive touch of Micha's hair against her fingertips.

"S'all right." June's voice slurred out of her, but she didn't know if she'd actually spoken. "Best thing that's happened to me in a long time. Not leaving."

Lights flashed above her, streetlights through the window. Someone was talking, fast and panicked, the words running together. Her body started to reassemble, and she became acutely aware of sensation. A pressure moved up her leg, up her stomach, onto her chest.

"Where the hell did that thing come from?" Sam asked.

Micha lifted his head from her shoulder. "How did she—"

A comfortable rumbling vibrated against June's ribs, and the soft, warm weight of a tiny body settled on her chest, over the wound. June lifted her hand, touched fuzziness with her wet fingertips.

"Dipster," she slurred. She tried to pet her, scrabbling weakly at her little form.

"Get it the fuck off her!" Sam said.

"No," Micha said. "Whatever she's doing, let her do it."

A gentle suction started in June's chest. Her breath was leaving her. The light at the corners of her vision renewed and eased in around her, embraced her, pushed the pain and fear away. Then everything dimmed.

She closed her eyes, calm, comforted, painless, and faded out.

Chapter 20

June opened her eyes to light. Not the same light she'd seen after being shot. The normal light of daytime. As her senses fell into place, she realized she was warm, lying on something soft, and encased in peaceful quiet. Since her memory was sketchy and completely nonexistent since she'd fallen into darkness in the back of the car, she assumed she might have died and taken up residence in some heavenly afterlife.

She turned her head, squinting, and took in her surroundings. A few things assured her she probably wasn't dead.

A needle was inserted in the crook of her left arm, a tube attached to it leading to a bag of clear fluid above her head. She was in a hospital bed, the railings pushed down and her head elevated. The tight, prickly ache under her ribs and a sensation of stiffness from the neck down also pointed to still being on the earthly plane, since pain after death would be rotten.

Micha sat at June's right side, arms folded on the edge of the bed and head resting on them, his hair spilling onto the mattress. While he looked an angelic sight, he wasn't naked, so she obviously wasn't in Heaven.

Confusion reigned, despite being comfortably assured she was alive. While she was in a hospital bed, had an IV in her arm, and judging by the ache in her side some serious excavation had been done, she wasn't in a hospital. Or if she was, it was the swankiest hospital on the planet. She didn't doubt the latter, being in Chicago.

She assumed they were still in Chicago, anyway.

A wall of windows to her right presented a dazzling, highly-elevated view of the city, the buildings outside reflecting and magnifying the sunlight. A little sliver of the lake peeked through the buildings in the distance. The windows reminded her of the hotel, but she was clearly in a spacious apartment with immaculate white décor. The walls were white. The furniture, white. The floors, where they weren't covered in white carpet, were gleaming white tile. A few tables, at least, were black with glass tops, adding some accent.

Maybe she'd landed in Heaven's waiting room. If God existed, He would undoubtedly pose some questions to her before He let her in. *If* He let her in.

She reached out and stroked her fingers through Micha's hair. After a moment, he stirred and lifted his head. He had a red mark on his cheek where his face had been resting on his arm.

He sat up straight. He was pale, but maybe that was the light. "You're awake. How are you feeling?"

"Like I've been shot." She winced. Taking too deep a breath made her chest burn. Her voice was thick and hoarse. She was also insanely hungry and thirsty. "Where am I?"

"Aaron's penthouse."

"How long have I been out? Did you guys bring me here from the hospital?"

"Two days. You've been going in and out." He touched her hand. "You were never in a hospital."

She was even more confused. "I…got shot in the chest?" she asked uncertainly. Maybe the whole thing had been a nightmare. "You didn't take me to a hospital?"

"Aaron has a very good private doctor."

"Oh…okay." She pondered that, and then stiffened. "My brother. Where is he?"

"He's all right. He's here. He's resting."

She relaxed. "Are you all right? I thought for sure they were going to kill you."

He said nothing for a moment. Then he whispered, "I don't know."

"Are you in pain?"

He shook his head slightly.

"Has anything…changed?"

"I don't know."

"Micha." She gripped his hand. "I'm sorry. I'm sorry I made you forget Rose. I'm sorry all this happened to you."

"How is any of this your fault? Don't apologize."

"If I hadn't messed up your head, you wouldn't have been involved in this. They wouldn't have caught you. You would have been grieving for your wife and you would have stayed out of it."

"Eric was preparing me, regardless. He would have come for me eventually." He paused, expression darkening. "And I'm not sure grief for my wife is warranted. She was apparently trussing me up to be Eric's guinea pig."

"I don't believe she was doing it on purpose." June lowered her voice. "A means to their end, that's what she said."

"She was a top researcher at the Institute, a place where the higher-ups are rife with corruption. Maybe I was a target from the day I met her. Maybe she was living a double life." Anguish shone in his eyes, the pain of betrayal. "Maybe it was her mission to get with me and make me ready for Eric."

"Do you really believe that? Maybe she didn't know she was giving it to you, or maybe she thought it was something else. Eric could have lied to her. He probably did."

Micha was silent.

June clutched his hand. "Micha, I don't think she'd be appearing to me if she really did it, on purpose. She wants me to clear her name. That's what her visits are about."

"I'm not so sure. The dead can be confused."

Footsteps approached. Sam, dressed in jeans and a black T-shirt, entered the room. The short sleeves displayed some impressive musculature in his upper arms. Probably from all that shotgun wielding. His hair rested smooth and gleaming on his shoulders.

"Thought I heard voices." He strode to the bed. "I knew this hot mess would come around." He stopped at the end of June's bed, hands on his hips. "Hey, Aaron! She's awake!"

"What's going on?" June tried to lift her head, but the strain on her chest hurt too much. "Did they close the Institute down? Have they been exposed?"

Micha gently touched her shoulder. "You need to relax. Your lung capacity is diminished. You have to stay calm."

June took his non-answer as a "no."

"What did you do to those guards?" Sam asked her. "They looked like they were stabbed in all their orifices with an ice pick. Did you have an ice pick on you?"

June swallowed. "Siren Song," she whispered.

Aaron appeared at her bedside, dressed in a pair of black pants and a white dress shirt tucked in and the sleeves rolled up. The light made his face smoother and younger, and he looked even more like Muse.

"I'll call the doctor," Aaron said. "If you need your morphine upped, just let me know."

"I would love my morphine upped. What the hell is going on?"

Aaron reached up to June's IV bag. "You've missed a lot, but you don't need to get worked up about it right now."

Someone else appeared at June's bedside—Muse, dressed all in white, of course. Her family had a thing for white. Before June could greet her, she bent over and planted a firm kiss on June's lips.

June gave her a half-smile when she stood back up. "I'm gonna let that one go, because I like you. We don't want Cindy to start a rumor."

"You're a hero." Muse smiled widely, the corner of her mouth jerking. "Thank you."

"You're a hero," June said. "The way you kicked Robbie's ass at that press conference. Is he alive? Does anyone know?"

"We don't know," Sam said grimly. "The police have raided his house, my sources tell me. He was amassing a library on the history of the paranormal, but they found a bunch of other stuff, too. Books on weapons and ways to kill people, stuff about serial killers and paranormal violence. Enough for the FBI to jizz over for years."

"Crazy bastard." June winced, fighting down the urge to cough.

"He's got his own little faction," Sam said. "I realized it as soon as he started talking about being responsible for all the violence. He can't be doing it all on his own. Problem is, I can't flush out his helpers right now, not while we're in hiding."

"We're in hiding?" June asked.

"We assassinated the head of the Institute," Aaron said.

He had clearly honored June's wish for morphine, because a sudden rush of euphoria spread through her limbs.

"Outside of our groups," Aaron said, "most people in this city— activists, the rest of the paranormal, the normals—think the Institute is a legit facility. We're not exactly heroes."

June didn't understand. Her body quickly became heavy, and yet she seemed to float at the same time. "What about the story?" she asked Sam. "Didn't Ethan run the story about the serum?"

Sam shifted his jaw. "He tried. He wrote it. He sent it to press. The head of his department pulled it and fired him."

"What!" June instantly regretted raising her voice. She gritted her teeth in pain.

"Let's not talk about this right now." Micha pressed a hand to June's forehead and eased her back down. "She's not ready for any strain."

"You have documentation." June was still stiffening against the pain. "And Micha is the proof. Can't you go to the police or some board that governs medical ethics? Isn't there someone you can tell?"

"We need an entity more powerful than either of those," Aaron said. "And until we find one, we have to stay under the radar."

"One good thing," Sam said. "Neither of our organizations believe we're cold-blooded killers. They're raising a lot of hell on our behalf."

"The police are unsure about you and Jason," Aaron said. "No one knows if you were involved, taken hostage by us, or killed."

"How awesome," June said.

June tried to relax, if for no other reason than she wanted to stop being in agony. Micha shooed everyone off. Sam stayed and leaned against the side of the bed.

"You're a force to be reckoned with," he said to June. "I knew you were powerful."

"I hear that's not a good thing." She looked up at him. "Muse told me why you helped me."

Sam arched an eyebrow. "Did she now?"

"I'm not a good poster girl, Sam. Unless, you know, someone wants a tattoo. Or a good wine recommendation."

Sam smiled, though it didn't reach his eyes. "I think there's more to you than you give yourself credit for."

"Sam, I know I owe you…"

"Let's not talk about it right now." He patted her arm. "However, how would you feel about joining the Paranormal Alliance?"

"Sam," Micha said, warning in his voice.

"Just striking while the iron's hot."

June smacked her lips. Her mouth tasted metallic from the morphine. "I don't wanna join any groups." She squinted up at Sam. "I think I'll stay freelance for a while. Sam Haain and June Coffin? That's too many kitschy names for one organization."

Sam chuckled. "My name is Samuel, I'm afraid. Samuel Marcus Haain. Not quite as fear-inspiring as the Celtic god of death. Unless you think all Arab people are terrorists. My father is half. Thus the last name."

"Oh, yeah?"

"His father came from Israel, but he married an American woman here. And my father married an American woman, so I'm quite a bit diluted. Still, you know how Americans feel about anything not pure white. Especially anything from that part of the world these days."

June pointed lazily at him, starting to get loopy. "Knew you had something a little exotic in you."

"And I knew you were pierced in other places. We had to take your clothes off."

"Sam," Micha said again.

A doctor arrived a short time later, tall, thin, somber-faced, and carrying a black bag. Like something out of the fifties. He checked the bandage on June's side and listened to her chest.

"Your lung is staying inflated," he said. "That's good news. And your sutures are holding. It was a clean shot, so you only needed a couple stitches after I took the chest tube out." He walked around the bed and checked the IV bag.

June was floating in a morphine haze. She felt a thump on the side of the bed. A brown and black fur ball trundled up the mattress.

"Dipster." She smiled.

"You do have a bullet in your chest cavity, though," the doctor said. "I don't have the equipment to do extraction in the field, and I don't think it's prudent anyway." He finished with the IV bag. "Don't panic, though. Contrary to what you see on television, most gunshot victims never have their bullets taken out. It's actually more dangerous to remove a bullet than it is to leave it in. You'll just be setting off metal detectors." He swept June's face with a critical gaze. "More than usual, I mean."

"Actually... Oh, never mind." She reached down to pet Dipity.

"And," the doctor said, "you're very lucky, Ms. Coffin. Lucky, ironically, that you almost died. You quit breathing for a short time, which actually saved your life. It stopped your injured lung from moving, which gave your blood time to clot and kept you from bleeding to death. I had to give you a small transfusion, but it would have been much worse had you been struggling to breathe and pumping blood out in the process."

Dipity rubbed against June's hand, eyes narrowed. "Is that so?"

"The bad news is your lung is going to take a little longer to heal than normal. I would suggest now is a good time to quit smoking."

"Crazy enough, Doc, I don't feel like a cigarette at all right now."

When the doctor left, June looked at Micha, still sitting at her bedside. "Her fur's all crusty and matted from my blood. Will you clean her up?"

"Yes. I'll make sure she gets a good grooming." He knitted his brow. "Where did she come from anyway, in the car?"

"She was in the duffel bag." June smiled at the cat. "The one Sam gave me. Turned out to be quite useful after all." June continued petting her. "Everyone really thinks we're the bad guys?"

Micha nodded, his face somber. He was definitely pale and had dark circles under his eyes. "We're safe here, though. It's Aaron's building. Just like the hotel is Sam's. I don't think they legally own either one, but they do 'own' them, in a sense."

"Is that part of the treaty thing? What's that all about, anyway? This 'territory' stuff?"

Micha scratched behind Dipity's ears. "When Aaron and Sam drew up the treaty between the Paranormal Alliance and the SNC, they made certain places their territory. Not the entire city, just a few spots. Members of the opposing group can't go on officially claimed territory without a concession, or else the owning group has a right to 'punish at their discretion.' There are neutral places, too, where members of both groups aren't allowed to inflict 'hardship' on each other. Sam is on the Parks and Recreation Board for the city, so he was given Promontory Point and a couple other parks as his territory."

June's astonishment increased. "Wait, what about Navy Pier? He said that was his too."

"He also has a seat on the Metropolitan Pier and Exposition Authority, which owns Navy Pier."

"I had no idea he was that powerful."

"Strong-arming and affirmative action might have had a little to do with it." Micha petted Dipity, the cat eating up the attention. "That's why people take such umbrage to him being the leader of an anti-Institute, anti-normal group, because he's so prolific outside the paranormal community. And that's why so much hell is about to be loosed at the idea of him 'assassinating' Eric Greerson." He paused. "A war is coming. I've expected and feared it for a long time."

June slid her hand over Micha's on Dipity's back. "You'll survive it."

"I've been fucked up. I don't know what's happened to me or what's going to happen to me. I can't promise you anything."

June squeezed his hand. "Well then, it's a good thing I like surprises."

When evening fell, June got another visitor. The pain medication had made her subdued and all her worry dulled in the fog. But when Jason sat down at her bedside and took her hand, her head instantly cleared.

"Are you all right?" June asked, clutching her brother.

Jason nodded. "I'm okay." His voice was gravelly. "I've been worried sick about you."

"What did they do to you?" She touched the marks on his wrist, rage and anguish rising, making her chest tighten and throb.

"Restraints." Jason pressed his other hand over hers. His eyes glittered, his form bright against the darkening windows. "When I wouldn't…use my power for them, they put a scope down my throat. I think it damaged my vocal chords." He blinked back tears. "They made me swallow stuff too, stuff that kept me from talking when they didn't want me to."

June wanted to scream, but the hot ache under her ribs kept her from making a sound.

"I figured they would kill me. I almost hoped they would, eventually. I kept thinking about you, hoping you got away, hoping they hadn't found you and brought you back."

June closed her eyes, but the tears slipped out anyway. "I never stopped trying to get in there and get you out. I did everything I could. Everything."

"I know that."

June opened her eyes.

Jason rested his head on her shoulder. "This isn't your fault," he whispered.

June pushed her face into his hair and kissed the top of his head. He smelled like home.

"Aaron said people think we might be dead," June said. "What if Mom hears that?"

"I don't know. We can't risk contacting her. She might come, and they might get her too."

"We can't let that happen. Maybe we can secretly contact her somehow and let her know we're all right."

"I just want to go home." He sounded small and lost. "It seems like I haven't been there in a million years. Like it's not real anymore."

More tears fell from June's eyes. "This is all my fault. I'm sorry I blew our cover. I'm sorry my big mouth led to them bringing us here."

"Stop it." He squeezed her hand. "We both agreed to it. They promised us a lot of money."

June sniffed. "I was gonna give it to Mom. To pay off her house."

He gave a wet, ironic laugh. "So was I."

"Goddamn, I hate everything." She brought her other hand up and mopped at her eyes.

"So do I," he whispered. "So do I."

Jason still had his head on her shoulder when Micha appeared. June didn't bother to wipe at the wetness that had leaked out onto her cheeks. The tears were unstoppable.

"Dipster is clean," Micha said. "But she's not very happy about it." He held up his hand, the back now decorated with claw marks.

"Ow," June said. "Cats and water. Worse than cats and blood."

Jason lifted his head.

"We haven't really gotten to talk." Micha indicated Jason. "We've just been taking turns watching over you."

"Micha," June said, "this is my twin brother, Jason. Jason, this is—" She paused. "Micha."

"It's overwhelmingly nice to finally meet you," Micha said.

The corner of Jason's mouth quirked, a knowing light in his eyes. "I'm not the least bit surprised."

June arched an eyebrow. "At what?" She didn't possess a hope in hell of actually pulling off the innocent act. Not with Jason.

"You're the only one I know who could pick someone up in the middle of a crisis," Jason said.

June snorted but promptly regretted it when pain settled across her chest.

"What can I say?" Micha shrugged. "She's a lovely lady. I see the family resemblance. You could both be movie stars."

"A lady," June said. She stage-whispered, "Are you flirting with him? Cause that's really weird."

Micha chuckled. "No. I'm a one-twin kind of guy. Also I only swung that way in college."

She didn't know if he was joking, but she didn't care.

She licked her lips. They were dry, and her mouth tasted like she'd been blowing Satan. "Do me a favor, guys."

"Anything," Micha and Jason said in unison.

"I'm hungry. The doctor said I have to start on liquids. Make sure no one tries to feed me any broth made with fucking flour or I'll *die*."

Micha laughed. "Vegetable puree it is. When you get a little better, I'll find you some veggie bacon."

"And wine. I want wine. That's liquid."

"I'm not sure wine is good for chest wounds," Micha said.

"No, but it'll be great for my mind wounds."

Chapter 21

Their drama stayed on the front page of the *Tribune*, and every other paper in the city, for over a week. Most of the articles included full-color pictures of Eric Greerson looking humble and munificent, followed by unflattering black-and-white photographs of Aaron and Sam.

None of the articles mentioned Eric's vampirism. An expensive and well-attended funeral was held, closed-casket of course. The search for the "assassins" was quickly blocked on all sides by furious marauding members of both the Paranormal Alliance and the SNC. Institute researchers were attacked and arson attempts made on the Institute. June waited hopefully for a bomb to go off, so she could head over and piss in the rubble.

Speculation on Jason and June's involvement, and their whereabouts, came up sporadically. The Institute initially resisted handing over surveillance footage to the police, claiming they wanted to conduct their own investigation once again. None of the footage, once in authority's hands, revealed the fate of the "disappearing Coffin twins."

"We sound like a sideshow act," Jason remarked when this hilarious title appeared. He read diligently every word of every article they printed.

June could only stomach the news in small doses.

"Of course," June said, "this whole damn thing is a circus."

"They don't really care about us, do they?" Jason said. "They're much more concerned with Eric Greerson's killers."

"That could be to our advantage. Gone and forgotten makes it easy to hide."

Aaron's doctor stopped by daily to check on June. Jason and Micha fed her vegetable broth and tea—*tea*—and kept her entertained. The doctor made her do breathing exercises, including coughing, which he told her she had to do or fluid would build up in her lungs and she'd get pneumonia. She wanted to stab him in the face with her IV needle, sound medical advice be damned.

The doctor also attended to Micha. At times, Micha seemed distant and lethargic, but when asked, he attributed the melancholy more to his mental than physical state. He cycled through various mild flu-like symptoms, but none of them lasted more than a day. The doctor didn't know how to treat him and told Aaron that without proper tests, he had no way of knowing what was going on inside Micha's body. He wanted to take a vial of blood, but Aaron wouldn't allow it, lest it accidentally fall into the wrong hands. Suddenly, Micha's blood was a precious commodity.

Then, something bad finally happened.

June was on her second day of being able to sit fully upright in a chair next to her bed. Micha sat in another chair nearby. His hair was rumpled, the white T-shirt he wore tight across his chest showing he'd lost some weight. He hadn't been eating much lately.

"You all right?" June asked him.

"I guess," he replied, his voice soft.

"I'm worried about you." She took a drink from the glass of water she had and put it aside on the table next to her. "I wish the doctor could do tests on you. Are you feeling anything weird?" She presented the question every day.

"What's weird? I don't know."

This was not the answer Micha usually gave. Most of the time, he replied with a simple monotone "no," or a mere shake of his head.

June frowned. "Are you feeling something?"

He tilted his chin down and looked at the table next to June. Uneasiness welled in her stomach.

The glass lurched, and June flinched. Her eyes went so wide they were on the verge of popping out of her head. Micha continued staring at the glass; it lurched again, water sloshing up the sides and splattering on the tabletop.

"Oh my God, it worked." June was half horrified, half relieved. If the serum did what it was supposed to, Micha might be all right in the end. Maybe it wouldn't kill him.

"That's not all," Micha said.

June watched, holding her breath.

Something started happening to the water. Little bubbles formed at the bottom of the glass and sped to the surface. Then the water began to churn. A thin wisp of steam rose from it. June dropped her mouth open,

Megan Morgan

but couldn't form words. The glass vibrated on the surface of the table, making a low thrumming sound.

"You're one of those—pyro things," June said. "Like your sister."

A sensation moved up her left forearm: warmth, initially mild, but the sensation quickly grew hotter, enough to cause pain.

June yelped and grabbed her arm. She winced at the sharp stab in her chest when she moved. Micha gasped, his expression turning horrified. The heat ceased, or at least it didn't increase. The aftermath felt like a sunburn.

"Oh shit, I'm sorry." Micha leapt up, rushed over to her, and grabbed her arm. "Are you all right?"

"I'm fine," June said, though truthfully, she was shaken. "It's all right."

"I can't focus it," Micha blinked rapidly, his eyes shining. "It started last night, in the bathroom. I moved some things across the counter. Then I melted a bottle of soap."

"It's all right," June repeated.

He knelt in front of her. "I'm sorry," he whispered.

She touched his face. "Welcome to the dark side, I guess."

"Please don't tell the others," he begged. "Not yet. There's no telling how this might work. I could develop more abilities. They might come and go. I might never learn to control or focus any of them. I want to know exactly what's happening before I tell anyone."

"I promise. I won't tell them."

"I'm sorry. I didn't mean to hurt you."

"I'm fine." She desperately wanted him to be fine too, for his mind to not be further broken. "We'll both be fine, Micha. We'll get through this together." She tried to force a smile.

Micha dropped his head in her lap, and she stroked his hair. He gripped her waist, shaking. Again, like the morning after breaking into the funeral parlor, she didn't know how to console, so she resorted to humor. She told herself not to bring up Hitler this time.

"Since you're down there…" she chided.

Micha sniffed wetly. "Doctor told you no physical strain."

"I promise I'll sit still."

He lifted his head. His eyes were glistening. "Thank you for coming back for me at the Institute."

She swallowed. "I couldn't leave you there. You didn't deserve what they did to you."

He sniffed again. "Maybe it would have been better if I—"

She placed a finger to his lips. "Don't you dare. Don't you say that."

He nodded, her finger still resting on his lips. She took it away.

"We both deserved to be saved," she said. "Things wouldn't be any easier without us."

He dropped his head back in her lap. She touched his hair.

"But seriously," she said. "While you're down there."

He lifted his head again. "I don't know where everyone else is..."

"I don't really care where they are."

June found out orgasms sucked when you had a bullet lodged in your chest.

Still worth it.

And so the situation became more convoluted.

An extraordinary number of people came and went from the penthouse considering they were in hiding: Cindy, repeatedly showering June with physical affection and making her yell; Muse, grim and twitching away like a rattlesnake, bringing Sam news from the front lines; Ethan, cocky as ever despite his unemployment.

"I can't believe they fired you," June told him the first time he showed up to see Sam. "That's bullshit."

"Any condemnation of the Institute is quick to put you under suspicion right now." Ethan actually sounded pleased he'd been persecuted by the Man. "I'll never sit down and keep my mouth shut, though. I'll find a way. I still have connections. And I can't let Sam down."

June narrowed her eyes. "You're a member of the Paranormal Alliance, aren't you?"

"No, but I want to be. I've been petitioning Sam for two years now. He's a great man. I want to serve him."

"Yeah, I bet you do."

"I'm damn lucky Robbie never targeted me, as often as I like to get the truth out there. Now there's a story I'd like to follow, his mad campaign. Sensational." He wandered off to find Sam.

"Right," June said. "Sensational."

Each day June got a little better physically. Mentally, she remained a wreck—a twenty car pileup, actually, complete with exploding gas tanks and body parts littered on the side of the road. She wanted to contact people back home. What had become of her shop? Was her friend and co-owner Diego running things? Did her friends think she'd skipped town? Did her mother think they were dead? Neither watching the news nor reading the newspapers—or reading blogs on Aaron's laptop—eased her mind, as each day the situation spiraled deeper into political and civil chaos. Only the patient, easy kindness of both her brother and Micha kept her from completely losing her mind; and poor Micha had his own problems.

Within a month, June was something like herself again. She had limited mobility in her right arm, and her chest still ached when she took a deep breath, but she got around well enough, as far as she could go, anyway. The penthouse was now their domain. She tried to give Micha some space, to work through the issues concerning his wife—who thankfully, didn't make any surprise visits—but this finally ended with a heated make-out session and some careful physically awkward sex late one night.

She didn't know if Micha wanted her, or merely comfort, but she didn't mind either way.

One afternoon not long after, they were sprawled on the big white leather couch in Aaron's living room. Micha was stretched out beside her and resting against her good side, so he was on the outer part of the couch, June wedged against the back of it. Dipity was curled on June's stomach, asleep.

Micha was reading from the little blue tour book he'd gotten at the hotel, about Jay Pritzker Pavilion in Millennium Park and the architect, Frank Ghery. Jason, sitting in a chair nearby, listened raptly. Cindy was paying them a visit and had planted herself on a stool in front of Jason, his bare foot in her lap. Of all things, she insisted on giving him a pedicure. She claimed her sister went to beauty school and taught her a bunch of things about grooming other people. June could use that line sometime, though she didn't want to play with anyone's feet. She liked seeing Jason focus on something besides the news.

"Read some more," June murmured, when Micha stopped reading. She played with his hair.

Micha turned a page. "The Millennium Monument." His voice vibrated against June's shoulder.

When he was through with that subject, he read about how the entirety of Millennium Park was funded by private donations.

"Just like the Institute," Cindy piped up, breaking the mood.

June scowled at her back.

"But a lot less sinister," Jason said. "I wish I could go see all of it." His voice had gotten stronger, though he was still hoarse at times, especially if he spoke too loudly. "Even though I get chills thinking about that place, I loved the sculpture in the courtyard outside the Institute. It's Harold Brenning's third public work."

"That's it." Cindy snapped her fingers. "I can never remember the sculptor's name. I think I deliberately blanked it out or something."

"You like sculpture?" Jason asked.

Cindy worked away with a nail file. "I went to college to be an art major. Dropped out, though. Couldn't afford the tuition. Became a bartender instead. But someday, I plan on going back."

"You want to hear some more?" Micha asked. "Crown Fountain was designed by Jaume Plensa…"

"Nah." June shook her head. "That's enough Chicago for now."

"I went to the University of Southern California for a liberal arts degree," Jason said. "Utterly useless. So I went to acting school. I wanted to make my mother happy by going to college since June had no interest in it." He had given June crap about this before. "But I eventually had to follow what was in my heart. Even in college, I was into theatre. I knew acting was my calling."

"You were in the right place for it," Cindy said. "Los Angeles is full of stars, so I hear."

"A whole sea of them," Jason said. "Hard to get noticed."

Cindy sat back. "I could give you a haircut, too, if you want. Slick you up a bit. You'll feel better."

"Can I have a makeover, too?" June asked sardonically. She hoped Cindy wasn't using her sex magic on Jason.

"Jason has a classic handsome face, good for the movie screen," Cindy said. "Shame to hide it behind scruff, even at a time like this. Your face is too unique, June. I couldn't do much with it."

"Are you calling me ugly?" June asked.

"I'm calling you unique. It's not a bad thing."

"Some of us weren't born with luscious lips and huge boobs."

"I didn't say a word about your boobs!"

Micha stretched up and kissed June's jaw. "You're not ugly," he whispered, "and I love your boobs." He then rolled away a little and dropped the book behind him on the floor.

A pile of newspapers were scattered on the coffee table parallel to the couch. Micha snatched up the ad section from one and settled against her again. Dipity gave a rumble of protest.

"Shut up, Dip." June patted her head.

"Let's look at fun stuff," Micha said. "I don't want to read the news today. Look. One hundred personalized pencils for five ninety-nine. I bet they don't have my name, at least not spelled right. I've suffered at the hands of the personalized crap industry all my life."

"You tell them your name, and they put it on." June snatched the ad and tossed it away. The paper fluttered to the floor behind him. She tugged at his shirt. "I got a better idea for fun stuff," she said. "Come here."

"Your chest."

"Just be careful."

Dipity angrily scooted off and cleared out. Micha got on top of her, delicately, not exerting pressure on her chest or side. June kissed him slowly. She didn't know exactly where they were going, but it had to be better than where they'd been.

"Please," Jason said, "don't mind us."

June waved a hand behind Micha's head. "Go court her with your feet somewhere else."

Jason sighed. "We better vacate. Otherwise we're going to see something nasty."

"Yes," Cindy said. "And something nasty might happen to all of you."

Left alone, their kissing intensified. June had learned from the last experience she probably needed to restrain from full-on sex for a while longer, but touching Micha, absorbing the warmth and weight of him, made her mind a little calmer. Being aroused and having the darkness driven back for a few minutes was bliss. They were lost in their own little, angst-free world.

That was, until she became aware of someone else uncomfortably close by.

June broke the kiss and glared at Sam kneeling next to the couch. He was like a dog under the dinner table, begging for a scrap, only a lot more aggravating.

"What are you doing?" June asked. "Get the hell out of here."

"Can I take a number?" Sam asked. "Or just wedge in between?"

"Go away!" June snapped.

"We do have bedrooms in this place, you know."

"What do you want?" Micha demanded.

Sam retracted and sat on the edge of the coffee table. His exaggerated pleading look disappeared.

"I thought you might like to know that Aaron and I have finally come up with a plan."

This was mildly interesting, but June didn't try to nudge Micha off her. Judging by what was pressing against her thigh, sitting up would be embarrassing for him. They didn't need to give Sam more fodder.

"And it couldn't wait?" June asked.

"It involves you, so we need to know if you're...*up* for it."

June rolled her eyes. "What is it? This better be really good. Better than what I'm doing right now."

Smugness oozed from him like Stigmata. She thought he should try out for the role of Our Lord and Savior of the Oppressed and Aghast.

"Who are the angriest, most vicious paranormal folks in this city?" Sam asked. "The ones who don't take shit and don't take prisoners? I mean, besides my people."

"I don't know," June said. "I'd love to meet them."

Micha furrowed his brow and shifted away from her. "The militant vampires, you mean?"

"They don't usually take sides," Sam said. "But what if we could convince them? They'd be a hell of a force for the Institute to reckon with."

Micha snorted. "They'll never side with you or Aaron. They despise both of you. You stand for everything they hate."

"They despise the Institute more than us. It's not really their rage we're hoping to bring on board, though it would benefit us greatly if we could get that too. They have certain connections. The FPS."

"The FPS?" June said. "Is that like a delivery service? Do you need to send a package?"

Micha looked down at her. "The Freelance Paranormal Scientists. Paranormal researchers who never trusted the Institute, so they work independently. When Rose made her discovery, the militant vampires enlisted them to counter her research. I don't think they've made much headway, though. I mean, Rose was right."

"Yet they don't like being thought of as bacteria-riddled disease factories," Sam said. "But if we could put the information we have about the serum in their scientist's hands, they might be able to do something with it."

Micha lifted off June's body. She wished he wouldn't.

"So what do you need us to do?" Micha asked.

"*Her.* We need a liaison to talk to the vampires. Preferably one who's been abused by the Institute. Sympathy points."

June, surprisingly, found she wasn't alarmed at the idea. She'd been shot, seen a man's head explode, almost lost her brother, maimed people with her voice, and nearly had to drink Cabernet Sauvignon with fruit crepes. Talking to some vampires sounded like a party.

"She could get hurt," Micha said. "They could make a snack out of her."

"She's proven she can hold her own."

"I'm not afraid of the vampires," June said. "I've seen a lot worse in this town."

"Does that mean you'll do it?" Sam asked.

"I don't see any alternative. It's better than rotting away here, waiting for something to happen. Just point me in the right direction."

"You really sure?" Sam asked. "Micha has a point. Militant vampires don't have a lot of morals about them."

"We don't have any other brilliant ideas, do we?" she said. "We've been here a month and it's starting to get old. I want to move. I want to get things in motion."

Sam got to his feet. "Aaron and I will talk to you later tonight. This can't happen until you're fully healed, of course. But in the meantime"—he reached down and ruffled her hair—"you crazy lovebirds keep swapping spit."

June scowled and smoothed her hair as Sam walked away.

"Sam?" Micha called after him.

His footsteps stopped. "Yes?"

"I think if anyone might be able to help us, it's the militant vampires. It's a really good idea, despite how dangerous it is."

"Thank you for the vote of confidence. I'll pass your approval on to Aaron."

"Good."

The footsteps started again.

"Oh, and Sam?" Micha said.

They stopped.

"If you ever put your hands on her again, or say some nasty perverted shit to her, I'll break every bone in your body from the neck down. And Aaron isn't going to care, because he's wanted to kneecap you for years, and much worse. I'll be doing him a favor."

A smile spread across June's face. Her arousal resurged with a vengeance.

"Noted," Sam said.

His tone held a dark sort of mirth though, and June got the impression he was up for Micha's challenge. She didn't see Sam and Micha becoming brothers-in-arms just because they were in hiding together.

When they were alone again, Micha dropped his forehead against June's, their breath mingling.

"Was that too much?" he asked.

"This whole damn city is too much." She dug her fingers into his hips and drew them down flush against her own. Maybe she *was* fit enough for sex. "Now, kiss me like the Institute just blew up."

"And chunks of it are falling down around us like rain."

"And then we'll bang in the ashes."

Meet the Author

Megan Morgan is a paranormal romance, erotica, and urban fantasy author from Cleveland, Ohio. Bartender by day and purveyor of things that go bump at night, she likes her fiction scary and sexy. She's a member of the RWA and trying to turn writing into her day job, so she can be on the other side of the bar for a change.